Evergreen Dread

Victor Marrow

Root Creates

Book Cover by Root Creates (rootcreates.com)

ISBN: 979-8-9901233-0-4 (Print)

ISBN: 979-8-9901233-1-1 (E-book)

This is dedicated to my son. You remain my hope for a better day amid the darkness.

Introduction

This project arrived to me through a news article from years ago. It was a simple story about nuclear worker accidents and secret animal carcasses. Agent Kelso was then born as a rookie U.S. Fish and Wildlife Officer, sworn to protect animals yet forced to become a beacon of hope amid places we pray don't exist. Conversely, many of the places you journey in this novel are absurdly gorgeous examples of why the Pacific Northwest is a mythical wonder. I remain awestruck each time I've stared at the Cascades, San Juan Islands, extraterrestrial greenery, and even the more desert-themed roaming golden hills of Eastern Washington. So, it was only fair to populate these beautiful areas with monsters, some from Northwest folklore and others my own creation.

To my nightmare police, your feedback remained vital as ever. Paul, Stacey, and Carly, my editorial supreme team, your patience is infinite.

Years ago, my friend was working on Stephen King's property, cleaning windows, and told him about my first novel. As the icon of horror fiction listened, my friend told him how I had taken roughly ten years to write my first novel. My friend offered many excuses: school, career, marriage, offspring, and life. King issued a simple edict to hurry the hell up and not take so long on the next book. Well, here it is, sir. My friend will try to smuggle this to you before he is forcibly removed by security.

Finally, to you, yes you literally staring at this page, I appreciate you giving this a try. If you fancy it, please toss me a review on the book's Amazon page, we can share this treasure forward. If you loathe it, then you still have options like gifting it to someone you dislike. I still thank you for giving it a spin.

Chapter 1

CASE: Trinity Terror

IT WAS THE SCREAMS that made Agent Kelso's head turn. Then the vomiting began. Gulps of terror mixed with explosions of puke against the concrete walls of the Trinity Nuclear site.

"Oh my god."

"What is that smell? What the fuck?"

The five radioactive remediation workers were grappling with something they hit during their dig. Two men continued to scream into the sky as coworkers huddled speaking Spanglish. A supervisor shrieked into a walkie-talkie. Amid the sprawling desert nuclear wasteland yet another mystery had been uncovered at Trinity. Three white vans pulled up with Department of Phobos (DOP) identification on the side. The summer wind billowed the chain link fences peppering the vast worksite spanning nine nuclear reactors, five plutonium processing plants, and over nine thousand workers spread across an area the size of a medium-sized city. Agent Kelso grew up, as a tribal member, mere hours from Trinity. Even as a little girl she heard her grandparents speak of the secret atomic city with caution.

"It burns! It feels like my skin is melting off my face!" a remediation worker yelped.

Trinity, one hundred and fifty miles southeast of Seattle, was created as a part of Operation Red Spear in response to the excessive security violations by communist spies at the nearby Hanford Nuclear site. Hanford was originally created by the U.S. federal government to contribute to building the atomic bomb. They evacuated a preexisting town and installed a company town to extract plutonium for the Manhattan Project. Across forty years, from roughly 1945 to 1987, the federal government's atomic quest produced lurking environmental problems. Amid that lust for victory the government had dumped waste into the Columbia River, some evaporated in fumes giving a cancer plume for a few decades, and the rest of this sludge raged inside evaporating concrete tanks. Hanford contained over fifty million gallons of radioactive waste with most of it, in the 21st century, residing underground in over a hundred tanks. Tanks built to hold radioactive materials for seven years were coming upon their seventieth birthday. Hanford, once called by newspapers as the most radioactive and dangerous place in the western hemisphere, had become a perpetual newsreel of worker injuries, delayed clean-up projects, and had burned through over two billion tax dollars a year with no end in sight. Just as famous was how Soviet spies infiltrated Hanford and stole essential atomic secrets.

Trinity, on the other hand, was built in 1950 as a dark sister site to Hanford. It was located one hour north of Trinity nested against the Columbia and Saddle Mountains. Trinity had the same layout, same purpose as Hanford, but with staggering layers of security and a complete lack of regulation. For example, the Department of Energy controlled Hanford while the mysterious DOP operated Trinity for over fifty years. The DOP, appropriately named after the Greek God of Fear, was set up to run domestic nuclear black ops sites during the Cold War but got shuttered in the late 1990s. It was only after a massive wildfire in 2015 that the press and watchdogs began to inquire about the collapsed tunnels and deceased remediation workers. It was rumored that for every drop of nuclear waste at Hanford there was an ocean of it at Trinity. After recent lawsuits the DOP relented, allowing waves of contractors and nuclear clean-up workers to try to patch up their deteriorating infrastructure. A corner of Trinity served as a military and civilian tactical training site. Washington, with its luscious western forests and ocean access, Cascade mountain range, and tech-savvy Seattle, still housed enough atomic poison to wipe out entire generations of the West Coast.

"Back up! Give them room!" a man in a white coat shrieked at the enlarging crowd. Several workers were dry heaving and one seemed to be hyperventilating.

Agent Kelso stood thirty feet away near some water tanks with mutated fish. Her dark brunette hair, tied in a ponytail through a U.S. Fish & Wildlife Hat, swung back and forth as she muttered to herself.

Sent to check out a creepy new type of salmon. Send the new girl to the nuclear site while others get to hang out in the Cascades hunting poachers. Now this.

"I'm going to check it out. I'll be right back," Agent Kelso told her DOP handler at the salmon tank. She zipped up her windbreaker and took off her sunglasses as the wind picked up. Sirens whined closer as an emergency medical service unit and Trinity police patrol jeep sprinted towards the area.

"Is it another vapor leak? They gotta clean that shit up, man. We aren't paid enough for that shit," a remediation worker snapped while holding one of the dry-heaving laborers.

"Fucking Trinity, just a year ago or so the goddamn underground tunnel collapsed. I knew this job was bullshit. I'm calling my union!" a man yelled at the Trinity DOP workers nearby. His supervisor mouthed 'shut the fuck up.'

Agent Kelso felt the sun beat down off the mountains in the distance. Inside her pocket she felt her cell phone vibrate. She knew it was her cousin texting updates from the races. This weekend was the boat races for the local areas of Richland, Pasco, and Kennewick, known as the Washington Tri-Cities. The cities soak in over three hundred days of sunshine amid a confluence of three rivers seated in the beautiful Columbia River Basin. Trinity, in contrast, was a concrete necropolis where clumps of workers like the ones screaming now worked in tandem to help clean, recapture, and one day move nuclear sludge from leaking tanks to newer tanks. With its northern rows of dead reactors and these two central tank farms it resembled a concrete cemetery with long stretches of desert roads between federal labs. Agent Kelso didn't want to know about the joy her cousin was having, mere miles away, on a beach watching boats and drinking. Sirens started to get much louder, replacing her drifting thoughts.

"Someone call a real ambulance. I don't trust Trinity with their medical quacks!"

"We signed a contract. If we get hurt they'll pay for it. You got insurance?"

Everyone continued to argue. Agent Kelso debated backing away so she didn't get caught up in the drama. She was just a guest to the DOP and facility. A mere check and report mission as part of her first six months on the job. She was still a probationary federal employee, subject to being fired anytime for any reason. She took this job to help pay for her grandfather's cancer treatments. Also, the past few years had become an endless fog. She hadn't found her place yet in life. College was working dead end jobs to finishing classes in a major that was forgettable. Her plans to serve in the military were thwarted by her doctor's concerns about her scoliosis. She escaped to working on some Alaskan commercial fishing boats, she liked the long hours and tough conditions. The crashing waves, strange crewmates, and travel gave her a quiet sense of peace away from home. Once her grandfather's cancer returned, she returned to care for him and find a gig. U.S. Fish and Wildlife waived any concerns of her back issues and she was half a year into learning how to best protect animals, preserve fishing rules, and feel out if it was a fit for her.

"Get your goddamn hands off me. I feel like the sun just took a shit on me!"

A pushing match began between the remediation workers and some DOP staff telling them to calm down. Agent Kelso used this as a chance to get close to the dig area. She had to know what triggered this whole situation. A terrified remediation worker sat silent against a concrete wall. His hands were shaking. Agent Kelso smiled at him and told him it will be ok in Spanish. He feigned a nod and looked down at his feet. The sun was setting, and it reflected against Agent Kelso's badge, installing curiosity in onlookers.

"Hey, you Trinity Patrol? Get this guy some help!" a worker barked at her.

Agent Kelso pivoted and nodded, leaning down to try to help another worker hyperventilating, and began to calm his breathing. In total, there were at least twenty workers and a crowd of forty assembled. It seemed to be a mix of scientists, environmental consultants, project managers, and frazzled construction workers. Someone took a double take on her badge.

"Hey! You aren't Trinity, you're...U.S. Fish and Wildlife? Are you even a cop?"

Agent Kelso chuckled. Months in, she was getting used to these jokes. "Yes, I am a federal special agent. I was working evaluating the salmon, over by Tank G when I heard the screams. EMS is arriving now, Trinity Patrol is behind them. You guys ok?"

Most of the guys nodded, but people were whispering and pointing beyond the hump of dirt into a pit. Outside of this central area, called 200 West, there was a huge nuclear storage tank and about a football field to the right was the area appropriately named 200 East. Both of these areas were trouble zones for Trinity nuclear waste reclamation. As the Trinity Patrol officers got out of their jeep Agent Kelso peered over the dirt mound adjacent to the 200 West Tank. She leaned forward to see, hoping she didn't catch the newest wave of radioactive vapors. What she saw made her gasp.

Carcasses. A mass grave of animal carcasses. Some were mummified, some seemed recent, piled across a basketball court sized area. The smell hit her. It was a mix of chemical solvents of extreme depths and delayed flesh rot. She felt her lungs seize up. Agent Kelso began to choke, coughing to get breaths.

Chapter 2

A PATROL OFFICER PULLED Agent Kelso back as she collected herself between coughs.

"Hey lady, what the hell are you doing? Where's your credentials? Get back with the scientists."

She flashed her badge. He seemed uncharmed behind his silver sunglasses. Sweat draped his military-cut short hair. His stocky partner was pushing back the other edges of the crowd yelling for disbursement.

"Officer?" Agent Kelso asked.

"Townsend."

"Special Agent, Alex Kelso. U.S. Fish and Wildlife," she replied.

"Great, why are you here?"

Agent Kelso explained that she was called out to identify a strange species of salmon that was discovered a few days ago by workers. Usually animals just die, they don't mutate right away or even within one generation. The salmon were taking on sizes and aggressive behaviors not observed in nature. She gave

Townsend her temporary DOP Trinity ID number. He told her to stay put as he ran it and continued to secure the scene.

"This shit ain't right man, I'm whistleblowing all of you!" a worker yelled as he was escorted from the area. A medical transport van had arrived for the affected workers. Out here, the slightest injury or breathing issue could mean a day off or death within a week.

Fifteen minutes later Officer Townsend returned and nodded at Agent Kelso. His partner, Officer Kennedy, joined him. Both had about a decade or more on Agent Kelso, in their late 30s with pudgy builds and a cold demeanor. Townsend had a poorly kept goatee.

"Well, you check out. Good news bad news." Townsend said.

Uh oh.

"Bad news is that your salmon case is deprioritized and DOP would like you to help us identify, classify, and close out this animal pit," Townsend stated to Agent Kelso. Back up officers had arrived. The crowd had dispersed into only a handful of remaining nuclear cops, emergency incident responders, and one protesting remediation worker being dragged out of the area.

"I'm going to have to check with my chain of command," Agent Kelso replied.

"Copy that. We have DOP and your regional Fish & Wildlife supervisor on the line now. They'll clarify. I'll get some tape up and will radio in a secured perimeter with some equipment. You'll need personal protective equipment and hazmat suit. We don't know how old these animal carcasses are or what is on them."

Townsend handed off his work phone to Agent Kelso. He turned back to Officer Kennedy and they began to shout into their radios. Back up patrol vehicles began to arrive as a leery Agent Kelso took the cell phone. Someone in a white coat was already handing Kelso some Area 51-looking garb to put on. She waved it away as she put the phone to her ear.

"Special Agent Kelso, this is Ron Ames, I'm the acting DOP Trinity incident commander for this situation here at Trinity. We are sorry you are involved, but we appreciate you and your agency's resources as we contain this matter. We'll get you anything you need, we just need tight angles on this. Wrong hands, wrong angle and the press could set us back a century on clean-up. God knows the Tri-Cities doesn't want that. Nor does the President, we are heading into mid-term elections."

President? There's no way in hell anyone on Pennsylvania Ave. cares about this. Not yet. I'm already stressed about my job, now this.

"Kelso, this is Commander Stevenson, I spoke with your field supervisor. Drop the salmon thing for now. You can double back on that after you assist with damage controlling this discovery for Trinity. What is it that we are dealing with? Anything to share with us?"

Agent Kelso stammered. Lack of tenure, experience, and any concept of the shitshow she just entered was apparent.

"Agent Kelso?" her second line boss, whom she had met for only seconds at her induction ceremony, asked again. His tone had grown sharper.

"Sorry sir, negative for now. Let me get another visual. I'm on it."

She threw her hands up at Townsend and Kennedy who were watching her. She walked back to the dirt pit. She held her phone and stared down at the clumps of various things. "I'm guessing animal carcasses. Some fresh, some old. I can make out possibly a few species: dogs, cats, turtles, maybe horses and some reptiles, maybe lizards? Some of these things are just chunks of bones and vestiges of flesh, sir. No idea on numbers. Could be a thousand, could be thousands. It's a massive grave, easily 300 feet wide and who knows how deep. Mr. Ames, since you are DOP maybe you can help out, what is this?"

Silence permeated the call for ten seconds. In the distance sirens rang out.

"This isn't to end up in your report or anyone in my staff, all I want is classification and quantity of what you find, understood?" the DOP commander stated. It was less of a suggestion and more of a career-ending directive if Agent Kelso disobeyed.

She agreed and asked again what she was staring at in that pit.

"Biological species impact studies. Before my time, but no different than World War II experiments to find out what conditions soldiers can endure to help prep them for battle. I'm still being debriefed, but in a program that has been terminated, the federal government exposed various animal species to plutonium to assess impact and survival rates. Given nuclear war is the future, we don't want to guess on this type of thing. Unlike the Germans or Japanese, we did not use humans, just animals."

Agent Kelso tilted her head at the incredibility of the swag of his statements. She realized he had also shown a card.

"Sir, what kind of species are in here?"

"Everything you named, domestic, foreign, zoo, and even an alligator or two. One got loose way back in the 90s, they had to chase, catch, and shut down the press on that one. Not too many alligators in the eastern Washington desert obviously."

"Yeah, so then everything I'm about to exhume and identify...has unknown quantities of radioactive waste and contagion on it?"

"That's why our DOP staff are here to help you. We have workers cleaning tanks full of the nastiest stuff in the western hemisphere and don't skip a beat. These are mere dead animals with some light frosting. If you aren't up for it then let it be known now Agent Kelso. Stevenson, you got someone else you can send within the hour?"

"Table that Ames. Look Kelso, I realize this is a lot to ask, but work this right and we might get you that Cascades field office position. Lots of impact on people hunting and protecting the remaining species out there. Who wouldn't doesn't like to hang out in the mountains and play tag with Bigfoot hunters?" Commander Stevenson lightened the tone. His manipulation was blatant, but he didn't seem to care. Beltway politics at its finest was on display.

Agent Kelso took a long look past the tanks. She could see the hollowed-out Trinity worker cafeteria in the distance. The Columbia River glistened against the dying embers of final sunlight. Fishing and protecting animals was part of her ancestral heritage clawing back thousands of years. She also came from a family of veterans, from World War II all the way to Operation Enduring Freedom. Service, to her family, tribe, and nation meant taking chances. This job provided benefits that helped her grandfather, sister, and her adorable niece Tia. This wasn't just about her, as much as she wanted to walk away from an invite to play in viciously toxic sludge.

So be it. This one is for the family.

Agent Kelso agreed to the case and thanked them both. They wanted a report within twenty-four hours, ideally twelve by the time they woke up tomorrow. Another agent was en route from the Seattle office to assist her. This was to be handled with highest security clearance. She motioned at Officer Townsend and handed the phone back to him. She grimaced and took the Area 51 nuclear costume. Townsend smiled.

"A DOP extraction team will come to close this out. We just need to double check there's no major leaks, you I.D. the animal mummies, and then we tarp this shut until that team arrives. We do this right, first round is on me at the Boat Race festival late tonight."

Officer Kennedy chimed in, “she’s a girl scout, I bet she doesn’t even drink.”

“I’ll be drinking through a tube if that shit gets on me,” Agent Kelso pointed at the raspberry and black water floating around the corners of the carcass pit.

“Keep your suit tighter than a condom on prom night,” Officer Kennedy yelled as helicopters bellowed in the distance. Townsend cracked up while Kelso took another long look at both officers and three other DOP workers.

“Kelso, none of this shit will kill you for like thirty years. Who wants to live forever?”

Agent Kelso cussed under her breath and suited up as nightfall began its descent.

Chapter 3

THIRTY LONG MINUTES LATER Agent Kelso was lowered into the pit by crane. Sides of the dirt pit were too wet and too deep to climb without the risk of collapse. The radiation suit felt like a suffocating blanket. She wished it had made her feel less terrified of the galactic levels of radiation she was about to handle in these carcasses. At least the god-awful smell was gone due to the respirator and layers of clothing.

Townsend and Kennedy were already in the pit scanning the southern perimeter. Two DOP workers were dipping their instruments into a corner of colorful goo. Due to the density of the carcasses, no one had made it to the northern point of this giant pit. It would require using some of their shovels and possibly the crane to knock some carcasses over for access. Agent Kelso reminded herself the goal was to identify the species, quantify how many were there, and write a report on it. *Touch as little as possible and get out.* A crew of tank cleaners were only hours out with construction equipment to physically remove the carcasses into a secured double-shelled tanker. In the far distance there was gunfire from the tactical training facility next to the Trinity police base.

"Any soil contamination, Kennedy?" Officer Townsend asked.

"How the fuck should I know? I'm a grunt not a scientist," Kennedy snapped.

The two DOP workers looked up and stated it would take more time to get a reading. Agent Kelso waved over Townsend and Kennedy to come help her.

"Whatcha got? Want me to rip some chunks off and make us some street tacos?"

Townsend elbowed Kennedy to shut up.

"Close, actually. Could you two beefcakes use those shovels to trench out a little alley so we can make it to the northern point. That way I can estimate numbers by row to make this quicker," Agent Kelso asked. They obliged and began to clank and thud shovels into the dead.

Agent Kelso began to see the bones and head carcasses of several cows, sheep, and pigs. Their bodies had whittled away, but the flesh around their heads had solidified against their skulls.

"Yeah, they used to have an animal farm out here from like 1950-1990 I think," Kennedy said between shovel loads. "Had to know what would happen if Stalin dropped the Tsar Bomba on us."

"Now it's North Korea. Guess nothing changes," Townsend offered while digging between two dog skeletons. The dead animals were scattered with manure making it harder to discern where one animal ended or another began. Due to the mixture of dried-up old carcasses and wettened newer ones, the officers made headway to within fifteen feet of the northern end of the pit. Already Agent Kelso had estimated at least a thousand animals were within the first rows.

"Look over there, that's a different species," Agent Kelso pointed at the most northern point near their current alleyway of death. She saw a strange assembly of bones and tail. She motioned for them to pause shoveling. She pointed at the greenish clump in front of them. It appeared to be the remains of a rather large alligator or reptile of some sort. It was a carcass bigger than anything she had seen except on those sketchy tv shows.

Hisssssss.

"What the hell?" Kennedy yelled. They had all heard a hiss from behind them. As Agent Kelso turned, she saw more movement under the dirty carcasses coming towards them. Dirt began to crumble and a black and green body appeared for a second. There was no time to react.

"Ahh!" Townsend screamed as he was dragged behind the northern stack of carcasses. Kelso, Kennedy, and the confused DOP workers couldn't even see what had taken Townsend. They heard Townsend release agonizing yelps and then saw his hands reach out past a column of dead animals. Instinctively, Agent Kelso and Officer Kennedy ran and tried to grab Townsend's hands. A strange wheezing sound like an air vent came from behind his hands and deep inside the northern pit wall. Both the sound and Townsend fully disappeared into the northern pit wall. The force of the exit was causing more dirt to cave into the area.

Agent Kelso grabbed a shovel and directed a DOP worker to start digging near the northern wall. Kennedy got on his radio to bark orders for help.

"We have a 30-20, repeat 30-20, something just took Townsend, we need help!" Kennedy yelled while realizing none of them were armed in radiation suits. He then began to take a shovel and hit it against the northwestern wall looking for clues.

"Oh. UGH. Help me! It's eating me!"

They could hear but not see Townsend. Agent Kelso swung her shovel against one part of the northern wall, it left her hands and fell into blackness.

Without pausing, Kennedy dove into the new hole in the northern wall. He reappeared seconds later.

"It's a fucking tunnel, those goddamn Pumex tunnels that kept collapsing years ago. I thought they filled these fuckers with cement. Someone get me a flashlight and a gun. I'm finding Townsend. He's not here, but maybe he fell and is down this tunnel."

"Tunnels?" Agent Kelso asked.

The two DOP workers looked at each other and said nothing. They began to get onto the crane to get out of the pit. Agent Kelso threw them a glare.

"Cowards, at least throw me a fucking flashlight," she yelled at them. They rummaged through the truck and threw one to her. She handed it to Kennedy through black gooey mud and told him the DOP workers were bailing on them. She offered to retrieve his gun, but he declined stating they didn't have time.

"I'm taking your shovel and finding my fucking partner. I'll beat whatever is down here to death before I wait for back-up. Meet me at the next opening for this tunnel."

Kennedy clicked on the flashlight exposing a tunnel that resembled a 20th century underground subway tunnel. Concrete and rusted metal walls lined an unending darkness ahead of him. Kennedy explained how this tunnel might connect their 200 West tank area with the also large 200 East tank area about a mile away. He took off running into the dark.

Agent Kelso took advantage of the caved in northern wall and began to crawl out of the pit. She fell several times but was able to pull herself out as three Trinity patrol jeeps pulled up. Even though it was likely that Townsend was dead, Agent Kelso couldn't let Kennedy stumble in the dark alone.

"Kennedy's in the tunnel. Two of you head down there and bring that rifle with you. Something has Townsend. It is hostile and presume it is predatory. I'm heading to the 200 East Tank, someone lead the way. Let's go, right now!" Agent Kelso yelled as she hopped into Kennedy's jeep. At least three Trinity Patrol officers slid down into the pit knocking over towers of carcasses.

Chapter 4

As Agent Kelso floored the jeep to its maximum speed, she put her phone in the center console. Within seconds she had gotten her boss on the line. He was pissed and eating dinner with his wife. Agent Kelso had to repeat herself three times before he stepped away to get Commander Ames on the line. Workers shouted at her as she and the entire three jeep convoy barreled past a worksite almost hitting workers taking a break. She could make out the 200 East Tank. She told Ames and her boss they had sixty seconds before she was hopping out and into whatever secret tunnel lies underneath them. Time was not on Townsend or Kennedy's side.

"Kelso stand down. DOP is on it," Ames barked.

"On it? Sounds like you have a goddamn gator loose and didn't tell my people or your own. Kelso, find that animal and put it down," Commander Stevenson replied at Ames.

The two authorities continued to argue as the darkness of the evening set into the horizon. A wall of white DOP trucks descended onto the old pit area in Kelso's rear mirror. Two Trinity police jeeps drove ahead of Kelso guiding her into the darkness of 200 East Nuclear Tank Zone. They had ten seconds left to sort out their issues on the phone. Ames was barking when he let loose with the intel.

"There's no gator. The animals we've been testing recently were completely farm domestics and nothing that can yank an adult officer. Are we sure this guy didn't fall into a hole? Those underground tunnels are full of metal. Some tunnels even lead to the Columbia River. Alert a boat crew to search for his body there," Ames said.

"Ames, are you telling me that DOP sent one of my wildlife officers into a pit that had recent animal testing?" Commander Stevenson snapped.

"Prior to this incident you didn't have clearance to know. Look Kelso, just contain this situation. You are Fish and Wildlife. If this is some rogue animal then fucking kill it. Isn't that your job?"

"Check your tone Ames!" Commander Stevenson bellowed into the phone. Kelso had arrived at 200 East Tanker.

"Alright, I gotta go. I'll try to find Townsend while neutralizing the threat. If I can contain the animal I will, if not I'll kill it. Update upon action."

Agent Kelso hopped out of the Jeep. The Trinity Patrol Officers told her no one had used this pit for a week or two. The nuclear remediation double shell concrete crew was running behind schedule on movement of the sludge. Scanning the scene nothing looked off and she hesitated to get into the tarped pit.

At least it had a metal stepladder for ease of entry and exit. Wind made the tarp flap.

"I know this is your facility so you can take tactical lead. Commander Ames wants us to find Townsend and neutralize any threat if it's biological," Agent Kelso said to the officers. Their faces tensed up.

"So far our team out in 200 West and that tunnel have found nothing."

"I'm sorry, I hope we can find Townsend and get him some help. Maybe he fell into some gross radioactive river."

Agent Kelso was doing her best to conceal, from her mind, the guttural screams and moans she heard minutes ago at the first pit. Working lethal animal attacks she knew the odds were not on their side. Someone had to conjure hope amid the weird situation.

After three officers yanked the tarp over the basketball field sized pit everyone took a pause and then descended. All five of them hustled down the ladder. Agent Kelso had tossed her PPE suit in order to have access to her service weapon.

One of the patrol officers yelled as he pointed down into the pit's eastern corner. Townsend's arm was quickly being dragged down along another dirt corridor in the pit. Two officers hopped down and the arm paused, turned, and a pair of fangs popped up.

Oh shit.

They began to fire at the fangs as Agent Kelso yelled to wait. No one knew if Townsend was still alive somewhere. No one listened to Agent Kelso as the officers all began to shoot.

She watched as a pair of jaws emerged from the dirt and snapped Officer Kennedy in two with one bite. Blood squirted all over the other officer as Agent Kelso, lost in terror of the situation, began to fire above the mouth of this monster. Kennedy was quickly pulled into its abyss of a mouth. Two officers behind her pulled out their shotguns and fired into its mouth. It did little to stop the Trinity monster as it took apart the other officer in three lightning-fast snaps of a metropolis of razor-sharp teeth.

Among the screams and shots a massive serpent-like head came out of the dirt. As it raised itself, it stood forty feet with blue reptilian scales adorning its sides. There were at least six rows of blood-soaked teeth. Chunks of its recent prey clung to its jaws as it hissed out strange triangular nose holes. Side fangs punched out of the side of its open mouth. Without eyes it lacked any form of social negotiation between human and predator. Razor sharp spires ribbed the end of its tail.

"What. The. Fuck?" a DOP Patrolman screamed.

Without a face the monster looked like a cross between a crocodile, serpent, and parasitic hookworm. Just one the size of a school bus with teeth like ten great white sharks. It snapped downwards at Agent Kelso but was met with shotgun blasts from the patrol officers. Three more officers had arrived and were firing into the beast's cavern of a mouth above them atop the pit. It wheezed and twisted in momentary agony but did not seem fazed. It blasted downwards into the ground and they felt the ground move as it took off towards an unknown northern direction underground.

Agent Kelso crawled back out of the tank pit onto dry solid ground. One officer hovered with a gun aimed at the hole where the monster last was observed. The radio crackled that the tunnel team heard movement but couldn't make out what had just passed them. Agent Kelso laid on her back as officers climbed down into the pit to help their injured. A few cussed and refused to get into the death pit. Everyone had questions and no one had answers.

"What in the fuck is going on out here? Anyone seen that before?" Kelso asked. By the officer's shouts and blank stares she knew they had lost their sense of control on the situation same as her.

"Titanoboa?"

"This can't be happening. I took this job to get into the State Patrol. They said nothing happens out here but pranksters and reporters trying to sneak in for a story."

"Shift Lieutenant said at least ten remediation workers had gone missing this past year but no one had details. Figured they got a better gig and hauled ass. Had no fucking idea we were food for an anaconda."

Kelso was getting no real answers from this group. They were rattled and looking to her for input. One officer was shaking and another was compensating by talking loudly. Kelso chimed in as she re-dialed the number to the federal authorities.

"Negative, this is at least double the size of any known species and the Titanoboa has been extinct for millions of years. Also, that thing had no eyes, all the snakes you are talking about tend to have some form of eyes. Whatever that is, it has been feeding off your animal testing areas for some time. Maybe even decades. Something like that doesn't grow fast. What is north of us?" Kelso asked the shocked DOP patrol crew.

She huffed as she got Commander Ames' voicemail on her phone.

"Nothing for like five minutes then you hit the 100 Areas," a sweating officer said.

"Ok, and that is?" Kelso asked.

"Sorry, ah, it is the reactor areas. Old northern tip of the nuclear site near the Columbia."

"The Columbia River? You mean this thing has free access to a river that has contact with eleven million people?" Agent Kelso asked.

"Nah. Those reactors are walled off from the river since like the 1980s. Plus, wouldn't it have left already if it could escape?" the officer replied.

The radio cackled. The team had cleared the west to east tunnels. Nothing. According to the patrol, the tunnels were shaped in a giant upside-down T. The bottom of the T was an east-west underground top secret tunnel to 200 East and 200 West nuclear tanks. The single north tunnel led from these tank farms up to the old reactors. There was a large entrance at the north sites for railcars in the 1960s.

"Commander Ames isn't picking up. Alert your chain of command. We need to flush this thing out somewhere in that northern tunnel. People are dying. No time for bureaucratic protocol. I know you people like to keep this stuff hush hush but its evacuation time except for us, your security team, and emergency personnel. All other civilians on site need to haul ass. Let's head to 100 Area and figure out a plan. Oh and for god sakes get more firepower into that tunnel," Kelso stated as she hopped into the passenger side of a patrol jeep.

As a youth, Kelso had been taken under by her Grandpa Silas, a military veteran on how to operate under stress. He shared everything he could with her about tactical awareness and survivalism with hopes of her becoming a Marine. Even though her medical status ended that dream, his training was paying off as she found herself pushed into informal lead of this rescue mission.

Within a minute a loud alarm, like those for tornados in the Midwest, rang out across the Trinity site. The evacuation code was being radioed site-wide and thousands of employees began to rush to their keys, bags, and cars. Kelso and her five-man crew were headed in the opposite direction, right into a nuclear demon's path.

Chapter 5

THEY PASSED AMBULANCES AND other patrol vehicles swarming the kill sites for Townsend, Kennedy, and the maimed patrol workers. Shift Lt. Colfax gave them an update that the military tactical training facility had a National Guard squad doing some drills. He didn't get official clearance through the bureaucracy but was sending them to assist with his team playing lead due to ongoing threat to human life. He warned that if this goes wrong these soldiers are acting on their own and is not an official operation of the DOP.

"Copy that sir," the officer responded. Kelso stared at the haunting but beautiful rolling golden hills surrounding the Trinity site. They took a more menacing shadow on the site now that the sun had disappeared. Houses in the far distance reminded her of the stories of the downwinders, those civilians who just happened to live downwind of this radioactive site and its mysterious vapors. She had grown up reading the media spin campaign to repeatedly remind people how the nuclear arms race helped finance the rise of this region both in population and commerce. Kelso's uncle even worked out here some years ago, joining the nine thousand plus that turned this federal-state perpetual cleanup program into a policy swamp. One that was apparently feeding a reptilian demon for decades through strange animal experiments and government coverups on worker deaths.

Ambulances and swarms of workers were cobbled at where Townsend was slaughtered a mile away. Little did they know what was sprinting underneath the ground.

Kelso's phone began to vibrate. It was her boss, Commander Stevenson.

"Kelso, are you ok? What is your status? Full disclosure, I have Commander Ames, a Pentagon rep, and liaison to the White House. We're getting very confused at what is unfolding there and why you aren't standing down? This isn't a Fish and Wildlife matter. Let DOP handle it. Their house their crew."

Kelso gulped and stared at the darkened skyline. A career born and killed in less than a few months. Least she'd have one hell of a story at her next job interview.

"Emerging situation, sir. Five dead. Threat ongoing and not sure what it is."

A bunch of people spoke at once on the conference line leading to static.

"Sorry guys but I can barely hear you. Signal is weak out here and we are hitting the reactor area. Some unknown Jurassic sized serpent creature has been living on-site feeding off your DOP animal experiments. Gunfire stuns it but doesn't seem to be enough yet to kill it. Commander Ames, how is it moving so fast between sectors? I thought all these areas were all sealed up but-for the radiation tanks? Wasn't that in the press last year?"

There was a long pause on the phone. DOP Commander Ames put up a fight he quickly lost about security clearances. The Pentagon and White House liaison commanded answers. Ames explained how there are still tunnels, called Pumex tunnels, where both nuclear waste and classified ongoing experiments were transported from tank to reactor and sometimes to railcar or river access past their alleged closure. Due to some tunnel collapses back in 2016 they had begun to block some tunnels with concrete but the ones leading to the 100 North area were still open, used, and lead to the Columbia River reactor. It was sealed with a steel gate but there were six separate reactors each adjoining the river. So if it got loose or through a gate, it had access to surface and lethal freedom.

"So this thing could or has been slithering across the central-northern chunks of your facility feasting on your workers and no one saw it? Is that what you are saying?" Agent Kelso asked.

According to Ames, the DOP tactical team did a sweep six months ago and found nothing but some old dead animals that they figured had fallen off the experiment cart. Trinity Patrol Chief joined the line and offered his rage into the conversation. It was his men that were dead. Quickly the debate centered around unleashing firepower on it versus capturing it for scientific study.

This monster's ability to not only withstand but grow in deadly radiation sludge held Pentagon interest for nuclear war preparations. A loud argument erupted.

"Why don't we just finish DOP's job?" Kelso offered amid the shouting and political angling. Ames snapped at Kelso what she meant.

"Look, at some point, you were using industrial quick drying cement to seal up these tunnels to protect workers, right? So just whip up every free hand you can find and every drop of cement and literally trap it in cement. It's in a tunnel right now. Why have us stalk the night for it to kill us all when we can just flood the tunnels with cement?"

"Kelso, this isn't a sci-fi movie. It is cement not magical elixir. It won't set immediately and do you know how much cement would be needed to cover the entire gauntlet of that northern tunnel?" Ames replied.

"It is an animal, so normal concepts still apply. Like maybe we place teams at the ends of each tunnel to pin the monster until cement fills up. Gunfire won't kill it but it travels like a snake so once the cement starts affixing it might slow it down for kill shots. I'm open to other suggestions. Recall I'm trained to issue fishing violation tickets, so if you all have something else?" Kelso snapped.

More arguing commenced, rebutting Kelso's idea.

"How are we going to encase an area the size of three football fields in concrete?"

"Do you know what kind of security clearance you need to even go in those tunnels?"

Various voices continued to trample Kelso's suggestion until a booming voice intervened.

"We are entering mid-terms. I can't have a walking nuclear monster taking out any civilians. Do what it takes and keep it quiet," the liaison for the white house stated.

"Given its desire for more food and eating habits, Ames are there any more animals located on site?" Agent Kelso asked Commander Ames. This thing could be drawn by its hunger. Each showdown in each pit gave it some food, but it was burning up energy it would have to replace one way or another.

An eternity of seconds passed in silence. Ames hissed out that there is a crate of dogs from a local shelter at 100-H reactor area arriving today for experiments.

What a creep. He knew this entire time. A box of poor dogs traded from one shelter into a dungeon of radioactive torture. Wouldn't mind tossing this monster Ames' address.

The Trinity Police Chief launched into battle plan mode.

"I'll have my people and their reinforcements start in the tunnels down near the 200 Tank Farms where you all last saw it and ensure it is pushed into the 100 H area. In the meantime Ames, get Trident Construction and whoever is left to get that industrial concrete equipment to that tunnel. Have them debrief patrol on how to do it."

"Since when does Trinity Patrol tell DOP how to operate? I understand you lost men, but I lose workers each year. Doesn't change chain of command," Ames stated.

Agent Kelso turned and looked at the patrol officer driving the jeep. With the call on speaker phone he heard this and almost swerved in hatred. He released a glare at the phone. The phone almost rattled as Agent Kelso's boss chimed in.

"Ames, since you created a fucking nuclear slaughterhouse, walking my new special agent and DOP Security's men into a goddamn dinner platter for a snake-monster! Not to mention your nuclear monster feeds on puppies and god knows what else you have running in those tunnels. Also if that thing breaches the 100 reactor area you will have unleashed not only a mass murdering monster, but enough radiation to kill millions who drink from that fucking river. Help us now or we skip the teamwork and I call the FBI right now."

The jeep next to us swerved as they snickered in quiet laughter listening to the top guy get verbally charred. The laughs were cut short as they arrived into the 100 area for the reactors. The seriousness of the near future hit everyone in the jeeps. This thing could be anywhere beneath them.

"We're here. I'm gonna head down into the entrance area of 100-H to await reinforcements and the concrete crew. Also, there's no way I'm leaving those poor dogs along with whoever their handlers are for DOP down there. Any updates, just let

Chief know. He has our radio channel. Hope this thing is cemented within the next hour or two. Kelso over and out."

Kelso clicked off the conference call and was handed a Trinity patrol radio. It allowed her to be in contact with both the patrol and any emergency security staff who know these tunnels. Dust began to billow up as the evening winds blew rattling off the rugged hills around them. Metal chain link fences creaked and waned.

"Concrete encasement team is en route. We got fifty guys already in 200-East Tunnels. They said it's clear so far. They even grabbed a flamethrower from our supply room."

"Flamethrower? Between the fumes and the chemicals is that really...fuck it," Kelso sighed. Policy, rules, and safety were barriers the situation had careened over. It was doomsday evasion time.

"Let's go. Trinity Patrol feel free to play point. Anything goes to save the river, people, and especially those poor dogs."

Chapter 6

THE TEAM OF TEN entered the 100-H reactor building where they immediately descended into a labyrinth of metal tanks, corroded valves, and meters in disrepair. Emergency lighting along with red wall lights gave an ominous gloom to the complex. The five lead patrol officers led Agent Kelso through a series of steel and heavily fortified gates. Each passing gate made her feel less secure given the direction they were headed. Once they got to the bottom platform where the Pumex tunnels began they radioed all clear for the construction crew to enter. The plan was to find where this tunnel ended, get the dogs out, and lock it down as cement clogged up both ends of the tunnel trapping the radioactive beast.

They heard the dogs barking behind them to the left of the platform. They also heard the whooshing of the Columbia River a mere hundred or so feet away separated by the concrete and soil.

"I see the dogs. About five; three black, two brown and... about five kittens?"

The radio cackled back at the patrol officer. A large crate of whimpering and barking dogs sat ten by ten on a railcar on the tracks. Some kittens meowed and licked one of the officers' hands as she petted them. Six others kept their AR-15s aimed at the darkness behind them facing 200 East sector. The glow from the lighting kept everyone on edge. Visibility was limited.

"Kelso, come over here and help us pull this crate back towards that freight elevator."

Agent Kelso glanced and saw that this subway railway ended at a yellow wall with a gray and blue freight elevator. It was dated, but had a thick and seemingly new security door with card access. To the right, and at the beginning of the entrance of the massive and dark 100 North tunnel, the patrol officers dropped glowsticks. Kelso began to push the crate railcar with four others. One black Labrador barked at them with a viciousness that signaled something was afoot- the type of barking reserved for real threats.

As the team of five pulled the animal crate off the railcar and pushed it into the corner of the elevator, they realized there was no way to make the elevator operate. It was a dual-security system where someone had to swipe and press their card inside the elevator and someone in a Trinity control room had to authorize the movement. As a patrolman began to radio for elevator power, a shadow jogged across the far wall.

"Freeze! Trinity Patrol, identify yourself."

"Whoa, don't shoot, it's me, Randall Reed. 200 West Experiments."

A man using his cell phone as a flashlight waved at them. He was one hundred feet out walking towards them. He wore a jean jacket with a Trinity ID card. He had a ponytail and glasses. The officers lowered their weapons and waved him to approach.

"What's with all the guns, man? Some earthquake drill or active shooter training?" Randall yelled at the officers.

Sgt. Colfax shook his head. "Negative, we have an active biological threat, five dead and we are here to contain it. Get over here."

Randall scrunched his face. He stopped in the dark train corridor. It curved beyond him. Sgt. Colfax kept motioning with his hands. Everyone wanted Randall out of their line of fire and sight.

"Well, I don't know about that but I heard some strange squirting sounds on the other end of this tunnel. Figured might be some fluid leak so hauled ass. So is this why those dickheads cut the power on my elevator? How am I supposed to get the subjects to experiment now?"

"Yeah about that...experiment is cancelled. Are you telling me you already made it down to the next sector, 200 East, and back?" Agent Kelso spoke up as the dogs yipped inside the elevator.

"Yep. Like I said, I heard some hissing-"

Agent Kelso shot a nervous glance at Sgt. Colfax. Several officers turned towards the darkness behind Randall.

"Squirting sounds, like concrete being poured or hissing? Be real fucking clear," Sgt. Colfax snapped.

Everyone paused pivoting towards Randall. It was so quiet that only the sound of the Columbia and breaths could be heard. Randall shrugged his shoulders and rolled his eyes.

"Hissing, whooshing, whatever. Fellas, in these secured tunnels there's a 'threat' every week. Now who is going to help me—"

Before he could finish his sentence the serpent had slammed its maze of razor wire teeth into Randall. The impact separated Randall so fast he didn't even scream. His bottom torso careened down the train hallway knocking Agent Kelso down. It felt like someone had thrown a couch onto her. No one had even heard or seen the monster creep up on them.

Eight officers began to unload their rifles into the beast as it took a moment to swallow Randall downwards into its gastric system. One radioed for help and alerted that it was here.

"Fucking take that!"

"Come get some! Yeah baby"

The officers were reloading their weapons. The monster was bleeding from several wounds made from the blasts. It recoiled backwards towards the tunnel but one officer kept firing, approaching it.

"Fall back. Let it go and get stuck in the concrete on the other end. What are you doing?" Sgt. Colfax yelled. The officer ignored him, screaming that this was for Kennedy and Townsend. The monster turned around swinging out its barbed tail at the officer knocking him against the tunnel wall. He screamed out but kept shooting as gray cement dripped off his face. The other side of the tunnel was already slowly filling up with cement on the base level of the rail tracks. It was mere inches of still wet cement but it was a start.

Two officers tried to unpin the officer from the barbed tail, but he was gored like a bullfighter to a demon in the darkness. The serpent slid back into their area coiling into a corner as seven officers surrounded it firing. Agent Kelso aimed and caught the monster's tail with a direct shotgun blast which caused it to hiss. Her positioning on the ground was helpful to keeping a firmer aim than others. It also left her vulnerable.

"Kelso look out!"

It was too late. Kelso had taken a direct hit to her legs by the tail. It ripped through her flesh like an alligator bite. She crawled against the back corner wall by the elevator. The officer radioing for help caught the next tail swipe. The direct hit to his head sent his body pummeling into the elevator. The dogs were gnashing through the crate's corners. Randall's bottom corpse half lay beside her oozing blood. She could see the concrete accumulating below him in the railroad tracks already creating a soup that within hours would be a trap. No one had hours now. Seconds, at best, before death.

The monster swung its tail and despite its own wounds took out two officers by crushing their skulls with its tail spires. Five officers; one female and four males all drenched in sweat and dread, backed into a staircase that had the access door going upstairs. While one swiped his card, the four continued to shoot aiming for the monster's mouth since body shots only made it bleed. At least mouth shots made it pause before striking. They were panicking at each other.

"Get that fucking door open. I'm about to run out of ammo. All I have left are grenades."

"Got it, let's go!"

Kelso watched from across the giant room as the men took off upstairs. She had used part of Randall's shirt chunk to tie a knot above her wounds to cull the bleeding.

Fucking great. They left me to die here with Randall's legs and a crate of dogs. Assholes. Maybe suffocating in the concrete is better. Can't stand up. Fuck it.

Chapter 7

THE OFFICERS HAD JUST shut the stairwell door and the monster began to slam itself against it. She could hear the officers bellowing as they sprinted up the first flight of stairs. Kelso looked down in defeat and saw Randall's access badge. She also saw two of the tactical vests on two slain officers near him had grenades.

Ah fuck it. Worth a try. Rather die trying to fight than become a part of the Trinity buffet.

Kelso launched her plan into action. She looked up to see the Monster careen through the door to the stairs. She didn't focus on the screams or stairwell gun fight as she dragged her bloody legs across the floor snatching Randall's badge. She felt herself want to vomit as both adrenaline and searing pain coursed through her system. Pained screams and moans with some final rifle blasts from behind the bunker walls of the staircase signaled doom. The animals were bringing unwanted attention to Kelso's elevator area. She had to do it now.

She swiped the elevator badge and huddled in the far corner parallel to the animal crate. She cobbled together a small pile of grenades, her last shotgun shells, and proceeded to rack and load. The elevator begun to slowly close its heavy steel doors secured with some concrete-like resin. The noise, along with the eruptive barking from the dogs, became a doomsday clock.

Within seconds she saw the monster's head which, at this point, resembled a decapitated gunshot victim. Several of its teeth were missing as its tongue dribbled out in rotten purple bubblegum chunks. Kelso didn't hesitate and began to shoot her final shots at the monster, hoping to push it back as the elevator closed shut.

It wasn't working.

The monster was dying so it no longer retreated as it bled out of several areas of its mouth, sides, and tail. It just kept moving towards Kelso and the animals. The kittens were hissing and meowing. Kelso threw her shotgun at it and resorted to her fatalistic plan two.

Oh well. Least it will be quick.

She began to pull pins and throw grenades into its Glasgow smile mouth. Her goal was to at least take both of them out before she had to experience being eaten alive. She had pulled the pin and tossed at least four grenades into its mouth when she heard gunfire behind.

It turned its head away from Kelso and the elevator.

"Yeah bitch, fuck you. Trinity Patrol motherfucker!"

The aggressive officer that took a tail hit had come to and fired heavy shots into the monster's side. He gave the monster the middle finger as he ran out of ammo and pulled out a knife.

Kelso kept her eye on the elevator doors which were approaching full closure.

"Ahh, ugh..."

The monster had turned and sunk its fangs into the officer's head.

Oh shit. The grenades.

Kelso braced herself against the animal crate looking up as the as the elevator doors closed. The explosion was temporarily deafening given the concrete walls ricocheting sound. She could no longer hear the hiss. The monster's mid-section and most of its body had exploded from the inside. All that remained was a divorced tail and its jaw-laden head. It began to crawl using its billowing jaws towards the doors as they closed.

The elevator shook as the monster launched its jaws onto the elevator's exterior doors. She could see the damaged talon-fangs had pierced through the exterior door.

How is this thing still alive?

Just then the elevator sprung to life as they began to slowly ascend up to 100-H surface level. Someone at command had realized the error or the staircase guys had radioed it in before they were slaughtered. Either way the elevator was finally working.

Five long minutes later, the 100-H elevator doors opened to the evacuation team. Three paramedics, five patrol officers, and at least nine DOP agents took in the sight. Kelso was covered in blood, a crate of dogs and kittens sat next to her, while part of an officer's torso sat in the corner. Kelso began to laugh. Fatigue and delirium sunk deep into her soul. Her hands shook as she pulled up her badge.

"U.S. Fish and Wildlife. We killed your pet snake. I wouldn't take the stairs if I were you."

Chapter 8

A WEEK LATER AFTER battling a variety of infections and horrific radiation exposure screenings Agent Kelso had emerged from her hospital haze. One night after family visiting hours, Commander Stevenson stopped by her room.

"Good to see you back from the dead Kelso. How goes it?"

"Docs say I was exposed to more radiation than a reactor. Leg will survive. I'll be able to walk fine in a few, but they won't know my nuclear contact issues until I get older. Am I fired?"

Commander Stevenson closed the hospital door.

"We haven't been able to update you. That thing is dead. DOP got it encased in concrete. They found its head with jaws locked into your escape elevator doors. They're studying it like it's a crashed UFO. With nineteen dead you think folks would be more solemn, but they seem pretty giddy."

Agent Kelso shook her head.

"Well don't get too forlorn Kelso, Ames and everyone involved via DOP is being federally indicted. Someone leaked the story and cell phone pics to the press. They're fucked. Everyone in that crew is going down. Worse, you are going to be asked to testify in front of Congress about the ordeal and if your actions while heroic weren't vetted, authorized, nor proper for a probationary employee and lead to deaths. That is...unless..."

"Unless what?" Kelso eyed Stevenson. Behind him a game show was on where people compete by eating insects until they puke last. A man had just choked down a spider while his wife cheered him on.

"Washington State has a remarkable amount of strange cases of rogue wildlife, to say the least. We, and the joint multi-district federal team of agencies, would like you to take lead on looking into them and getting results. In exchange for helping unclog these kooky unsolved cases, the feds won't make you testify. Plus, after a year any post you want."

Kelso smiled for the first time in weeks.

"Are we talking, like that one tv show?"

"Not exactly. No alluring partner to charmingly debunk you, and there's no vast governmental alien conspiracy. Give or take douchebags like Ames. Mainly these are just random patterned sightings of strange things usually on some cell phone. Mostly it will be horribly reported animal or unknown creature cases that FBI and state-related stakeholders don't have resources to waste time on. Fighting cartels, terrorism, and domestic militia threats is the focus, understandably. Yours would be separating fact from fiction, and containing optics on strange stuff. Ninety nine percent of this will be the town loon but other times, like Trinity, you might find something that really does go bump in the night. If so, debrief us, contain it, and take appropriate action. Think of it as Fish and Wildlife on steroids, you in?

"Does Godzilla shit in the ocean?"

Stevenson pursed his lips.

"Get it? Because Godzilla woke up due to atomic testing and I just was in a radioactive-"

"Work on your jokes Kelso. Rest up, we'll talk."

Kelso nodded and turned the volume up on the tv show.

Chapter 9

CASE: A Thousand Teeth

The two lovers clung to each other against the harsh fall breeze. Walla Walla, set in the beautiful southeast portion of Washington's wine country, was in full late autumn bloom. The rolling hills and nearby fields of onions, asparagus, and grapes were receding. Marc and Lisa, two Whitman College kids on their date night, were profoundly underdressed for this weather. They had just walked across Lowy Park Bridge over the Waldo Creek. Marc led her to a patch of cement stone seats on the riverbanks. They leaned against it as they began to kiss. Amid pick-up trucks with modified mufflers in the distance, Lisa heard a soft howl. Like a growing whisper from the darkness.

"What the heck is that?" Lisa asked, snuggling against Marc's thin sweater. He rubbed her back and held her tight.

"Ah just the wind coming off the Palouse hills and Blue Mountain range. Means we should keep kissing," Marc replied smiling. Lisa laughed and kissed his chin.

Lisa leaned up and kissed Marc as he held her closer. Water bubbled and coursed underneath them heading towards the mountains. They were on the edge of town far from the college campus, winery crawl downtown, and even lights of the Washington State Penitentiary. Five minutes away the regional Walla Walla airport tossed lonely flights up into the night sky.

Lisa heard the howl again, this time closer. It had more of a snarl.

"Ok dude, it's go time," Lisa stated as she gave him a quick peck. The wind, darkness, and mountain howl were not turning her on.

"No problem, let's hit Hamada's for some grub."

"Sounds like a plan sweetie."

He held her close as they walked back onto the bridge. Marc noticed something red out of the corner of his eye. He turned and it seemed to dart behind the trees.

"What's up?" Lisa asked.

Marc said nothing. He picked up the pace as the wind matched in rhythm. They rounded a series of trees and found relief in seeing Marc's car in the parking lot. He held the door for her as she heard the howl getting closer.

As Marc leaned down to get into the driver seat he could see something red across the trees, bridge, and near the spot they had just left. Looked like a blanket caught in the branches. Probably some other lovers who tried to make a sleepover of Lover's Corner. Lowy Park had become quite a common place for romantic picnics, hookups, and tweakers to smoke meth. He shook his head and closed the door, started the car, and took off for Hamada's Mexican Cafe. Lisa turned up the music to drown out the noises echoing in her head. Red blinking lights blinked at them across the dark night sky, although they were just windmill lights, it gave a strange ambiance to driving west on Highway 12 at night.

Hours later they were cuddled in Lisa's bedroom, talking about post-graduation plans. He was pre-law but expressed concern about whether he'd get into law school. She was eyeing a Ph.D in psychology to help teens who suffered sexual abuse.

"So then it's settled, we move to Portland or Seattle, yes?" Lisa asked.

"Seattle is amazing but I feel like Portland's vibe matches us more," Marc replied.

"Good point, I just know some people up in Seattle, could be a big help in starting with the homeless youth there."

"There's homeless in Portland, abundant ones, and they need someone like you."

Marc got up to use the bathroom. The bedroom was adorned with movie posters and Italian ads from the 1960s. Marc's gold coin lay on her bookshelf next to a picture of them hugging by a waterfall.

Lisa heard a low hum. It sounded familiar, but she couldn't place it.

"Are you shaving?"

"Ah, no silly. It's 3 a.m. I don't care what I look like."

"Using the electric toothbrush?"

Marc laughed and shook his head no as Lisa stared at him from across the bedroom. The hum had gotten closer.

"Ok this isn't funny, what is that?"

"Baby what in the world are you talking about? Is this some type of psych assessment you are trying on me? Not working!"

The hum had converted into a growl. It felt like it was coming from within the room, if not beside the bed. Lisa began to tighten her grip on the covers as she felt it elevate into a high-pitched scream.

"Marc! Can't you hear that? Oh god, it's so loud, what is that? Marc!"

As Marc looked up to glare at her in the bathroom mirror, he saw it. There was a seven-foot red blanket standing upright next to the bed. Something was standing under the red blanket, and it wasn't Lisa. He clenched the bathroom sink by the sides. Marc blinked again and saw the blanket turn revealing a face, but something wasn't right. It was a skeletal elderly woman's face, centuries spoiled, eyes gouged out. Its eyes were bleeding all over his floor. It was screaming at him, but he couldn't hear anything.

Marc began to weep. He tried to call out to Lisa, but his voice was gone. He saw the ghoulish face open up revealing massive alligator-sized jaws which were nestled against Lisa's ear. A long fingertip pointed at Marc as the jaws turned towards him. He felt his body go limp as Lisa grabbed a set of keys off the nightstand and began to jab.

Chapter 10

THREE DAYS LATER, AGENT Alex Kelso was confused. *Was it a goat? Was it a man?*

"Look Kelso it was half man half goat. I'm in the air force, I could be dismissed for lying. It's a goddamn goat man on my airfield!"

"I think it was like more of a Minotaur. He galloped across A-4 field, we almost had a crash. Serious shit."

Agent Kelso was nodding while writing down each story. The two air force staff were sensing her skepticism, which pissed them off. She was sent to the Fairchild Air Force Base right outside of Spokane, Washington to close out a goat man case. For some time, the Air Force had been accumulating reports from their staff about seeing a goat man at night running across their base. Now that Agent Kelso was known in the region for exploring the bizarre her caseload was bursting.

"So, have you ever taken a picture of this thing?" Kelso asked. Both men shook their heads.

"Ok, does this goat man thing talk? Act aggressive? Does it appear to be friendly?" She had to bite her lip as she asked this last question. The two air force officers remained serious and shook their heads again.

"It just kind of runs around, staring at us, with glowing green eyes, crazy man."

Since her Trinity mission, it had been one month of recovering, two months of expedited FBI training, and in her first weeks as a cross deputized federal special agent. Her official assignment was working Atypical Investigations Unit cases or AIUs, an attempt by the FBI to avoid the embarrassing reality that they did have strange cases that had to be worked. No one wanted to work them since crime assignments got you the promotions, not interviewing sketchy rural witnesses talking about Mothman sightings. Agent Kelso welcomed the new job since her boss said she could still work Fish & Wildlife cases once it got old. Plus, Washington state had some really bizarre stories. Her grandpa used to tell her the darkness holds more truth than the light, but today's goat man case didn't validate that theory. She was just hungry and tired.

"Dude are you fucking listening to me? I got a half man half goat thing running around. I want some Pentagon guys to come down here and wipe it out. When is that happening?"

Agent Kelso smiled and stopped writing.

"I am here to take your information, evidence, and then we'll see what we can do, sir. The Department of Justice takes this stuff seriously and knows this is a security threat. We're on it."

As she placated them her work phone vibrated. She excused herself and saw it was her boss, Commander Stevenson. Although he was a US Fish and Wildlife regional commander it was his idea to share her with the DOJ to clear out neglected fed cases. For this favor he was rising in the ranks and was able to have rare managerial control over her new caseload.

"Kelso, how is goat man's pasture treating you?" Commander Stevenson asked.

"Great sir, there's no forensics, no corroboration, but they want some predator drones to nuke him out."

Stevenson laughed, he noticed her jokes were improving. He was able to sell her for this AIU project given her ties to both the tribal world and her handling of the Trinity matter with stateside figures. Many of the sightings of strange creatures intersected with reservation lands and having someone who can engage with cultural respect is an authentic edge Kelso had on others in the DOJ.

"Good news, you can put goat man to bed. Bad news, we need you in Walla Walla by nightfall. Unofficially the local police want some creative brainstorming on a situation out there. And guess what? No goat men and no nuclear snake monsters."

"Yes sir. I'm game, what is it?"

"Five dead. Across two months. No signs of foul play, no suspects, no charges."

"Serial killer?"

"Negative, Kelso. Due to Bundy and Ridgeway, cops have departmental resources on serial killers. They did call up the FBI wanting a profiler, so you gotta love TV's effect on law enforcement. After the FBI passed, Tom Winters, the Assistant Special Agent in Charge (ASAC), asked us to help calm down the locals with theories. No shooting, no drama, just using your fresh federal law enforcement training to see if there's some exit strategy on closure for these families, the colleges, and mayor concerned about winery tourism issues."

"They know I'm a Fish and Wildlife Officer right?"

"They know that the DOJ has a new AIU program that is regionally helping Washington's various unique occurrences. Like five dead people with no suspects, forensics, or foul play."

"They try the EPA? Epidemiologist? I read somewhere that after four people got sick in different parts of the country, they had medical teams investigate. Mere days they narrowed it to a strange floral bottle that had rare bacteria in it. We sure AIU can help?"

Agent Kelso bit her lip and watched a plane take off. She didn't mean to overstep her rank but did not want to end up on some documentary about how a serial killer wasn't caught because of a rookie working the case. High profile cases have a way of rearranging careers when you don't get it done.

"Listen Kelso, the victims have reported seeing weird things down there. And we aren't talking a guy in the bushes with chloroform. Each death was a suicide. Four suicides and the fifth took out his entire family before turning the gun on himself. All construction workers, now we got two normal college kids clawing apart the mental hospital. Serial killer is out, our new bizarro specialist, you, has been asked to help. Thus we deliver."

"Ok, copy that. Any info on the college kid situation?"

"Police have two very pissed families of the two college kids caught in the mix. The couple went on a date, got back at her apartment, they both end up in the local mental ward. She has come close already to offing herself, he's shown more restraint. Local PD tells me the other five had similar fact patterns prior to suicide. So they want to see if you could get fresh eyes on it, talk to the victims, and try to figure out a plan to curb these suicides."

"Strange. Ok, I'll get packing-"

"One last thing Kelso, the mayor and police chief aren't jazzed about us stopping by. We got this from under-the-radar requests. One, Barron Morris, a local winery CEO, wants the drama ended. And my naval buddy's daughter, Lucy Stone, is a newer cop out there and caught the case. She's feeling the pressure. Media is all over this and if enrollment drops at their three colleges, the town will pay the price. Not to mention the biggest players are now the wineries which employ most of the city alongside the prison. Mayor and Chief are on board as long as we are ghosts in the case. Goal is to help Lucy with some leads, and we'll move onward without any press, formal case work, or federal involvement."

"Copy that sir. And Goat Man case?"

"Pass it to Agent Platt. Any ideas you'd like me to share?"

"Honestly I think the goat man thing is just stress, some of these witnesses were working gruesome shifts at night. I noted in my report that they have a decent slice of their fence compromised. Meaning I'd give it a 1% chance of demonic goat creature to something like a Pronghorn Antelope. Might fit the nighttime sightings. Please text me Lucy's number and I'll get started on my drive."

Chapter 11

THREE HOURS LATER KELSO arrived in Walla Walla. Officer Lucy Stone asked her to meet at the Bledsoe Burger drive-in. Kelso ordered an overtime chicken sandwich and found Stone's patrol vehicle parked on the edge of the darkened lot. Officer Stone rolled down her window and invited Kelso to sit in her passenger seat.

"Agent Kelso, thank you for coming. I appreciate it so much."

Officer Lucy Stone shook Kelso's hand and smiled. She was college aged, with curly hair pulled back into a bun, with sparking green eyes. Agent Kelso smiled back and eyed the officer's green fingernail polish.

"You can call me Kelso. I'm happy to help out, and girl they let you wear those green nails on patrol? Lucky!"

Officer Stone sucked her teeth in then smiled, "It's something I'm trying to hold onto, I gave up on my hair, eyeliner, lipstick, so I convinced them might help me curry favor with locals. As a Latina, community policing is real, and has value. When I roll up on a scene sometimes I can sometimes deescalate things fast. I might be able to really help folks out here. Plus let's be real, my nails are still worn down from searches, wiping up spit, blood, and cuffing college drunks as they try to swing on me. Thank god for my brothers rough housing, those college dudes don't stand a chance!" Officer Stone snickered.

Agent Kelso chuckled, "I know what you mean, few months ago I had that incident at the Trinity Nuclear site. I've always been too restless for a hair stylist, but my aunt luckily forces me to let her upgrade my hair every decade. Fashion isn't my scene, just ain't my thing. So how you end up a cop?"

They traded stories about being younger and women in law enforcement. Kelso's journey was to work with animals, hunters, and serve. Even during her tenure at the Alaskan fishing ships, when on break, she'd explore and meet local villages. Many Pacific Northwest and Alaskan tribes held sacred their fishing rights so the enforcement of them, she learned, can be life or death for a small local economy. Kelso's dad died when she was young via drug addiction, and her mom had similar struggles amid periods of sobriety. She got to see her mom once in a long while. Her grandfather, Silas, was her real parent and so that was the magnetic force, as well as her niece, that had her sorting her life out again. Officer Stone's choice to become a cop came unexpectedly as she just found the first responder role more fulfilling than post-grad jobs in marketing. It had the added bonus of making her father anxious that she didn't have a husband yet, given her four sisters had already cranked out babies. Her mother was delighted and bragged about her brave cop daughter at their local parish church. Both had grown up Catholic.

"So, can I take a look at the apartment? That seems to be where the call came in from and after that each of them, Marc and Lisa, didn't even see each other again, that ok?" Kelso asked.

Stone nodded. They dropped Kelso's car off at the hotel and proceeded to Lisa's campus apartment. Rain started up, heavy and fast. The apartment building was in the heart of campus and had heavy foot traffic around it. Brick, older, and full of college tenants it lacked the profile for a quiet home invasion. Within minutes they had ascended to the top floor and into the apartment. The front door was busted open due to police entry.

"Stone, what type of call was it again?"

Agent Kelso scanned the room and saw two chairs overturned, holes in the wall, and bloodstains circling the main room and the bathroom. Given it was an apartment with only two rooms one with living, kitchen, and small bedroom, with a side bathroom it was hard to discern where or what started. Walking in further she noticed the bathroom mirror was broken, shards of glass covered the floor.

"Well it was four different calls, none of them were from Lisa or Marc."

"Wait, they didn't call the cops themselves?"

"Nope, all of the people below and across the way called once they heard the screaming. At first they figured it was just loud sex but then it took a heavier form. Police knocked, heard screaming, no one answered so they made a forced entry. Came in and saw Lisa on the floor weeping, blood covered her clothes with Marc in the bathroom punching the mirror as well as those lovely blood caked holes in the wall."

Agent Kelso saw no signs of an intruder, maybe domestic violence, but most likely some type of drug situation. Reminded her of some bath salt cases she had seen in the news.

"Any abuse claims or prior domestic violence stuff?" Kelso asked.

Stone shook her head. She pointed out the blood pattern for Marc started in the bathroom and never left that room. Same for Lisa in the main bedroom area.

"So they both have self-inflicted wounds without even crossing paths? You already tested them for drugs? Especially that lethal shit like bath salts and meth mixes right? This sounds like those MK Ultra experiments with soldiers and LSD."

"Yep, no drugs. I mean now they are both pumped full of Thorazine and a factory's worth of psych meds but at the time they were stone sober. Same alleged profile for most of the prior suicide victims. Her injuries were to her ears, and his were to his eyes. Both refused to give statements, to be honest, it is only within the last day that they have gotten them under control. She tried to kill herself again but they stopped her. He keeps laughing all night long. I'm glad you're here, I welcome the help at interviewing them."

Agent Kelso continued her walkthrough and asked if they could try interviewing at least one of them tonight. Stone made some calls and got blocked on Lisa, but Marc was able to chat prior to bedtime. Both Stone and Kelso were quiet on the drive over. The rain hammered their vehicle.

"Hope this doesn't keep up, we've had flooding issues recently. Like entire parks and streets roped into waterflows from several creeks that run throughout Walla Walla," Stone said.

"Yeah I thought Seattle had it bad, this is something else," Kelso replied. They signed in, flashed their badges, and were escorted to a visiting room.

"Heads up, I don't know how many interrogations you've done in Fish and Wildlife, but if you don't mind I'd like to play lead. Maybe you can be his cheerleader and I'll keep him focused?" Stone asked. Kelso nodded and Marc was walked into the room with a hospital security attendant. Kelso's mouth dropped. He had bandages over both eyes and had sunglasses on. He stumbled into the desk and was helped into a chair facing the two female officers. He had a nice set of thick blonde hair and muscular build.

"Ah, good evening Marc, my name is Lucy Stone I'm with Walla Walla PD and with me is Alex Kelso a federal special agent. We'd like to talk to you, is that ok?"

The hospital attendant took a seat in the corner and started playing on his phone. Marc mumbled something and began to laugh. Kelso and Stone shot each other glances but then let him continue for about a minute. Stone asked if he could take off his glasses. His laughter stopped.

"No point. On or off, it's all black now. Everything is black. Better that way."

Stone repeated her request to chat. Kelso kept her eyes on his hands and the useless hospital security guard.

"Yes yes, we can chat all day- wait it's night, we can chat all night but it won't stop it. Won't stop her."

"Do you mean Lisa sir? We haven't had the chance to chat with her yet."

His laughter returned. It was more of a hysterical laugh than a comical one. He began to roll his head towards parts of the room.

"She's probably here. You know. Staring and yelling. But now I don't have to care. I'll never see her again."

"Well Lisa is not in this room sir, so it's safe to chat, please tell me what happened that night."

"No. No. No. Not Lisa, Officer Stone, the other one. Kelso was it? Tell me have you seen it? Can you tell your partner here she's not doing herself any favors."

Agent Kelso nodded and told Marc that she had seen it. Whatever he wanted it to be.

"Oh you have? You saw her too? Was it as beautiful as when I saw her? Did you see her in the apartment or at Lowy Park?"

"All I saw at the apartment was blood Marc, tell me more about that?"

"Hmm. So the park eh? Gotta watch out I give it about a few hours to a day before she comes to visit. Oh just wait. It will be worth it, look at me now! Look. At. Me. Now!"

He began to tear off his glasses and started on his medical bandages. Both Kelso and the ward guard grabbed at his arms. He was too fast and got the bandages off and began to pound his vacant eye sockets causing blood, fluids, and scabs to rip off onto the floor. Officer Stone gasped. Kelso pinned him to the ground and got him into a cuffing position. The guard borrowed her cuffs and secured him. Marc began to slam his head into the ground as several guards sprinted into the room to help him up.

"Heyyyyy Kelso...look at me now...I'm all better. You will be too...just let her in. LET HER IN!" Marc's screams became guttural as they dragged him out of the room. His skull and eye socket pockets were oozing things that made even Agent Kelso dry heave.

Marc's treating psychologist arrived within twenty minutes to debrief the officers. She declined to let the officers meet with Lisa since their presence was obviously triggering patients already on the thread of suicide. As a brokered deal she agreed to relay what information each patient had revealed to her and her staff as long as the officers leave until both are doing better. Stone and Kelso agreed and the psychologist shared her notes.

"Marc said that he saw something at the park, and later it came to visit them that same evening. Lisa hasn't spoken since she got here so all I have is Marc's account. He laughs, she cries uncontrollably, it is quite a situation. Marc's account starts to get hallucinogenic, so I don't know what to make of it. In short, he says that a middle-aged woman appeared in that apartment and proceeded to scream into Lisa's ears while pointing a long fingertip at him."

Agent Kelso's mouth opened but she said nothing. Officer Stone asked if he gave any details about the woman.

"Nothing that should be of use to the real world. Or to law enforcement. But across a few hours the unit attendants said he kept mumbling about an alligator mouth and red cloak. All I got."

They thanked the psychologist and climbed into Stone's vehicle. An awkward silence was pierced by Stone.

"Well that was fucked up, we don't have big city crime here so I can't say that I've had that happen in an interview before. Usually I have DUI drivers or klepto rich kids falling apart about their parents and caving into confessions."

"Prior to this special unit gig, my investigations involved hunters acting like assholes to the animals or people illegally fishing. Can't put words to what that was up there. Or even the psych's helpful info. Is this Hansel and Gretel? We chasing a hallucinogenic witch?"

Stone began to laugh as Kelso joined, "I mean so far Marc up there sounds like he ingested some hardcore psychotropics then wants to blame their meltdown on a woman-alligator thing running around in a red jacket. Sounds fair."

"Stone, I know it's late as hell, but before I head to the hotel can we hit that park? Is it close or?"

"I figured you were going to ask, I'm on the same page, let's check it out. We'll need heavy flashlights given it has zero lighting. If I see our wicked witch I'm out, I like my eyeballs where they are," Stone replied shaking her head. Kelso thanked her and they began the short journey to Lowy Park.

The police SUV cranked down the muddy park road. Already puddles of rain were collecting in pockets around the pitch-black park grounds. Trees hugged the sides of the parking lot. They both got out and clicked on their flashlights. Wind shook the trees as rain shattered against their jackets. Aside from some picnic tables and the bridge across Waldo Creek the park held little clues. Agent Kelso almost slipped into a small stream next to the walkway. Lucy caught her arm.

"This park really isn't much more beyond these tables. That's why I think Marc's full of shit. Take a look do you see any roaming witch thing?" Stone said.

Kelso nodded and jogged to the bridge walking halfway across it. Waldo Creek was in rapid movement underneath them. Her light shone onto the cement seats on the opposite side of Lowy Park.

"What is that?" Kelso asked.

"Ah just the new river seating and jogging path. Been a long project, zoning, and construction crews. There apparently was a major sewer tank underneath it so delayed it for awhile, year I'd say. Been up for like a month."

Stone's radio cackled. They needed her to help back-up a traffic stop with multiple people. She told them she was five minutes out and would respond.

"I'll drop you at the hotel, it's on the way right off the highway. Tomorrow I'll come back and do one more sweep including the area for any drug paraphernalia or such. It is strange but I've had a Professor Pendleton blowing up our station on this case. Willing to take that heat off me and meet with him while I hit this park again?"

"Sure, but is he like a drug expert or psych guy or?"

"Anthropology, specifically mythology. I know I know, but his class is one that is always packed. It's a way to tell the families we covered every lead and chief might like it for Whitman College to feel heard. I would but I want to speak with prior victim's families."

Kelso agreed and muttered to herself, "great another goat man session." She took one last look at the darkness and saw nothing. *It has to be drugs, preexisting mental illness, or maybe some environmental induced hallucination*. After the Professor meeting she would circle back to the apartment to check for gas leaks, carbon monoxide, or weird ecological variables.

Chapter 12

THE NEXT MORNING THE sun and rain took turns exposing themselves in the sky. For the brief moments of sunshine the nearby mountains, hills, and rolling clouds created a gorgeous day. Kelso had given an update to Stevenson. It wasn't much to go on, but he liked the idea of some tainted drug shipment or possible local environmental issue either at the residences or park. It was a short drive to Whitman's campus. A small private liberal arts college but a prominent one with an accomplished set of departments and an alluring close-knit campus. Professor Pendleton's office was in the new Tyner building. Adorned with strange sculptures and an eclectic lobby Kelso made her way up the staircase to his office. He had offered the police his phone number, two e-mails, and all of his office hours. His significant interest in the case peaked Kelso's skepticism. The recent FBI training had taught her that some interested parties are wacky innocents while others are involved voyeurs with motives. Time to find out which he is. She knocked on his door.

"Yes? Come in."

A man in his late thirties, slightly gray hair, and medium build turned around in his office chair. He had a light amber complexion, much like Agent Kelso, with a warm smile. He motioned to an empty chair in his office. Bookcases bursting with books surrounded them. Papers laid in disheveled piles across his desk. He had turned back to his laptop and was typing out an email.

"My apologies, just let me send this e-mail. Conference of the Gods. They want to know if I'll attend and give a keynote."

"Gods?"

"Yep, think ComicCon but with mythological deities. We each come dressed as a selected god and give a speech about it. Some even do a contest in which the gods compete using only their historically supported powers to see who wins."

Agent Kelso furrowed her brow but released a slow smile. He chuckled.

"Yep, it's nerdy and weird but supremely awesome! Sorry, I know you aren't here for that. Ah, how can I help you? Trying to get into my advanced class or see if I can push you up the waitlist for 'Entry into the Eternal – Death' class?"

"Nope. Actually I'm Special Agent Kelso with DOJ/F&W assisting Walla Walla PD with a case. I've been told you have some information?"

His eyes lit up. Professor Pendleton got up and ran to close the door. His face was beaming.

"Oh my! I'm so honored you stopped by! Hell yes!!! Yes let's talk about this situation. I think I know what is going on. Tell me, how much do you know about Walla Walla history?"

Agent Kelso shook her head and relayed that she grew up in Wenatchee. All she knew about Walla Walla was mostly what others across Washington knew, Whitman College, wineries, and sweet onion country.

Professor Pendleton nodded. He then pulled out one of his own books, *Beneath the Glow*, about Walla Walla's history. He handed it to Kelso.

"You can keep that. So you are right, but underneath that farming and super-recent winery trend lies an amazing history. So let's take the Idaho gold rush. This area was a massive area for people trying to find, mine, and secure some gold fortunes. Given the rougher clientele this area also became a roadhouse of prospectors and villains. Enter McGrady and his gold. Various reports confirm that McGrady had hit gold and was traveling westward to share it with his wife and kids. He takes a pit stop here, too many drinks later, shared one too many stories and all of a sudden he finds himself inside a noose, courtesy of a local lynch mob. He pleaded and begged but the rascals wouldn't listen, nor the local sheriff and they killed him out way out near what is that new Lowy Park Bridge area. Anyways, they got the gold on his person and in his hotel but it was rumored he had entire wagons of it hidden at a camp site."

Kelso paused in taking her notes and looked up.

"So how does this factor into our case, sir?"

"I tried protesting Morris from putting up that grotesque cement park, which really is just a marketing scheme for his wineries. I went to city council and tried to get it listed as a historic site, but Morris has very powerful friends. Rumors emerged he came into some wealth and all of a sudden, even amid worker deaths, this monstrosity of Walla Walla was built."

"Monstrosity is a bit much, it's just a cement park, two picnic tables and that statue of the settler dude."

Professor Pendleton shook his head, "No, that's a bronze statue of Morris himself. As wine god to the region, if you take a selfie with it, his company will send you a case of his newest wine. It is quite the spot now for the self-indulgent."

"Not a wine fan. Got it. What's this about worker deaths?"

"I think about five died, all Morris construction crew, it was quite the talk of the town. Four suicides, one killed his entire family, Morris' money kept people quiet. Even more bizarre now that we got these two kids in the mix."

Agent Kelso's eyebrows shot up. *The gas leak theory.*

"Anyone do an environmental impact or inspection of that site? For a gas leak or like benzene, ethylene, anything that could cause that type of behavior?"

"Ah the Oracle of Delphi you mean?"

"Come again?"

Professor Pendleton pulled up a recent paper presented in Rome on the history of the famous Oracle of Delphi. It is one of the most sacred sites of ancient Greece where people from around the world would come to get advice from God Apollo. This was delivered by the oracle, called Pythia, a series of women serving the higher calling in the temple. She would enter into a trance and would predict the future affecting the outcomes of wars, economy, and politics of her time. The paper was an update that previously people had speculated she was high from inhaling noxious fumes from deep fissures under the temple. At first scientists thought it was ethylene due to traces of it in the temple walls but made no sense to induce the level of hallucinogenic trances, so a new paper posited it was a combination of carbon monoxide and methane both of which were abundant on the temple site.

"Long story short Morris shut down any environmental teams and paid off all the families with binding non-disclosure agreements," Pendleton said.

"And wouldn't the effects of any of these gases reduce as people got further away from the worksite? I doubt any of these suicides or murders occurred on-site, right?" Kelso asked.

"Yep, which is why I have another theory-"

Agent Kelso's phone rang and she mouthed 'I'm sorry' and held up her hand. It was a call from the local police chief. She was being summoned to Baron Morris's home thirty minutes west, where the Walla Walla River meets the Columbia. It was a request by the mayor's deputy who thought it would help the investigation. He repeated how her supervisor also thought it was important to occur right now. A veiled threat that irritated her. *Send me out to chase goat men, gas leaks, and now meet with a wine snob. Time of my life.*

"Professor Pendleton, I'm so sorry but I have to go, thank you for everything. I'll circle back around if I need more info. Please keep this quiet as it is an active investigation. Take care."

"But Agent Kelso you need to hear my theory, just hear me out!" Professor Pendleton begged. Agent Kelso apologized and promised she'd be back.

She stepped out and closed his office door, so that a poster of Saturn eating his own son was staring back at Professor Pendleton.

Chapter 13

ACROSS TOWN OFFICER STONE was wrapping up an investigative interview with one of the deceased worker's families. They weren't keen on letting her in but working her charm along with a promise to try to knock down a recent case on their cousin for receiving stolen property, got it done. The older lady gave a rather uneventful story about a construction project, some transporting of the dig materials, and how all of the deaths occurred after the project was done. She repeated how amazing Barron Morris had been to their family, at their funeral, and stated she has nothing bad to say about him. It was only as Officer Stone was leaving that she mentioned the gift boxes that Barron Morris had given each worker that piqued Stone's interest.

What was strange was that these were given about one week after the dig was complete and that is when her husband began to hear voices, screaming, and wailing at all hours. Eventually he stopped going out to eat, shop, and couldn't work. He would lock himself into his shed praying and yelling. They went to Father Prosser but the priest couldn't seem to help beyond praying with them. He had an ear nose throat appointment the week she came home to find her husband dead from a shotgun suicide. She hasn't touched that room or the gift box since. It was a simple small square box big enough to fit cuff links or some type of jewelry. She opened it and saw it was a large gold coin. She picked it up and was mystified.

"May I borrow this? I'd like to see where this came from and if maybe there's something on it, chemicals or such," Stone asked.

"Ah, um, sure. The legal agreement says I shouldn't open or show anyone but...if it will help make sense of this thing...it's worth it. I miss Juan more than life itself. Do you think my husband was poisoned? Or like a gas leak? That's what Barron Morris told us, it was an unfortunate gas leak that he has now sealed."

"To be honest, I have no idea. I'll do everything I can to find out what happened to Juan. So can you please share with me the address on Ignacio?"

The widow handed over the address but warned that it is a cabin way past a mountain town in Oregon thirty minutes southwest. He doesn't like visitors. She got it from his wife who has been asking local police to check on him but no one will return her calls.

"Well I guess I won't tell dispatch that I'm headed there then," Stone replied, "we'll figure this out, thank you for your help hermana."

Chapter 14

STONE MADE GOOD TIME heading south into Oregon splitting her way through Milton-Freewater and then down across Weston, heading east towards the Blue Mountains. This pocket of southeast Washington and northeast Oregon was gorgeous but little time was available for taking it in. She hit the Weston-Elgin highway and turned off onto a dirt road hugged by ample forests. Before she lost her cell signal she left a voicemail for Kelso updating her. In her voicemail she told Kelso about the strange gift boxes, gold coins, and how no one from local PD had checked on the sole survivor of the worksite suicides. Her police vehicle slowed as rain began to fight against her uphill drive towards the lonely cabin nestled to the right. Ignacio's truck was parked outside. *Good sign, least he's home.*

She flashed her brights onto his cabin and flicked them on and off. She got out and unholstered her service weapon. There were no signs of other people as she walked up the steps. She announced herself as she leaned against the side of the cabin. Not taking chances with some rifle shots. Might be hard given all the windows are boarded up but anything is possible with an unstable possibly armed guy hiding in the mountains.

"Ignacio, Griselda sent me. I'm Officer Lucy Stone with Walla Walla Police Department, please tell me if you are in there. I just want to talk."

Silence. Sound of soft rain peppering the leaves and ground around her.

"Sir, I am not here to arrest you or remove you from your cabin. I just want to talk, make sure you are ok. I'll be gone within five minutes."

No response. Officer Stone decided to take her chance.

"Nacho, I've seen it. The woman. The demon. I need someone to talk to..."

Within seconds of mentioning the monster she heard movement. A large sound of wood moving from behind the door. She peered around the corner of the cabin outside wall and saw the front door was now open.

She continued yelling as she entered his cabin with her weapon drawn. It was illuminated on every inch of the interior. Bedroom, kitchen, living room, and small bathroom. The smell hit her of feces and spoiled meat. Her glare went to the bearded man sitting at a wood table. His lack of grooming, along with the smell and his paunch body gave him the appearance of a wild lawn gnome. A shotgun lay about five feet away from him. He wasn't giving it any attention so Officer Stone lowered her service weapon. He extended his hand for her to sit across from him.

"How long you been seeing her?" Ignacio asked.

Lucy shifted in her seat and told him about a week.

"Try a month out, you'll soon be out here."

"I think your wife might have an issue with me moving into the cabin with you."

Ignacio didn't smile at her joke.

"So tell me, when did you first start seeing it? Or is it a her?"

"A week or two after the job was complete. At first I saw her from far away. She would crawl or run towards me then disappear. Thought I was going mental...then all of my friends died from the sight. Knew it wasn't a fucking joke."

"Has she ever spoken to you?"

"She doesn't speak. She just appears, stares, and then points at you screaming. She doesn't need to speak. Have you seen her fucking mouth? A thousand teeth."

Officer Stone nodded keeping her eye on the shotgun.

"So has staying up here helped? She not come up here?"

Ignacio grinded his teeth and frowned. His glare pierced her face.

"Course fucking not. She can pass through walls, she's a fucking demon. Least there's light inside here. As well as the shotgun. No sleep, but least I can manage my corners."

"Is she afraid of the gun?"

"Is an eagle afraid of a worm?" Ignacio shot back. His eyes darted around the room. A slow smile began to form. Officer Stone was distracted by digging in her pocket. She told him she had something that she had a question about. She reached in her pocket and pulled out the gold coin from Juan's widow. His eyes froze on it.

"Tell me about this. Do you have one as well? Who gave it to you?"

He sighed.

"Fuck me man. You like to party eh? Pinche Rick Baldacci gave it to me and all the guys. It was a gift from the big boss man. Fucking trap, man."

"Rick Baldacci is?"

"Barron Morris's business manager. He paid us shit wages for the job but after our little favor, they figured toss some scraps to the migrants, right? Fucking wineries are new age plantations, man."

"What favor? Barron Morris's manager gave you a gold coin like this for what?"

Ignacio grimaced and then smiled some more tapping his fingertips on the table.

"Fuck it, no time left why not share eh? The fucking kilos of gold we found man. I've never seen anything like it except in like fucking pirate movies. Real deal gold man. Right out the fucking ground. Had us move it from the work site into the Blue Mountain Bank vaults. At night, with the fucking bank manager opening the back door. Felt like I was moving coke for the cartel or some shit. You know I didn't take any home. Some of the other fellas did but not me."

His breathing was accelerating as his voice began to raise.

"And even when I got that fucking gold coin I gave it to my Tia, told her to sell it and try to give money to the little cousins in college. Doing better things than us. You don't see her, do you?"

Officer Stone ignored his question, attempting to calm him, "that was nice of you."

Tears began to slowly drop down his face. Officer Stone stared, trying to track.

"She was dead, from a heart attack, within a week of getting one of those coins. I've been waiting but I'm gonna pay Barron Morris back, real good. Wait a minute, you don't see do you? You lied to me. You've never seen her. And yet you bring this into my cabin?"

"I'm sorry for your loss, Ignacio. Did anyone ever find out where these coins came from, I mean besides the ground inside the worksite?"

He began to growl as his tears flowed faster down his face. Officer Stone reached back down by her hip and service weapon as well as her pepper spray.

"Why don't you ask your friend?" he softly hissed at her.

"What friend? Agent Kelso? Chief Connelly?"

"No. The fucking monster that is behind you, pointing right now, at your hands."

"That's not funny. I need you to calm down Ignacio."

He leapt up from the table and grabbed the shotgun as Officer Stone hit the ground. She drew her weapon and yelled for him to stop. She saw nothing in the cabin but them.

"Oh Dios Mio, Oh fuck. It's mouth is opening, she's showing me those teeth. Fuck her and fuck you!"

He let out several shotgun blasts whose noise ripped through the small cabin. Officer Stone crawled away from the table taking cover behind the stove. His shots were in wild directions as he spit and cussed at emptiness. He still had at least four more shots left as he sprinted around the corner towards her. She begged him to stop but he raised the shotgun at her.

"You brought her back, you are with her, fuck you!"

Officer Stone hit him with five shots through his face and head. He dropped to the ground as she began to hyperventilate. Everything was moving slow for her. It was her first time using her service weapon outside the firing range and also the first time she had seen a dead body.

"Oh god, fuck, you crazy bastard."

She was wobbly but got to her feet and kicked away his shotgun. She took his pulse and knew he was dead. She had to be sure. She grabbed the gold coin, put it in her pocket, and headed to the front door. For some reason, she turned around due to a feeling someone was watching her. Nothing. Just what was left of Ignacio.

She started to dry heave outside. Stress and adrenaline were racing inside her as she made her way to the police SUV, switched to a local police signal, and called it in. Officer under fire, one suspect shot and no pulse, need EMS and back-up. Walla Walla PD.

As she began to try to catch her breath, she saw it. A red and black figure crawling out the front door. It was feminine but also without human features beyond vacant black eyes and a long protruding mouth, like some type of demonic alligator. It was walking towards her as she drew her service weapon, rolled down her window and fired five shots. Its mouth opened revealing the thousands of teeth Ignacio had warned about. A long swampy arm emerged from the red shroud pointing at her. She put her vehicle into gear and pressed the gas. She drove right through the monster and into the cabin, without a seatbelt on, cracking her face into the windshield as she fell into trauma-induced unconsciousness.

Chapter 15

AT THE SAME TIME, on the opposite side of the region, Agent Kelso barreled down the semi-busy rural highway turning off at a gated road that led up a massive hill to Baron Morris's mansion. Agent Stone's voicemails were helpful but left more questions than answers. Why was Barron Morris handing out gold coins to migrant workers? Was there some environmental conspiracy afoot? Why in the hell wasn't Stone with her on this meet-and-greet?

Wine orchard trees surrounded the estate. It took almost ten minutes to drive up to his parking area. As she got out, she turned and saw storm clouds to the right and golden mounds chiseled against the massive waterways. Railroad cars in the distance headed to the nearby dock and she could see hundreds of workers picking grapes. Stone, wood, and stylistic postmodern features clutched every inch of his mansion. It had to have at least twenty bedrooms and five floors. It reminded her of those east coast tycoon places. An attendant greeted her and escorted her to the back balcony where Baron and the mayor's deputy awaited.

"Welcome, Agent Kelso, thank you for stopping by." Baron Morris shook her hand.

"Don't know how much choice I had in that, but happy to meet. How can I help you?"

"Tsk tsk, you rez girls are all business, let's talk about some things first."

Rez girl was a slur Agent Kelso had encountered growing up as a tribal member. It creeped up at stores, restaurants, with unkind people tossing such taunts. It would peak if, even as a teen, she didn't respond to men catcalling her.

"Unless you are selling my new favorite wine, Pale Face Douche, you'll not call me 'rez girl' again. But I am happy to see if the flavor of your blood will mix well with the dirt, once I knock your teeth out."

Barron Morris laughed and the mayor's deputy gasped.

"Fair enough, my apologies. I did pull your background, quite a fighter, I like that. Former state champion women's basketball player, disappeared to Alaska for three years, bachelor's in criminal justice, rookie fed fish and game cop, now temp FBI agent stalking snake monsters in nuclear sewers. Too bad Marines didn't take you, saw that too. Interesting moves."

"You forgot volunteer at women's shelter, caretaker of cancer-stricken grandfather, Catholic, proud lesbian, ghost hunter. If you want to go there, we can go there. Let's circle the wagons, as your people liked to say, right?"

Agent Kelso's voice began to rise.

I am sick of qualifying my tribal identity at home because I got a fed job. And I'm tired of people needing to know who I choose to date. Morris has about thirty seconds before I'm done with this case. I'll do twenty goat man investigations instead.

"You forgot to mention, monster-killing newspaper-star of the Trinity Nuclear site," the mayor's deputy chimed in attempting to broker a de-escalation. "Sir, that led to at least fifty charges against twenty high level federal defendants, quite a debut. The mayor is honored to have federal support. We apologize for Barron's manner, his family is involved and victims of this case."

"Alright alright, Kelso calm down, I'm the reason you are here, shortcake," Barron said.

Agent Kelso glared at both men. *One more goddamn remark like that, just test me.*

"You asked for me? Commander Stevenson-"

"Commander Stevenson is a nobody out here. This isn't a situation where you are giving someone a ticket for illegal fishing. Fish and Wildlife, really? We need a fish and game rookie cop to come and solve a date rape situation? Give me a break. Nevertheless, I asked you here for a reason, Agent Kelso. I do like how you operate."

This guy has some balls.

Barron Morris nodded, "True, I was told you saw things you never spoke of, even when the U.S. Congress came knocking with warrants. I need someone with that type of discretion here. Are you that type of person still?"

Agent Kelso placated him and they began to walk along his back deck. Baron Morris described how his family had run the slaughterhouses for generations here but until a year ago hit hard times. Since the wine business had been good to the local Tri-Cities of Kennewick, Pasco, and Richland he tried his hand at it a year ago. He snagged the project at Lowy Park hoping a statue and park for local college kids and tourists would drive business. By mere chance his work crew dug up giant amounts of gold. He had it moved into the local bank, no one laid claim to it, and he gave each worker a gold coin as a thank you. All of the money was going to further his investment in Walla Walla and the region becoming the Napa Valley of the Northwest.

"And the deaths that began afterwards?" Agent Kelso asked.

His boots sunk into the mud as they walked onto his groves. He got quiet.

"Yeah, I was horrified by it. I figured with the first one or two, construction crews can be rough, those migrants have tough lives, I know I employ and feed over a thousand in my wineries here. Maybe it was stress or drugs. Then Carlos wiped out his own family and turned the gun on himself and I reached out and had my lawyer take care of all of the families. Paid for their medical, grief counseling, and such. These things can grow legs unless you rip the head off early. Ignacio abandoned his family and took off for the Blue Mountains, he was always weird. Two weeks ago, I lost my business manager, Richard Baldacci, to a heart attack. Horrific tragedies. Then-"

Agent Kelso stared at the workers picking amid the growing storm clouds.

"Marc started dating that wacko and now we're here. I think that is a red herring, I'm Marc's stepfather, we don't get along much but hey who does anymore? He has returned back here for college hoping to get a sliver of my new wealth. So far all he's gotten is a gold coin, just like those migrants."

"You have a charming way about you, I still don't follow how I play a role in any of this."

Barron Morris released a smile. An attendant walked up to him and began to speak into his ear. Morris' smile widened then faded patting the attendant on the back. He motioned the mayor's deputy over to them.

"So Agent Kelso. There isn't a snake loose for you to shoot nor is there some witch monster running around town. Lisa didn't hear shit but probably something about him getting bored and slipped him a fucked up roofie. No, why you are here just got that much more important. Lucy can fumble around with the college kids bad romance case, I want your federal connections. The cartel is in the nearby Tri-Cities and they've been expanding into our region as of late. Small pockets but fruitful ones I've heard from local task forces. I have a growing suspicion, as the region's wealthiest man, that the Cartel is plotting to rob me. In fact, I know it for a fact, and I'd like your help, behind the scenes, to interrogate the players and find out more. You can say you are contacting them because of the boogeyman story crap, those migrants love their Gods. Whatever keeps them picking those grapes works for me."

Agent Kelso grimaced at the proposition.

"Sir, I think you are confusing me with ICE or the DEA. While I do enjoy hunting, fishing, catching dirtball poachers, and protecting natural resources means a lot to me, but hunting down cartel members isn't really my strong suit. Pass. Thanks for the offer."

Barron Morris figured she was going to decline but then shared an update that left her speechless. Officer Stone is in the hospital and on administrative leave from police duty after a horrific shootout that left Ignacio dead. Oregon isn't pleased nor is the Walla Walla' Police chief that she played detective out of state without coordinating with anyone.

"I have it on good authority Ignacio had retreated to that cabin to team up with cartel to come and get me. Come rob me for my Fort Knox stash. Probably same fate as other workers who told cartel about the gold, and they closed their eyes to firm up any gaps of witnesses. So you can pretend to hunt monsters but unless you get real smart fast, you might find yourself up against the most demonic monster you've ever seen, the cartel."

This guy is something else. If he had seen the serpent at Trinity he'd think otherwise, Agent Kelso thought.

"Plus, if you've learned anything from this conversation be it that what came to Lucy will come to you. It has eyes on you and unlike the mob they don't hesitate to behead the feds. Give me a call if you want to be in the game or you want to keep thinking like a...rookie."

"Roger that, sir. You've been a joy to meet."

Agent Kelso turned and walked fast to her vehicle. She turned the engine on and sped out of his driveway causing dirt and rocks to fly all over as attendants stared on. She called Stevenson on speakerphone as she barreled her SUV towards the Walla Walla hospital.

Chapter 16

STONE WAS STABLE BUT in and out of it due to her concussion. Face was cut up. Internal affairs as well as Oregon State Patrol had just left her when Agent Kelso arrived. They hugged and Kelso joked there goes Stone's chances at getting a husband now. It made Stone smile amid the beeps and wires.

"Kelso, it isn't looking good. I'm worried girl."

"Ignacio shot at you. I heard it will be cleared as a justified shooting. Some time off, counseling, and you'll be back on patrol in no time. Don't let the investigations mess with you."

"No. That's not what I'm talking about. I'm scared for real. Reach over there but be careful, don't touch it."

Agent Kelso dug around the container by Stone's bed until she came across a gold coin. She pulled it out and held it as Stone warned her to use a glove.

"Ah is it like covered in blood? How the hell didn't the investigators take this as evidence? Oh Barron Morris told me about his little gold treasure trove, thinks the Mexicans that he builds his fortune on are teaming up with cartel to get him. He's about one pointed sheet and a swastika from leading a rally. He's a peach as far as your local mogul."

"No girl. Be careful. I got that from one of the worker families. They had never even seen it and Ignacio lost it when I showed it to him. Started talking about the witch monster with teeth and shot up the cabin and almost me."

A nurse walked in to check on Stone and they paused. Switched topics to places they'd like to eat once she gets out. Once the nurse left they resumed their conversation as Kelso held the gold coin under the light. Unremarkable and without much inscription. Not much help.

"Like I was saying, after I shot Ignacio I was calling it in and I saw it."

"What?"

"It. The thing. It was horrible. No lie. It was exactly as Marc described it. Red shroud, older woman without eyes screaming, mouth like an alligator, with enough teeth to swallow a shark. It crawled out of the cabin and ran towards me, which is how I ended up like this."

Agent Kelso took this in and stared long at Officer Stone.

"Look girl, you've been through a lot, hell I didn't even shoot anyone at Trinity nuclear site. I just shot a massive serpent. Saw people die and took me months to process it. Hell, I'm still having nightmares I don't talk about. How can I help you?"

"Go see Professor Pendleton. Tell him what I saw and ask him what he thinks."

"Oh god Lucy, that guy wouldn't stop talking. He invited me to a MythicCon thingy. I mean he did mention McGrady's gold and some lynching like 400 years ago but I don't know what he'll do to help us."

Officer Stone shrugged but her eyes revealed fear.

"Look, I'll go to him, but don't get too hung up on it. Could be some toxin in these coins, could be stress from Ignacio losing his mind at you, and so if it will help you I'll do it. Girl, keep this quiet though. If you start talking about monsters to internal affairs, you'll never be released for duty again. Or...maybe to hunt monsters with me?"

Officer Stone sniffled out a laugh. Somewhere deep beneath her smile was a level of worry that made Agent Kelso sad. She leaned over and squeezed Stone's hand to comfort her.

"We'll sort this out Lucy. Monster witch, noxious chemical, or the cartel of wineries one way or another. You do know that just four days ago I was investigating a roaming half man half goat that haunts an Air Force base right? And I thought that assignment was crazy. Keep your phone handy, I'll keep you updated. Let me know if I can pick you up any food or stuff. I got you."

Agent Kelso spoke with the doctors, after some hesitation and flashing her badge, and got that it was a mild concussion at best. Agent Kelso asked the treating doctor if that would cause the level of anxiety and hallucinations that Stone is reporting, and the doctor said anything is possible given the double trauma of the shooting and crash on Stone's brain. She would be released in the next twenty-four hours to home care and should be fine in a matter of weeks.

Chapter 17

Agent Kelso arrived at the café about five minutes after Professor Pendleton had already ingested two latte's and it showed. He was rambling in full light speed about rumors of the shooting and that the cartel was afoot in Walla Walla.

Barron Morris really does have some long media fingertips.

"Well Professor Pendleton, I'm sorry but I'm not here to talk about the cartel. Also could we move to that back room, no one is in there. We need to have a very confidential conversation. One that could put you in harm's way if you share it or people know about it."

After they moved into the back room, Agent Kelso laid out the situation. The shootout, ramblings of Ignacio, appearance of the monster to Stone prior to car accident, Barron's admission about finding gold and paying off workers, now fearing they are interlinking with the cartel to come get him. She finished by pulling out the gold coin from Stone's possession. At first Lucy had put up a fight about Kelso taking it, but Kelso promised to handle it and any consequences of possessing the stupid gold coin. Professor Pendleton admired the gold but only touched it for a second.

"You are creeping me out Prof. For the first time since I've met you, you haven't said a word now for five minutes."

He looked around the room and took off his glasses.

"You left before I could warn you. God I'm so sorry, Kelso. This is all my fault. I knew I should have just grabbed you before you left my office yesterday. Fuck. May the gods forgive me."

"Ok I'll bite, what in the fucking hell are you talking about?"

"What do you know about Banshees?"

"The car?"

Professor Pendleton didn't laugh, his gaze remained serious.

"Celtic mythology. A spirit, usually young woman, maternal, or old hag form, appearing to wail and warn of impending familial death."

Kelso stiffened slightly and stared at the professor with a curious gaze.

"Varies per sighting but often she is wailing so loud that it can break glass. Other times she is weeping, washing blood-soaked clothes in a local water source, eyes leaking blood. A few horror movies have really taken liberties with how they look, but same concept. A warning of death. McGrady, as they were killing him, cursed his Walla Walla townsfolk that anyone who took part in his death or stole his fortunes would find tragedy."

"Ok, but that was what one hundred and fifty years ago? This is 2018. I'm still not making a connection here. I know I killed a radioactive snake but this is still a long leap, even for me. Snakes exist, radiation exits, Banshees?"

"Agent Kelso, this is a small town. Everyone talks even if they shouldn't. I know for a fact that Marc has matched this description of what he saw. The construction workers had made similar statements prior to their suicides, and now even Officer Stone's account matches. You can't deny we have a pattern with consistency."

Agent Kelso sighed.

"Banshees are unusually tall maternal woman with ghoulish features. Eyes sunken out. Mouth agape with almost reptilian layers of teeth. Some type of red shawl or dress. And fingertips long as an arm's length with a scream or glare. Tell me I'm wrong, I'm just trying to help. These two, Marc and Lisa, are Whitman's own. Officer Stone is a friend as well." Professor Pendleton pulled out a book, flipped through pages, and showed Kelso some pictures of Celtic Banshees. They ranged from slightly scary to quite unnerving.

Agent Kelso grimaced and said nothing. She stared back at him assessing his demeanor and credibility. He seemed genuine even if insane. Stone seemed sure of his theory.

"So, let's assume I believe this, no noxious fumes, no cartel, just a wild Banshee. And like a psychotic leprechaun I assume the motive is it wants McGrady's gold, which Barron Morris stole, and everything will return to normal? Or how does this play out? How do you make a Banshee go away?"

"See, that's the weird thing. In classic mythology Banshees don't kill people they are prophetic warnings to the mortal world of impending death. Even some Irish families welcomed a Banshee as a way or sign of time to pass into the next world. Ever heard of the Mothman of Point Pleasant Virginia? Various sightings of prophetic creatures who aren't actually agents of harm but just help tell mortals what is coming down the existential pipeline."

"Nothing you just said helps me."

"Let's just use logic and maybe circle back to it. Has anyone died yet, citing a visual of the Banshee, yet they haven't touched one of these gold coins or had it in their possession?"

"Construction workers, Ignacio, Officer Stone, all saw it after handling it, check. But, oh shit, Marc..."

"What?"

"Barron told me Marc is his stepson and although they hate each other he tossed him a gold coin to get him off his back. That means presumably Marc and Lisa handled or at least have a gold coin in their place, hence the visit from yours truly, Banshee."

Reality set in at the moment Agent Kelso finished her sentence. She now was holding the gold coin and had been for hours since leaving the hospital. Professor Pendleton kept the conversation going.

"Try returning it. It is clear that removing the gold set off a chain of supernatural events. See if returning the gold does something for Officer Stone or such."

"So you want me to drive to Lowy Park, dig a hole, and just randomly dump a gold coin, evidence from an officer-involved-shooting mind you, into the park hoping a magical Banshee will dance her way to another city?"

"Great Oracle of Delphi! I am not, but I'm not hearing any other good ideas."

Agent Kelso told him she needed to go to the bathroom. As she sat in the stall her mind was racing and overwhelmed. All of a sudden a silence hit her and she felt very uncomfortable. She looked under the stalls and no one had opened the door or come into the bathroom yet she could tell something had arrived.

"Die. Die. Die. Now. Now. Now. Die. Die. Die. Now. Now. Now. Hahahaha."

Something was whispering into her ear over and over. It was so close that she felt like someone's tongue was against her eardrum making her shiver. She yelled back they weren't funny and busted out of the stall. Absolutely no one was in the bathroom. She peeked up at the bathroom mirror and saw only her face. The voice returned.

"Die. Die. Die. Now. Do it. Die. Now. Do it. Now. Hehehe."

It was laughing in her left eardrum as she felt her skin crawl. Terror seeped through her soul as she figured she was losing her mind or this was really happening. She began to walk back to the table as the voice disappeared. She excused herself and told the Professor she was going to head to get some sleep, they can reconnect tomorrow with a plan.

As Agent Kelso got into her vehicle, she texted Officer Stone to see if she was up. Stone replied she was but she wanted to tell Kelso something.

I saw it as you visited me. I was too afraid to say anything. It was pointing at you. You've seen it now, haven't you? I'm so sorry. I told you I didn't want you to hold that gold coin.

Agent Kelso read that sobering text and felt hope leave her.

Heard it. Not seen. It apparently wants me to die and right now. It repeats it every few minutes in my ear. Either that or this case and sleep deprivation has driven me into madness. Please don't do anything crazy and if needed put something on your eyes so you can't see it, Professor Pendleton said that either you see it or hear it but never both. Can't believe I'm operating under mythology rules now.

As Agent Kelso sent that last text the voice returned.

"Silas dies. Next. Next. Next. Now. Die. You. Now. Silas. Die. Next."

Hearing her grandfather's name uttered by this demonic thing only made her enraged.

"Fuck you! Come and kill me you coward! Piece of shit. Stay away from my family!"

She fought off tears as the voice wailed and laughed in her eardrums at her words. Agent Kelso now fully understood why Lisa manually removed her eardrums with needles. Marc ripped out his eye sockets. She was now part of the Banshee victim family with her grandfather apparently next in the crosshairs.

"Ok, I'm done with this shit."

Agent Kelso peeled out and drove into the early morning direction of Lowy Park. Within a half hour she had removed dirt with her bare hands, had pulled out the coin, screamed at the empty sky about returning the gold, and told the Banshee to fuck off. Nothing responded as she drove home. It gave her some limited sanity and limited hope. Things changed the next morning when she woke up.

Chapter 18

"More. More. Where is it. More. Die. Tomorrow. More. Where is it? More. Die."

The voice had returned and now it was giving clues that gave Agent Kelso her dangerous plan. She phoned Professor Pendleton and Officer Stone telling them on speakerphone her concept. After ten minutes of Kelso brainstorming her big plan, Officer Stone was the first to speak.

"Kelso I can't see anymore, like for a second, but I refuse to stare at that demon again. So how am I supposed to help given I'm temporarily blind?" Officer Stone asked.

Officer Stone admitted she put eye patches on her eyes out of terror. She repeated that she has no medical issues with her eyes, but until this thing goes away she never wants to see it again, she can't sleep, eat, or function with it creeping up on her. She asked for an extra month off from work and has kept the news from her family. She lied to them stating she needed the eye patches due to migraines from the shooting.

"This is astoundingly exciting, I'm like Indiana Jones! Wait, run that last part by me?"

Professor Pendleton was impressed but horrified that Kelso's plan involved several felonies not to mention a high chance of being killed. He asked why not alert more cops or Kelso's chain of command, why is it just them?

"Prof, you technically touched the gold coin, the other night, so the same reason you have my eardrums exploding from torment and Stone blinding herself, that thing is coming for you. Quite soon, might be there right now if you turn around. Next, because we have seen or heard the Banshee, but all the other cops we tell haven't, we will just end up roommates with Marc and Lisa in an asylum. And worse yet, we won't be able to do a thing about the Banshee stalking us, we can pull it off. Even if we fail, we are good as dead if this is our new normal."

Agent Kelso repeated her warning just so they knew what they were signing up for. None of them had much choice or a better idea. Professor Pendleton, after hearing it a second time, suggested a major twist and after another hour of debating it, they all agreed on the modified plan.

"First, I think we need to stop at the local boutique store and upgrade your current wardrobe, ahem, if you are going to play the role," Professor Pendleton offered.

"Yeah girl, if you want to do that thing, you need to wear a dress. A real one, and you know I am right," Officer Stone said.

Agent Kelso looked down at her dirty cardigan and jeans, rolling her eyes. She put up no fight since her work phone began buzzing.

"Fine, whatever. Gotta go explain to my supervisor why I need to stay here a few more days, gotta keep him happy, he might be important at my parole hearing in forty years after our little operation."

Chapter 19

HOURS LATER, AGENT KELSO was sitting in the Blue Mountain Bank manager's office staring at the clock. It was 4:45pm and they had fifteen minutes before the bank closed and four hours until nighttime arrived. Outside it was pouring and the flooding of several streets had already sent many bank tellers home. Local police were securing streets and declaring a safety curfew.

"And Walla Walla was the largest city in the entire Washington territory, an anything-goes town in the early 1860s, which reminds me, what brings you here?" the bank manager winked at Agent Kelso. He eyed her form-fitting black dress with intentional cleavage with delight. She winked back but hid her dry heaving deep within her battle-focused mind. With the excessive make-up, hair extensions, and dress she was wildly unrecognizable from anything resembling herself. She did like the heels, though, that she might keep.

"Like I said, I'm here regarding gold options. Barron Morris stated you were the man to ask for if I wanted...access," Agent

Kelso purred her last words at the bank manager, "Perhaps we can have some privacy?"

"Yes of course," the manager replied, shutting the office door. His was the last corner office before hitting the bank vault with the safe boxes.

"What about these cameras? You wouldn't want this to go from private to public and lose access to all of this? I hope it isn't sent to some nerds in an office somewhere?"

The bank manager let out a deep sigh and told her it was a closed circuit. He hit a button and the cameras turned off and his shade was drawn across his windows. Agent Kelso had strutted to the desk where his chair was and sat in it with her legs spread under the table.

"Oh my god. Yes."

"On the floor, crawl to me." Agent Kelso commanded. The bank manager complied and began to crawl towards the desk opening.

"I bet you want a deposit, don't you?" the bank manager cooed.

Agent Kelso stood up, towering over him. She put her heel into his face.

"Actually, a very deep nasty withdrawal."

He looked up confused and saw her gun pointed right at his head.

"Barron would like to make a withdrawal, so please dispatch the remaining workers after they close, to help load up a van parked outside. Barron has lost confidence in Blue Mountain and is going to search for a new place to store his funds. Ask too many questions or make too many phone calls and you'll get visits from our friends down in Juarez. We don't want that, do we? Barron has enough issues, you don't need to get in the way right?"

"No. I just don't understand. We have been making the various payments and no one is saying anything. I never even told my wife!"

"We understand, just have your people load the van. Keep it calm, keep it routine. Cut the guard loose and have your tellers load the van. Tell him something about the flooding and not to worry. Both Barron and the family will reward you for your diligence. Obviously you are going to need to wipe those digital camera files."

He nodded and got up from the carpeted floor. He asked permission to leave the room and she told him to first let her leave so that everyone knew to take guns off his family at home. It made him gulp but her eyes signaled no weakness nor deception. Agent Kelso sauntered out of the bank past the guard who had no ability to look beyond her breasts.

Agent Kelso made it outside and walked around the corner into the van. Officer Stone and Professor Pendleton were in a rented white industrial van with armored transport uniforms on. Poorly assembled ones from a costume store. Professor Pendleton was overflowing with excitement as Officer Stone looked tense with her blacked out sunglasses on.

"What's the status?" Stone asked.

"He went for it. The whole thing, the porno dialogue stuff, cartel cliché stuff, the fact that he didn't hesitate only confirms Barron is super dirty," Kelso replied.

"Ohhh yeah. We are stealing gold! Not even just flecks but full gold bars, kilogram bars! I'm like Butch Cassidy and and and...wait until I tell this story at MythiCon."

"Pendleton, no stories. You realize the gravity of what we're doing here?"

"Yes. I'm sorry. It's just...exciting! Where is my ski mask? Isn't that what they wear?"

Kelso and Stone exchanged anxious glances.

"Pendleton, Stone is serious. If he, that quickly and easily, destroyed camera footage and is hauling gold bars at the threat of a cartel you do realize that Barron is likely backed by some cartel or tethered to something we don't want in our lives?"

"My Zeus, when you put it like that why are we doing it then?"

"Because on the other side is a Banshee, demon, whatever the fuck it is. And it won't leave and just you wait until it arrives. You'd be willing to burn this city to ashes to get it off you before you off yourself. Believe me."

Officer Stone threw Kelso a look.

"What about him calling cops or FBI?"

Kelso shook her head, "no way this is way too sketchy operations to do that. Also, take a look around, we are fighting a flood with monsoon tides of rain. No one is looking for anything except a canoe and paddle right now. Only one person that bank manager is going to call once this van is loaded, and he ain't calling the cops either."

"Barron. Hope he knows what is coming."

Pendleton was mumbling about how gold was replaced by wheat as the number one valued crop in the region. He whispered how he wished he was stealing wheat which made both of the women laugh.

It was then that the voice resumed. Repeating in Kelso's eardrum in whispers and screams.

"Die. Die. Now. More. Find it. Find it. Find it. More. Die. Tomorrow. Die."

The Banshee's taunting screams confirmed why she was willing to get fired, arrested, shot, or spend the rest of her life in federal prison if somehow this fucking thing would fixate on someone else and spare her grandfather. It was like a fever she couldn't shake.

One hour later their van was stocked with gold bars. Pendleton and Stone had stayed mainly hidden in the front passenger area while Kelso sat in the driver seat waving at the bank manager. He signaled when the last bag was loaded and they drove off. There would be a very narrow window for the second part of their plan and the weather wasn't on their side.

"It's safe, you two, I'm a few blocks out. Pendleton, you are my eyes for tails."

"I don't know why she came then?" Pendleton asked. His nerves getting the better of him.

"Hey, if you had seen what I've seen watching and waiting, mountains of teeth with a scream, you'd wear blacked out glasses yourself. Want me to hop back there and drop a gold bar on your lap so you can join the party early?" Officer Stone replied.

Pendleton apologized repeating he is nervous. Kelso hit a road that was completely flooded. Part of a park small shrub floated past them. She put it into reverse and began to drive away avoiding police blocked roads.

She had twenty minutes speeding to make it to Barron's estate to get the jump on him. If this didn't work he'd likely put a bullet into all of them, but she didn't share that lovely concept with the group.

Chapter 20

THIRTY MINUTES, AND TWO detours later, Kelso pulled the white van onto the final county road leading into Barron's estate. Just then two black SUVs shot past them and turned around. She already knew they were his security detail and gunned the engine. They began to hydroplane a bit which made the temporarily blind Officer Stone clutch the ceiling bar.

"Fuck. It's on. Stone, its game time."

Every time Stone was tempted to take her glasses off, either from motion sickness or curiosity, the memory of the Banshee's cackling death teeth made her take her fingers off the glasses.

One of the black security SUVs was ramming Kelso as she gripped the wheel. Rain continued to slam into the windshield blocking most of her view. She saw Barron's estate road and jerked the wheel causing the wheels to lose traction as the wind almost tipped the van.

"Grandfather. Die. Now. Now. Die. Die. Gold. Die. More. More. More."

Kelso blasted the van up the hill towards Barron's muddy estate as the Banshee continued to taunt her eardrums. A tear started to drop down her face as she felt her sanity slide off her grip. It wasn't even just the words, but how they were whispered then screamed right into her eardrum. The reality of what she set into motion, robbing a bank, instigating a cartel security team on them, and all while being teased by a demonic force. She drove past the mansion and down into the winery acres. The two security vans gave chase without hesitation. They were going uphill, but the mud was stalling her tires. She hit a rut and was stuck. She pulled out her federal badge and held it out the window.

Immediately the two vans stopped and replied with gunfire.

Both women yelled. Stone hit the floor as Kelso leaned downwards. The security detail had shot out the tires and windows. Four men exited the two vans and slowly circled the front of their van.

"Get the fuck out. Right now. Hands up or I'll shoot you in the fucking head."

"Ok. She can't see so I'm going to guide her out. We are not armed. Search us."

Kelso helped Stone out of the van into the mud. They separated them, searched them, and put plastic ties onto their hands. Two security detail opened the back of the van and began to transfer the gold from Kelso's van into theirs. One security guard kept a gun on the girls making them kneel into the mud while another picked up his cell phone.

"Barron, yeah we got the gold. Ah, I don't know sir but at least half of the van is full of gold. There's two girls not one. Yeah the fed and the local cop. I'm in the north sector field. We'll hold them here until you arrive."

"I'm a federal agent, Deputized FBI Special Agent Alex Kelso. You hurt or kill me and you will be pursued by every corner of this nation with federal force."

The security guard said nothing in reply. The other two men kept unloading the gold. The rain made tapping sounds on the trees as Officer Stone fell over from having her hands tied in a muddy trench. An ATV peeled from around the grove corner and barreled down into their area. Kelso could see it was Barron Morris, in a black waterproof jacket and sweats, smiling.

"Ladies, you are in some serious trouble. Naughty naughty. Agent Kelso when I asked you to step up and become useful I meant in protecting me, not robbing me. I like the dress though, Dot's Boutique on Fifth, right? I like the mud look. If we had more time I'd make you both mud wrestle for me, but we have stuff to do. Like get all this gold back to the bank, calm down the bank manager, and also the Veracruz family. Kelso, you really know how to party eh?"

Kelso digested this update.

"Didn't know that did you? Nor did your dumbfuck federal superiors did they? Yeah. I found gold at that construction site. Yeah I hid it in the bank. But obviously I want to diversify my money. Do you know how easy it is to use a wine operation as a front for drug trafficking? Not even I knew until Paulo Veracruz laid it out. Same transport routes, same containers, hell even the same fucking migrants or their younger smarter cousins."

"You wanted me to find out if your competitors were creeping on you," Kelso replied.

"Winner winner chicken dinner for the rez girl. Instead now you have alarmed the fucking bank and now my Mexican friends need reassurance that we are still on track. Gold goes back and I find out who you spoke to, and the natural order restores itself."

"We didn't talk to anyone, we just robbed a fucking bank. Who are we going to tell?" Stone snapped.

Barron Morris sneered.

"Stone, take those ridiculous glasses off. Lowden and Finley yank those stupid fucking glasses off."

The two security guards pulled Stone's glasses off as she yelped. The bright dusk sky plus mud and rain made it hard for her to see. Kelso whispered something into her ear. Stone nodded.

"Oh no, go ahead. Final prayers and words are welcomed. You'll soon be dead."

Silence in both women as Agent Kelso waited for it. Barron picked up a gold bar and held it.

"Never had time to hold the gold before today, my workers had good reason to steal some, it is something else. By the way, Kelso, what the fuck was your plan anyways? Is this some Thelma and Louise play or what? Doesn't matter. Mother nature made this easy on you both. Going to give you two options, I like options, don't you?"

"You can get into the van, we'll place you there with a cement block on the gas so you can fly down off the pier over there, right into the river and drown peacefully for people to find. Or you can elect to take a shot to the head and we'll just dump your bodies into the river with a rock so fish can decompose your body. Either way it will be a tragic end to two brave law enforcement agents who got swept away in the flood. I have calls to make so choose now. Bullet or drown?"

"Drown," Agent Kelso replied. The two security guards began to push the van out of the rut and repositioned it towards the pier. As Kelso and Stone were being pulled up a scream emerged.

"Now!" Stone stated trying to close her eyes.

"What the fuck?" a security guard shrieked and began to fire his gun into the tree line.

Agent Kelso ducked down pushing Stone into the ground.

"She's right over there, coming fast, ahh," Stone replied. Kelso nodded as she heard a whisper reemerge into her ear.

Barron Morris took cover and yelled to stop firing. He fired warning shots into the air to no avail. He emptied his magazine realizing his gun was empty. The guard did not comply and began to shoot wildly. One guard was hit while another started to cuss and shot at the vans, trees, and in every direction.

"What...is...happening?" Barron Morris hissed pulling out his gun and aiming it at the guards. It was pointless. One put the gun into his own mouth and killed himself after seconds of hearing her whispers. The other two guards dropped their guns and began sprinting away down the grove lane. Before Barron could command them to stop they leapt off the cliff.

Their bodies cascading off rocks, mud, and hitting the water with the pressure of falling off a skyscraper.

“Die. Die. Gold. Now. More. More. Die.”

Agent Kelso whispered back, “That’s him. He has the gold, he took your gold, get him.”

Officer Stone looked up to see the jaws near her face howling. She reached up and pointed at Barron.

One hundred feet away Barron Morris saw the girls pointing at him and he hopped on his ATV and took off. As he motored away twisting in the mud, Kelso grabbed Stone and they began to run up the winery aisles as Stone stumbled. Kelso had kicked off her heels and was running barefoot.

“Come on Stone we gotta get there. We have to see if this works. I’m sorry girl.”

They arrived at his mansion ten minutes later as darkness began to set around them. Barron Morris was on his second story balcony with an assault rifle. He was aiming it all around his perimeter until he saw them.

Stone and Kelso ducked behind a pickup truck and shed. Barron had not let them say a word before he started firing rapid shots at their location. Kelso looked around for better cover as Stone looked disoriented.

"I don't know what the fuck you did to my men but you won't get inside my house. It's locked down like a prison. You fucking thieving pieces of shit."

It was then that they saw Professor Pendleton from far away giving them a thumbs up. He was laying on the ground hiding behind the side of a barn, far beyond Barron's focal point.

"And guess what ladies, I got my fucking gold! Right here in my hand. No one is taking my fucking gold. This...huh?"

They knew the Banshee had caught up to him once they heard the screams, and then the thud. His voice had echoed as he fell off his balcony twenty feet away from them. His groans showed he survived the fall.

"I got to see this," Kelso said. She stood up and watched under Barron's night flood lights as he tried to move but had sustained massive injuries to his legs and back. Professor Pendleton was standing up now pointing to the side door. Kelso looked but couldn't see anything. She could hear yelling in her eardrum.

"Gold. Die. Now. Die. Now. Him. Him. Time. Time."

Officer Stone stood up and began to cry. She told Kelso what she saw. The Banshee was opening its jaws and snapping at Barron who could now finally see her.

"Holy shit. Pendleton did it. He actually snuck into Barron's mansion and hid some of the gold while we distracted his goons. Stone it worked! Why are you crying?"

Kelso couldn't see it, but Officer Stone watched as the Banshee's jaws opened extending a massive continent of serrated teeth dripping with blood. She looked away unable to take the visual. Barron's screams were tunneling into primal grunts.

Agent Kelso watched as a strange giant wind gust pushed Barron up and out onto a nearby winery downhill sloping road. Barron's legs wildly crumpled as he began to yell and slide downward out of their view. Pendleton and Kelso gave chase to look down the hill. Both of them could not see the Banshee, but each heard its screams.

"Mine. Mine. Mine. Time. Time. Die. Die."

Professor Pendleton spun around but saw no one talking into his ear. The Banshee had caught up to him.

The black security van loaded full of gold, a few fields away, began to slide downward as well and careened right towards Barron. The wind was so intense that Pendleton and Kelso hugged onto each other against a nearby tree as they tried not to get pulled downwards.

"Oh my. What is happening? Where is that wind coming from?" Pendleton asked.

Before Kelso could answer, the SUV pummeled Barron splitting his head from his body and sending both Barron and the gold deep into the flooded river waters on his pier.

Agent Kelso and Professor Pendleton were left speechless at the horror they saw unfold. Little time for processing occurred since behind them they heard a van start up and both turned startled. It was just Officer Stone.

"Stone, it's ok. Barron is dead! Kind of gruesome...actually. I can't say that I will miss him. Turn that van off, what are you doing?" Kelso asked Stone.

"Do the math Alex, most but not all of the gold is now back with her. We have to return what Pendleton hid in the mansion. We put it in the other van and toss it into the river. Banshee gets her gold, so hopefully that bitch stops with us, and the flood accident story makes more sense," Stone replied. She had taken her eye patches off and was adjusting to nighttime visuals.

"Did you hear what I said? Barron is dead. We're home free," Agent Kelso repeated.

"If you saw what I saw, you'll never be home free. Just help me load this gold."

Pendleton and Kelso exchanged glances. Professor Pendleton grumbled but agreed to help load the van with gold.

Hours later all three watched as the last black van was sent careening into the dark river waters. The taillights of the van peeked out at them as darkness consumed all of it. Stone retreated inside Barron's mansion to wipe down any of their prints and to destroy his surveillance camera footage. Agent Kelso's plan had worked, two vans, one with Kelso and Stone caught by Barron to allow Pendleton to sneak into the mansion and put the stain of the Banshee firmly on Barron. Professor Pendleton pushed Kelso and Stone's rental van into the river since the tires were shot out from the previous gunfight. The hope was that it would float far enough to not be associated with any of Barron's disappearance. Pendleton's van was parked safely around the corner from Barron's estate. They piled in, unable to capture into words what their situation was, settling on silence for thirty minutes.

"So ah, what now?" Pendleton asked. Stone was staring out at the horizon.

"Let's drop Stone off at her house, she was never here. Nor were you, Pendleton. You rented two vans and lost one in the river loading up some stuff. Whatever insurance story you need. Walla Walla is taking a beating so it won't be that insane. I'll put myself here, will update my superiors that I came here for a meeting with Barron but he was nowhere to be seen, so I left. Cartel will want a new leader for this winery, mayor and bank manager can't risk exposure or cartel repercussions, and I plan to say nothing about anything criminal in my report. Rest is up to fate. Honestly, I care less about the FBI or cartel as long as that...thing...never talks to me again."

"Well I don't hear it anymore. Strange. Wish I could have recorded that," Professor Pendleton remarked.

"Hear what?" Stone asked.

"Stone, you got to see her, but we only could hear her, a wild pulsating scream to whisper that repeated really nasty things into my eardrum. I guess either you see her but can't hear her or you hear her but can't see her, honestly I don't fucking care long as it's gone," Kelso replied.

"I finally heard it after I stashed the gold. But now I can't. Hope?" Professor said.

"Maybe," Kelso replied.

"I'll take it," Stone said as she stared at the moon, eyes still darting side to side scared of what might sneak out of the corners of the darkness.

Chapter 21

A WEEK LATER AGENT Kelso got a call from Commander Stevenson.

"Kelso, this is one peculiar report. Two weeks in Walla Walla, met a kooky Professor, Officer Stone is involved in a shooting, you ended up on the wine baron's property, but did not witness five men drowning by flood with entire vans missing?"

Kelso remained silent.

"Kelso how exactly do five grown men and their SUVs just flop into the river like that? Am I missing anything?"

"Sir, it was a tragedy. I'm lucky I didn't drown myself, the streets had become oceans even in town. It was horrific. I still think it might be like a gas leak or something from the ground, about the college kids and suicides. I could stay here and meet with more witnesses?"

A few moments of silence passed. Stevenson was the first to speak.

"Nope, you're all done there. Lisa has recovered, doing amazing they say. No more weirdo voices. Marc, still on the mend but no more visions of boogeymen, they are seeing if they can restore any of his vision but locals are focused on cleaning up the flooding. Families are as satisfied as they can be. They already forwarded your theory about toxic vapors at Lowy Park to the local environmental teams. They'll secure the site and take a look. Sometimes closure has weird faces."

Stevenson thanked her and told her to get some rest.

Chapter 22

Intermission: Demon Detox

Agent Kelso pulled up to the Catholic Church on the outskirts of Wenatchee. The yellow walls and profound greenery in the driveway made her smile. In the distance some kids played on a rusting playground while three people were working on the north side of the exterior of the church. Kelso parked her car and stepped outside, as one woman turned her head and smiled at her.

"Alex! Oh my god!"

The lady, with rubber gloves on, ran over to hug Agent Kelso. It was a deep-set hug that melted Kelso's anxieties, at least for a second. Aunt Susan filled the void left by Agent Kelso's mother. A powerful advocate and heroine of the local community, for decades she had not only helped mentor Kelso, but cared for victims of abuse and domestic violence. Her weeks were spent in homeless shelters, hospitals, and courts giving protection to those without. Her hair blew as she took her sunglasses off to stare at Kelso.

"How you doing Aunt Susan?"

"Blessed, especially now you're here! How are you hun?"

Agent Kelso waved to the priest in the distance. He was on his knees looking at something on the church wall.

"I see Father Harrison and you are working on a project?"

"Something like that, come over and see."

Aunt Susan was still hugging on Agent Kelso as she made her way around the corner to see her childhood friend-turned-priest, Tommy Harrison, scrubbing the brick on the side of the church.

"Father, you should just let me use the pressure washer, we can blast this out faster."

"I googled it and it says we are supposed to sponge it first. Right? Kelso, care to solve this one?"

Kelso hugged Father Harrison and stared at the wall, "RAT CHOKE", was graffitied onto the church brick wall. The large purple letters were curved and matched a few RC's also on the playground the children were on.

"Sounds like one of those metal bands you used to play in before you joined the church," Kelso teased Father Harrison. All three of them began to laugh. Agent Kelso picked up a sponge and began to rub the purple letters.

"So what's happening Kelso? I know that look. What's up?" Father Harrison asked.

"First of all, Susan is right, this medieval sponge approach isn't going to work with this type of paint. Use the pressure washer, and second, I don't get it. Is it that he's choking on a rat? He's a rat that chokes?"

Kelso's smile faded and she dropped the sponge.

"Can we talk inside? I always found St. Michaels comforting, the walls signaled a moment of peace. Something I can't find these days."

They went into the nearby metal door and walked into the open empty church. They sat on an empty pew, Aunt Susan next to Kelso with Father Harrison in front turning back to listen to Kelso. She shared her last two cases and how they each took a toll on her. The Trinity Terror monster had killed everyone but her and the Walla Walla Banshee had pushed her sanity beyond its limits. While she was getting lots of praise within the AIU she wasn't sure it was worth all of the time she spent away from home, especially her grandpa Silas and niece Tia.

"Not even my boss knows the truth about the Banshee, just Professor, me, and Lucy."

"Uh oh, who is Lucy?" Susan cheesed. She knew Kelso when she was crushing on someone. Father Harrison kept the focus of the conversation tilted towards Kelso's mental state.

"While I spent summers stacking boxes at the cherry plant, you did Alaskan ice fishing ships. Remember those girls? They made fun of you for not having a dad and you unleashed a can of whooping on them. Although I don't condone violence, the physical world is something you've had a grip on. Now this Banshee creature, it's of the spiritual world, and those are different rules, but there are still tools, if you look for them. Is it still around, this Banshee?"

"I haven't seen it or heard it, but every now and then...well I don't even know if it is a memory or it talking into my ear. I can hear it every so often whispering things. It's embarrassing. Lucy won't even do night shifts anymore and it is getting her in trouble at work. She actually saw it before we returned its gold to it. I sound like a loon even saying all this..." Agent Kelso looked down at the bibles in the back pockets of the church pews.

"I'm sorry you went through that, it sounds horrible. I knew some priests who had done exorcisms and it changed them. Made them see things others shouldn't know about." Father Harrison patted her on the arm.

"Tell your boss you need time off to heal. You've earned it, you shouldn't even be working cases right now. You just need some time to refocus, to heal. Remember why you even became a Wildlife Officer? It wasn't demon hunting, right?" Susan asked.

"Of course, Susan. Service. Nature. Wilderness. Not having a desk job. Our people's history is centered on fishing, hunting, and land rights or lack thereof after it is stolen away. All that sounds cute until you watch a nuclear serpent chomp on people. Or a gold obsessed demon cackling at you. Makes the idealistic concepts melt away into...just dark pointless oblivion," Kelso stated without looking at Susan.

"If not for what you did, sweetie, thousands of people could have died, if that snake had gotten out. Not to mention the radioactive effects on the water. So you are suffering, but it is not for nothing, I'm proud of you. I know some good therapists in the area. Many warriors have stood where you are now, it isn't just parades and happily ever after, these sacrifices take a toll, no matter the noble purpose. Just know those scars aren't for nothing, right?" Susan offered.

"Yeah, true. I think Tia and Silas are making me second guess it all."

"What about Tia?"

Agent Kelso detailed how her niece, Tia, had written her a long text a few weeks ago stating that she missed her auntie. While her sister, Leticia, had been around, really it was Kelso and Silas who made sure Tia was on track in life. Leticia was loving but had a wild streak that led to some questionable choices in romance, partying, and left holes for Kelso felt compelled to fill same as when Susan had in Kelso's wilder youth.

"Now that I'm getting cases all over the state, I am not there to help Tia with her homework, read to her before bed, and play planet attack. Silas raised me and now I'm only there for like half of his chemo trips to the hospital. So what is this for?"

"Alex, you spent your entire life railing against where you grew up. Each weekend you'd say Wenatchee sucks, too small, everyone dated everyone, nothing to do, citing no real purpose here. And you found any and every way out, now you are out and long to be back in? The unhappiness is bigger than that, Kelso, hun, you've spent a lot of your life running, maybe time to slow down and process."

Agent Kelso took in Susan's words while staring at the ceiling. Father Harrison spoke.

"Also Tia and Silas are fine, I'm often bored and join him on those treatment visits. But I love you, if you feel you can't take it anymore, you can come home. We'll take care of you, and that will be the end of it. But give it a week, month, and you'll be restless, give it years to a decade and you'll likely be soaked in regret about not seeing where this road leads. You wanted the U.S. Marines, you wanted adventure, here it is. The universe put you in this story, I believe you are strong enough to finish it. Least for rest of the year then you can take the cozy regional job nearby, and then you can rest knowing you gave it your all. Want to know real haunted? It isn't a Banshee, it's people at the bar, talking about 'if I had only' or 'one day I'll get it together', that's haunted. Not chasing your dreams turns your life into a slow nightmare."

"Plus, Lucy doesn't even live up here, so you know you'd be gone every weekend to see her" Susan joked.

Agent Kelso broke out in a smile. Father Harrison nodded, staring out at the Cascades as they spoke.

"Alex, very few people can do what you do. To walk that spiritual plane between real and spirit, and not fall into evil ways. Just know your limits and recall why you are doing it. When that gets foggy then it's time to fall back. One of those priests who handle exorcisms shared with me that the power you give to the demons is the true power. It isn't the windows breaking, doors closing, or in your case, the demonic whispers. It's the straying from God, and knowing that we each have a purpose, you, me, Susan, Tia, Silas, and within God's fingertips. These evil men, monsters, and demons may seem terrifying, but in the end they will all kneel. Love and goodness will always win. No Banshee can change that."

"What about Rat Choke? From the graffiti he seems legit, let's throw him into the mix."

Susan and Father Harrison gave Kelso a soft glare.

"Oh you two know I was listening, why do you think I came out there? I get it. Can I please sit here for a few alone?"

Kelso stared around the church, taking in deep breaths. Her left eyebrow was twitching from lack of sleep and stress.

"I'd like to gather myself before I head over to surprise Tia and Silas, gonna grab them a pizza and see if I can find a book on Saturn for Tia. Soaking up my free time before my next case, whatever the heck that will be."

Susan kissed her on the head and whispered how proud she was of Kelso into her ear. Father Harrison hugged her and said he keeps her in his prayers.

Agent Kelso took a long deep breath and stared at the crucifixion art. Sacrifices. The candles and organ all reminded her of the warmth of the universe. Their words sunk deep into her soul and she nodded. She looked around and pulled her phone out, her home screen of Silas holding Tia in a Saturn costume made quiet tears come down her face.

Time to get going. Tia will want to read all thirty solar system books before bed. Guess I'll keep chugging along until I'm knocked out of orbit.

She put her phone away, said a prayer, and walked out to her car. Father Harrison and Aunt Susan were still arguing over how to get Rat Choke off the church as she pulled away waving.

One week later, the phone began to vibrate. Agent Kelso picked it up, it was Commander Stevenson.

"I hope you got some homecoming rest. Something else came in and it is hot. We're bringing in another agent to help you. You'll be thrilled, guess who you have to find?"

"No idea sir, who?"

"Bigfoot. Well, not exactly, State Senator Logan is missing in the Cascades, out by Mt. St. Helens. Three other civilians missing, one surviving witness, and our misplaced senator. Senator Logan is a Bigfoot enthusiast who was partaking in an expedition to hunt Bigfoot with a team of cryptid scientists. Whatever they call those people hunting for the Chupacabra."

Kelso released a grin, Commander Stevenson could sense her elation.

"Yeah I know everyone wants a Bigfoot case. But Kelso we have a missing Senator, they don't care about the monster part. It's fed lands, forest jurisdiction park service people, we work with them often so play nice, got it? Most likely a bear got him but kind of strange for a bear to eat three people right? That's where you come in, go find us a Senator and his entourage."

"Copy that, sir. I'll grab a car, just text me the coordinates."

As Kelso hung up she looked down at Officer Stone and repeated her mission. They were cuddling on the couch in Kelso's apartment. Stone had night terrors and sometimes preferred wearing her eye patches when she got scared. It was a struggle to shake the vision of a thousand toothed grin from her mind, even though no one had heard or seen the Banshee since the case closed weeks ago. Stone had traded time at Kelso's apartment and her own but rarely alone.

"I gotta go, please rest up, and this place is yours. Eat and use whatever you want. You're gonna be ok. Even if not, I'll still watch horrible sci-fi movies with you. Also, if Aunt Susan stops by, don't believe any stories she tells you. That cop car set itself on fire in 2003. One final tip, don't go collecting gold coins anytime soon."

"Promise me you'll text me?" Lucy asked.

"I'll send a pigeon with a poem," Agent Kelso winked and kissed Stone goodbye. She grabbed her keys, phones, and service weapon, and headed out into the darkness.

Chapter 23

CASE: Cascade Tiger

12:00 PM SEARCH MISSION DAY ONE

Agent Kelso stared at the terrain shifting underneath her, desert flatlands to escalating mountain range. The helicopter billowed fast across the rising Cascade mountain range. Mt. Adams on her right, Oregon's state border on her far left. The pilot informed her to brace herself since the winds were increasing. Mt. St. Helens' lopsided peak emerged as they sped towards the landing point at the Ape Canyon. Agent Kelso was born a decade after the Mt. St. Helen's eruption in 1980 and she grew up hearing the stories, but never got around to visiting it until now.

Kelso still remembered the sobering documentaries that filled her with awe about it. The 1980 eruption ash traveled across eight states, blocked out the sun, turning the Evergreen state into a gray gloom. Fifty-seven people died that day. A hot stone-filled wind had surged north at speeds over 300 miles per hour and temperatures of 660 °F. This lateral blast toppled or snapped off trees over a 230-square-mile area north of the volcano, which later became known as the blowdown zone. On the outer fringes of the blowdown zone, the force of the lateral blast had diminished and trees remained standing but were seared by the hot air, leaving a band of standing dead trees referred to as the scorch zone. Beginning about noon and lasting for several hours, super-hot, fast-moving, pumice-rich pyroclastic flows poured from the crater and covered six square miles north of the volcano with pumice many feet deep. This sterile, desolate terrain was later called the Pumice Plain. Heat from the eruption melted snow and glaciers on the volcano's slopes. The meltwater picked up soil, rocks, and logs, forming mudflows that traveled for tens of miles. The towering column of ash rose for more than nine hours and reached a height of about 80,000 feet. Wind carried ash mostly to the northeast where it darkened skies and covered the ground with gray, volcanic ash. Some ash remained aloft, and this part of the plume circled the Earth in 15 days.

"Wow, I expected it to be more barren, it has really recovered, eh?"

The pilot nodded, pointing out the different zones around the moody volcano. The landscape where the lava had ripped through the area restructured the plants, trees, and wildlife in ways that make the area seem like a Martian planet on the north side. Nature reclaimed her territory on the southeast side where Kelso was meeting the search party. Her contemplative viewing of Mt. St. Helens was pulled to an immediate halt.

"Hang on!" the pilot yelled. The helicopter swung heavy left and made Agent Kelso take deep breaths. She was doing her best not to puke as the turbulence ramped up in their final approach.

She looked down and saw Ape Canyon trailhead, dotted with two black SUVs and a jeep. A dozen people looked up as the pilot struggled to get balance to land the helicopter. A little journey north was the actual famous Ape Canyon, the Roswell of Bigfoot fans. Winter had not yet arrived but the October winds were punishing the helicopter's final moments. Kelso's battle with her nausea was a lost cause, she tried to breathe and swallow it down. She forgot to chew some mint gum, which usually helps her on these aerial trips. She never had sea sickness on the Alaskan fishing boats but softcore vertigo always tested her nerves when on small propeller planes and helicopters. Beneath them the barren rock of Ape Canyon reflected with the dying sunlight of the day.

"Sorry, those winds are a bitch, but we're almost done," the pilot said.

"No problem, I hope you like Mexican food since my lunch is coming back up," Kelso replied. She contemplated flinging the door open and leaping to hurry the end of this trip. Certain decapitation from the helicopter blades kept her from taking that adventure.

"Famous Ape Canyon! Best bike trail out there! Bigfoot!" the pilot was shouting over the noise of their landing.

Across the gray and green eastern fingertips of Mt. St. Helens was Ape Canyon, the most famous of all bizarre Bigfoot lore in the United States. Here in 1924, miners were staying in a cabin that was attacked by mountain demons or ape men, depending on who you ask, which threw massive rocks at their cabin. One miner even claimed to have shot one of these mountain demons and watched it fall off a cliff. Almost a century later the truth was as confusing as the origin story. One man claimed it was him in an ape suit playing pranks, another claimed a bunch of teens being jerks, and the most coveted theory was a tradition with boy scouts from local Spirit Lake camp tossing rocks as part of a ritual, with no idea miners were way at the bottom. The cabin was gone but the Ape Canyon trail was a beloved trail with unrivaled views of not just Mt. St. Helens but Mt. Adams, Mt. Hood, and some cool captures of post-eruption terrain. Secretly Agent Kelso always had a soft spot for Bigfoot and Sasquatch tales. She knew the miners were probably full of shit but loved the Ape Canyon story.

The helicopter eased down just as a huge wind gust made their window rattle. Agent Kelso thanked the pilot and hopped out, ducking underneath the helicopter blades. She saw a familiar man walk out from the tree line smiling. She ran up and hugged him.

"Our monster hunter, how goes it? I heard you had a fun time in Walla Walla?" Special Agent Martin Gaucho asked. His brown and green uniform was adorned by a rifle, tactical vest, duty belt, and tattoos across his forearms. Shaved gray hair dotted around his camouflage hat.

"Oh god, don't get me started. It was a real mess. What you been up to?" Agent Kelso replied. She had met the elder Fish and Wildlife Agent at a seminar and immediately took a liking to him. He had a positive attitude and had served with some special forces units prior to his career in wildlife enforcement. Of the cliques and crews of mainly men he had been one of the few people, early in her first weeks, to treat her with respect. She befriended him also to enjoy more wild stories of his adventures in Santa Fe, Argentina. Making use of land and mastering animals were life and death for his farming uncles, aunts, and grandfather.

"Ah, I'm happy. Other day I caught an illegal shrimping boat. Mostly get to cut people loose and relax. Fishing without a license, help out local police on tracking folks, as well as animal control. Rich city people dump their exotic pets quite often, so I make sure to find them homes. Every now and then I still assist in a bear rescue and release upstate. I can't get around as fast as I once used to after that black bear attack in '09. Still got a soft spot for those furry critters though. In life you have to earn your scars."

"Earning mine," Kelso showed him her scar from the Trinity Terror nuclear monster case.

"I like it! Today should be a walk in the park compared to that."

Agent Gaucho began to walk her through the thicket of rocks, dirt, and thickening forest trees. They both heard the lawnmower-like sound of the helicopter blades gearing up and watched as the helicopter disappeared back into the vacant western sky.

"So, we don't have aerial support? Wouldn't that speed this up, order up some federal or even local military copters with thermal imaging, track heat signatures, and scoop this lost group up?" Agent Kelso asked.

Agent Gaucho nodded up the trail towards a man yelling into a walkie talkie waving at them to come over.

"Agent Kelso, just in time, come on over. I'm Tim Gilroy with U.S. Forest Service, Special Agent-in-Charge (SAC). We've got a search and rescue team over here. I'll go over the briefing as we walk to the camping and trail site. Thank you both again, for agreeing to help us out." SAC Gilroy stated as he almost walked into a puddle on their uneven trail. He was a heavy set man, with sunglasses, and warm demeanor.

"Since Mt. St. Helens is a National Monument this is a USFS operation. I'm the SAC, but as you all know we have the funding of a middle school bake sale so I welcome all of you in helping track down the Senator and his crew. We're hoping for a quick and successful op here. Call came in some hours ago from Senator's wife and a few others in that crew."

"So how many are in our search party?" Agent Kelso asked.

"Five: you, me, Agent Gaucho, two USFS rangers here at the camp site. I got some local Skamania County Deputies scouring the woods to the far east and south, just in case they headed to nearby Cougar or Lava Canyon."

SAC Gilroy ran through the thin background known so far: Senator Logan, a massive Sasquatch enthusiast, had organized his annual Sasquatch hunt. Usually in the Northern Cascades, this year moved it to Mt. St. Helens' Ape Canyon region. Four expedition members, three Pacific Northwest Sasquatch Protectors Organization members, and State Senator Ronald Logan. Senator Logan's wife stated that for two days her husband and crew had planned to camp out near Ape Canyon and return two days ago. Upstate, near the towering Mt. Rainier, some geological scientists fell into a collapsed crater so U.S. Parks Service and some state conservation officers are helping with that rescue mission. Gilroy confirmed that there is no aerial support but tomorrow is a possibility. That included at least one helicopter with geothermal cameras to scan for heat signatures. Today would be old school tracking and search and rescue by foot.

"One last catch, although it is a bit early, winter wants to peek its head out of the climate and so we have forty eight hours to get this done before a wicked snow storm arrives. Unless these guys packed for Alaskan camping they won't survive well, exposed to this storm. Maybe a cave but the Ape Caves is the opposite direction of where we think they are located," Gilroy said.

"So we are canvassing this massive area, for four guys, who are lost, without aerial support, and with a blizzard sprinting towards us?" Gaucho asked.

"I didn't say blizzard, but sure," SAC Gilroy replied.

"I got $20 that they are out on Spirit Lake hammered, and just blowing off steam," Gaucho chimed in.

The two USFS rangers laughed. Agent Kelso didn't mind the mission since it didn't involve radioactive monsters or screaming demon banshees. Three mountain bikers passed by staring at them.

"Strange that none of these bikers have found them, no?" Agent Gaucho asked.

"I suspect their campsite is probably two to three klicks northwest. Either that or way out almost by Smith Creek some three to four klicks northeast is a cabin. I have to chase some teens out of there every so often. You want to see Bigfoot, you won't want to hang around these bike trails. Too busy."

"Sounds good, let's get started. You got a trail? Last known point?" Agent Kelso asked.

"Yep, their wife texted us an update of a possible campsite one click north of here. The Northwest Sasquatch Protectors group has been awaiting their footage but haven't heard from them."

Chapter 24

2:00 PM SEARCH MISSION DAY ONE

The team of five descended onto and then quickly off the Ape Canyon trail. Sounds of the trees and unnerving quiet followed them. They mined the terrain with the park rangers leading the way. Mt. St. Helens disappeared behind tree lines as both the mountain bikers and signs of human encroachment evaporated. Agent Gaucho kept his eyes low and scanned their path non-stop.

"Famous west coast tracker in action? My grandpa taught me some stuff but I haven't been able to really apply it. Any tips?" Agent Kelso asked Gaucho.

"Imagine your quarry. No human can move through wilderness without leaving signs. Roughly a walking person will leave signage of passage every eighteen to twenty inches, that's a crime scene of thousands of clues per mile. Some obvious, some not so obvious. Signage here could be bent grass, broken twigs, flattened soil, disturbed bushes, compressed stones, and of course for these dudes, literal trash and prints. Also beware of what might seem human but could also be large mammals or other humans not the focus of the rescue operation. Ahem, like our lovely rhinoceros fellows up there charging through probably a ton of signage and clues."

"Do you want me to tell them to stop?" Agent Kelso asked.

"Nope, I'm just warming up the senses for later. We know where their campsite is supposed to be. Once there, we'll probably need to be more sensitive to not ruining tracks. I'll take point and you can be flank with SAC Gilroy. For now, let them barrel through. This is their area anyways."

Across the next thirty minutes the team continued to descend into the thickening national forest. Along the way Agent Gaucho pointed out some prints to Agent Kelso, noting their gait and stride as well as some compressed branches and bruised vegetation, most likely created by Senator Logan's team. Various scat showed that elk and the black-tailed deer were nearby residents of this part of the National Forest. A clearing emerged, seemingly out of nowhere, and a tan box appeared from afar on a hill amid thundering Douglas Fir trees. SAC Gilroy updated the deputies that they were moving in to investigate.

"Bingo, we got the campsite boys...sorry and girls, Agent Kelso," SAC Gilroy said.

"It's ok, I sit down to pee like the rest of you," Agent Kelso replied causing the group to cackle.

They climbed up and SAC Gilroy opened the tent flap. It was a large luxury tent, a Yurt, that seemed out of place for the area. It was big enough to house ten people and had more room than most of Agent Kelso's family homes growing up on the edge of the reservation.

"This had to be a bitch to haul up here, this thing is fucking massive," a park ranger with blonde hair observed.

"These fellas might not be savvy on survival if this is their tent, reminds me of those hunters who shoot deer with assault rifles."

"About as camouflaged as a Cadillac. If I were Bigfoot I wouldn't come near this thing, they're geniuses," another dark-haired ranger replied.

Inside the luxury tent, three sleeping bags were unfolded, one left untouched. A variety of food was left dangerously around, a temptation island for nearby black bears. Laptops, cameras, and clothes. Outside was a fire pit that was used within the last few hours.

"Folks got some strange ideas," the blonde ranger stated as he pointed to a book in the tent. *Bigfoot-Roswell Nexus: Doorways to the Beyond* was the title.

"Theory is the government is hiding the connection between often aligned UFO sightings in the same areas as Bigfoot sightings so keep people in the dark."

"Dark from what? Fucking stupidity?" the ranger asked.

"Inter-dimensional space travel. Bigfoot is really a traveler from another dimension" Gaucho stated.

"And who is covering it up?" Agent Kelso asked, not actually caring about the answer.

"Essentially, us," Gaucho replied smiling.

"We can't even agree on the lunch options, yet somehow we are swooping in and snatching flying saucers and Sasquatches?" the ranger retorted.

"Team, we got prints outside headed northwest, let's hit the trail, I got Skamania County deputies heading up here to secure and canvass this tent for more clues, any signs of where they might have gone. One of my rangers is going to hang back here to wait for them, the remaining four of us, let's see if we can find what these fellas are up to," SAC Gilroy shouted.

"Gilroy, I got blood," the dark-haired ranger shouted as he touched near the blood drop on the rough trail upwards into the forest.

Everyone began to jog faster up the trail, until they all stopped.

"Oh fuck, is that what I think it is?"

"Yeah, but where is the rest of him?"

Chapter 25

4:30 PM SEARCH MISSION DAY ONE

All four agents stared twenty feet ahead where a severed human hand lay on the ground, clutching a cell phone, amid a dried blood pool.

Several agents drew their weapons while Gaucho and Kelso approached to look at the hand. SAC Gilroy was on the radio updating that they had a hand and possible casualty.

"Thinking bear? Mountain lion?" Agent Kelso asked Gaucho.

"Maybe, Grizzlies are rare even in the Northern Cascades so could only be Black Bear, but we should have a body or remains of one, survivor, something. He's gotta be nearby, the human and maybe even the bear. Bears like to go for the face since they attack what is most powerful for other bears, the jaws. That one horrific Black Bear attack decades ago in Vancouver Island had a Black Bear go crazy feasting on humans. Still a bit extreme, maybe these dudes scared or shot the bear, pissed it off?"

"Yeah, bite marks don't seem bearish, maybe it was your inter-dimensional Sasquatch. Either way let's check out the perimeter. I'll take north and you take south," Kelso replied.

As SAC Gilroy barked commands on the phone and radio, Gaucho went south into a pool of trees to see if maybe someone was hiding. The park rangers took the path upwards to search for survivors. Kelso carefully lowered herself down off a small cliff, beneath the severed hand, using a rope tied around a tree. She landed onto the forest floor and smelled something.

Her allergies had been bothering her so she couldn't make it out but it smelled off, like when she passed by an industrial farm. She was surrounded by a strange pack of collapsed and broken trees, with some sharp rocks adorning the collapsed tree area. It was as if someone had punched down the ground from the normal elevation of the path above them. She scanned the ground as Gaucho had taught her to assess if she was tricking herself and it was a dead end or not.

A rancid, foul-smelling scent hit her again with a wind gust and she followed its horrible depth towards its source. After carefully walking around several trees she saw a stack of animal feces at least six inches high. Mystery solved. She saw another stack as well. Either a pack of animals or one animal with digestive issues.

Not radioing this in, how embarrassing, I used top shelf tracking skills to solve the mystery of an animal taking a dump in essentially a forest port-a-potty area.

Kelso saw across the collapsed tree area a giant tree that had fallen from above, creating a natural bridge up and out of the pit. She began walking towards it when another smell hit her, and she leaned around a tree to make sure she wasn't going to walk into it.

Great, another pile of shit, this one smells even worse than the rest. Forget the tree bridge, I'm going back to my rope and climbing out of this shithole.

When her eyes hit it, she didn't know what it was, at first. It was like a backpack or mannequin had been thrown onto a spike. Whatever it was had landed onto the sharpest rock in the pit, creating a natural spike, and was stuck onto it. It reminded her of marshmallows on a stick over a fire, except this was much more sinister. As she got closer the smell and blood informed her what she was staring at, the fragments of a human carcass. Stumps of thighs, arms chewed off at the elbows, dried blood surrounding the five-foot-tall pyramidal rock. After covering her mouth she circled around the carcass and saw a male face, eyes bulged out in horror, long dead, and far from a peaceful exit in this existence. She pulled out her service weapon and stared around to make sure she was still alone.

"Gaucho, I found him!" Kelso screamed upwards. She also turned to their selected rescue channel, seven, and radioed in for back-up. Within minutes the five federal agents and four county deputies were in the pit staring at her grisly discovery.

"How in the hell?"

"Is this Senator Logan or someone from his team?"

"I've seen fatal fall victims but I can't say I've seen this type of shit before. What the fuck happened here?"

Questions and theories were being tossed about in rapid fire succession. Gaucho had climbed out of the pit and found a trail of blood that led from the severed hand to an edge of the cliff, then it stopped. SAC Gilroy was demanding more help and delegating securing the evidence for an investigation. From the visual leftovers before them it didn't match the photos provided to the team for Senator Logan. It could be Rodney Fischer, one of the Bigfoot Expedition team members, based on a chunk of what was left of his face. He worked in information technology at a hospital in Bellevue, Washington. SAC Gilroy delayed notice to his family until someone could come extract the corpse. Gaucho was trying to piece together what happened.

"Something, let's assume bear but not confirmed, struck him up on the path, boom. So he takes off running, missing his forearm and hand, and leaps, or is pushed, into this pit. Ends up impaled on the rock, can't get away."

"And something turns him into a five-course dinner and takes a bunch of dumps? What the fuck kind of animal can leap twenty feet down and then jump back up?" a deputy asked.

"Well, the tree bridge would allow something to come down here, athletic human, smaller bear, or maybe mountain lion. Ate what it could then returned back up. We should take a look at what prints or tracks there are at the top of that fallen tree.

Although I'm the first to admit it, these bite marks look a bit too big for an attack by a mountain lion."

"This doesn't seem like bear scat," a park ranger offered.

"Poor guy, this is not the way to go," a deputy replied. He couldn't take his eyes away.

"One thing is for sure, these guys are in trouble. I need a pair to stay here and secure this as a possible crime scene, albeit from animal fatal attack. I need a team to go northwest, if the other two guys and Senator Logan outran this thing they hit that cabin three klicks northeast. Let's hope they made it," SAC Gilroy barked.

"I'd like to take Kelso and try the northwest route, just to make sure there isn't another straggler out there lost, good with you?" Gaucho asked.

"Good with me, keep your radios on, and stay alert. I don't want any of you to be its next victim. Find the survivors and let's get the fuck out of here or set up camp, storm isn't slowing down."

"Oh, one last thing," Kelso remarked. She kept her eyes on the chewed off hole that once housed Rodney's extremities.

"Yes?" SAC Gilroy replied.

"Before you bag that severed hand, try to unlock that phone with his thumb and see if we have anything on it. Rodney was trying to phone for help or, let's hope, maybe recording when this thing got him. Worth a shot, right?" Kelso asked.

SAC Gilroy agreed and got two county deputies to work on that with him. He promised to share anything they found with each search team. Agent Gaucho and Kelso agreed to radio in updates as the sun set creating a new challenge of nighttime search and rescue.

As they began their northwest forest trail, Gaucho pulled Kelso aside.

"I'll take point and we're going to move slower than that other team. I hope I'm wrong but many times when untrained folks hit crisis or get lost they go for landmarks. I don't know of any other massive landmark than our friend, sister Mt. St. Helen's. So us moving towards her peak or at least gorge might mimic at least one of these survivors if they got split up. It's obvious they didn't go south back to camp, so let's try to find and help these folks. Signage is key so look for hidden clues of human passage. Given the fear of that last scene it should be obvious if anyone came this way."

"Got it, not thrilled to be canvassing at night. Least with your cologne you'll be the first snack so I can get away. What is that anyways, Olympia Musk?"

"Capital Mall's finest, makes my wife swoon," Gaucho replied. Kelso revealed a microscopic smile and they began their rougher trek across the forbidding terrain towards Mt. St. Helen's peak. Kelso noted some branches but otherwise was not in rhythm with identifying any tracking evidence. She listened to the silence of the trees interrupted, at times, by nearby mountain bikers blasting across trails. Their dialogue and grunts gave her comfort that civilization was still nearby, even if an unknown wild animal was hunting. The deadfall tree debris pulled at their ankle giving them lots to trip on as they made their way across the landscape. The smell of pine and decomposing leaves trailed them.

After thirty minutes of trying out various paths, Gaucho had followed a line of disturbed foliage that intrigued him. They came across a hidden path deep within some heavy bushes and towering trees.

Footprints.

Gaucho had found a trail of footprints. He radioed it in and got confirmation that the northeast team had crossed the suspension bridge and found a trail headed towards Bear Lake, an area east of both Mt. St. Helens and Senator Logan's campsite. The northeast ranger team had animal and human prints. SAC Gilroy confirmed both findings from trailhead headquarters and wished them luck. Just then a gust of wind hit Kelso making her zip up her coat.

"Guess an old man can still nail it, every now and then," Gaucho replied.

"Least we only got human tracks. I'm quite fine with just a search and rescue."

As the sun bid goodbye and fell off the horizon, they pressed onward hoping to help whoever was left out here all alone.

Chapter 26

6:30 PM SEARCH MISSION DAY ONE

Two hours after their big find, they hit a wall. No branches, no leaf litter disturbance, trail had gone dead. Gaucho and Kelso tried going back a little, retracing prior clues and signage. There was no evidence of a campsite and yet the human footprints they had been tracking had evaporated. Night had arrived early along with the first chilly breezes of the storm front. The distance from the original campsite, wind, and storm front had begun to make radio communications challenging. Their phones had satellite coverage, but the smothering tree lines dropped any attempts to make calls.

Kelso looked around and saw they were at least in a small clearing amid hordes of trees reaching upwards towards Mt. St. Helen's top peaks. Beyond them was an array of heights, rocks, and the forest began to thin out as it hit where the eruption lava rivers had spewed their apocalyptic spit.

"Let's camp here, just for a few hours, get some energy do a few more rounds, then turn back and meet up with the team to warm up. Feds have those decked out SUVs with heaters. It is getting so fucking cold out here," Kelso said.

"Sounds like a plan, too early in the season for a real snow but prefer a little light regardless. Someone was out here, I'm not going to give up on them just for comfort. If the snow really picks up we'll have to haul ass to make sure evidence isn't covered up. I just need a little rest. These things can drag on for god knows how long."

They set up their tents and Gaucho built a fire. It took a few attempts given the conditions, but once it was crackling it helped the ambiance. In the distant sky the stars were populating but were being slowly enveloped by a snowy fog that threatened their fire. Just then the radio came to life.

Repeat. NE team inside cabin with a survivor. He's bleeding but secured. We got noises outside. Copy. NE Team engaging. Weapons free. NE team on the move.

Shots! Shots! Aim for the head!!! Fuck.

Gaucho said nothing and stared at Kelso whose eyes were widening. It was like listening to a movie with only her imagination to fill in the blanks.

Hoo rah! Target down. Target terminated. What a large sucker. Copy SAC Gilroy? NW Team?

Copy that. This is SAC Gilroy. You are breaking up NE team, run that by me again, copy. Any casualties?

Negative. Zero casualties and target is out. Survivor Joey Medina secured, en route to EMTs standing by at nearby Smith Creek.

Senator Logan is likely around here. We are going to camp in this cabin for a few, then do a wide perimeter sweep to rescue him. Medina had injuries to his throat so he couldn't talk. This thing really took some bites out of him.

Outstanding work fellas, what was it? SAC Gilroy copy.

An absolute monster of a black bear sir. It took three of us engaging to slow it down. It has to be easily 900 pounds, if not bigger. This thing is the size of a small car, mini cooper or some shit. Wohoo!

Not too bad for some park rangers! Guacho and Kelso here, NW team, we hit a wall of footprints. Taking a breather and will pick it back up in a few hours with more light. Sounds like a real man eater you put down, saved a ton of biker and hiker lives. I owe you a six pack. Copy.

SAC Gilroy here, based on today's findings we might be on track to get Herschel and Senator Logan by early morning tomorrow. Stay warm and tomorrow we'll connect here at headquarters. We'll have aerial support after the storm passes, around noon tomorrow. Over and out.

Even the last bits were hard to follow as the storm winds ramped up.

"They are lying!" a voice shouted above them.

Kelso pulled her gun aimed it near the sound, "Who the fuck said that?", instantly bringing back memories of the Banshee. Its horrific whispering took a toll on her peace of mind whenever things got too quiet.

Gaucho told Kelso to lower her weapon.

"Oh yeah? And what were they lying about?" Gaucho asked the darkness above. His eyes began to adjust to his visual search of the upper tree lines.

"It's not dead. And it's not a bear. Trust me. I saw it."

"Come down here so I don't have to shoot you," Kelso barked into the sky.

Gaucho nudged Kelso and pointed at a tree where halfway up, easily fifty feet up, was a man clutching the tree lodging on a branch and the trunk. He looked cold and had leaves tied to his clothes. Signs of both urine and feces surrounded the lower tree trunk parts. He hadn't left that spot for days, it seemed.

"Hershel? That you sir? Come on down man, we have a fire, some protein bars, and guess what? Tortillas and beans! I literally will make you some delicious eats so come on down man," Gaucho yelled to the camouflaged man.

Silence. Kelso waved at Hershel and offered to come get him with some rope.

"No! It's not safe down there. He's out there, watching and waiting. He took Senator Logan out past here. Medina took off the opposite direction, I ran towards Logan. Your team won't find a thing."

"Who is out there?" Kelso asked. Gaucho frowned.

"Bigfoot man, he took Logan. It's all our fault. Tell them I'm sorry. I can't come down. Logan is probably dead. Oh my god I'm going to lose my job, go to prison, and oh my god."

After some more bargaining, Gaucho and Hershel struck a deal. Agent Kelso felt bad for him and gave her coat and as much of her bedding to Hershel so he could survive the night in the tree along with some food. In exchange for letting him stay in the tree, Hershel agreed to come down in a few hours, with sunlight, so they could evacuate him and return for Senator Logan.

Hershel gobbled up the protein bar and sipped their water, thanking them for their coats. He had tied himself to the tree so that even if he fell asleep he wouldn't fall off the tree, but the tight ropes had taken its toll on his circulation. The storm was beginning to release the first wave of snow which worried Kelso, but she kept smiling at Hershel.

Gaucho radioed in their discovery, which SAC Gilroy confirmed with congratulations. Medina was in critical condition but alive for now. No statements yet from him on what happened. Gaucho told Gilroy he'd get some intel in the morning and share with him and the NE team for plan adjustments.

Despite a few attempts, Kelso couldn't make much sense of Hershel's ramblings, but in the morning she hoped to nail down some more facts to help them find Senator Logan. With one dead, two rescued, progress was in their hands but Hershel's story worried her. She had seen what lies beyond the normal world; with the Trinity colossal nuclear serpent and a demon Banshee, she held out hope that this was all a bizarre bear attack, nothing more. She also knew Hershel could be entirely delirious due to days without movement, food, or shelter beyond imitating a tree branch.

"Good night Hershel. Since it's already 12am, the sun will be up early in like four-to-five hours now, so we'll take turns on watch and keep this fire going until the storm snuffs it out. Need anything, just say it, we'll come get you. We're here to help you. Hang in there bud."

Hershel nodded and was already fading into sleep having finally gotten nutrients. Kelso took the first shift to let Gaucho recover himself. The light snow was beautiful even if her mind drifted to the bloody crime scene she had stumbled across hours prior. She hoped that the monster black bear didn't have any hungry cubs or a vengeful spouse on the prowl.

Both Kelso and Gaucho got some rest and held night watches without any signs of Senator Logan or the ravenous Bigfoot Hershel spoke of in his tree ramblings.

Chapter 27

5:00 AM SEARCH MISSION DAY TWO

The radio crackle woke Kelso as Gaucho chomped on some jerky talking to SAC Gilroy. Hershel was also already awake and had begun his slow descent from his Cascade treetop condo. His body seemed frail and she hopped to her feet to make sure she could catch him if he fell. She grabbed him once he had lowered himself within arm's reach and guided him to the ground. He reeked, but the colder temperature helped reduce the wastewater treatment smell he was basking in.

"Ready for breakfast? Gaucho just built another fire for a quick bite of his beans and tortillas. "I'll toss in some jerky to really give us a five-star meal, you game?"

Hershel nodded but kept his eyes swiveling around them. No signs of distress, but the snow had come releasing a thin set of three inches dusting the trees, grass, and paths. The sun's light was still muted by the clouds and light snow fog blowing around. The soft symphony of nature forfeited the ability to hear anything moving in the forest. Hershel sat down on a rock near the fire and felt the warmth cover his body. Gaucho handed him a tortilla bursting with beans, jerky, it was so warm that it looked like it was smoking.

"Fuck that tastes better than anything I've eaten in my life," Hershel said.

"You welcome bud, Medina is in surgery and hanging in there. Rodney, I'm sorry, didn't make it, did you know that?"

Hershel almost dropped his food. He started to cry. Kelso put her arm around him.

"What happened, did you see what happened to Rodney?"

Hershel shook his head. He continued to eat through his tears. Hunger had made him primal. He was gasping in between bites sobbing and chewing.

"First of all, do you believe in Bigfoot?" Hershel asked.

"Nope, but I'm sure you do, which is fine," Gaucho replied.

"I do, maybe not in the traditional sense. I'm entirely open to meeting whatever it is, with a gun," Kelso stated.

"Exactly, it's on cave paintings, police, senators, and military members have all seen it. Zoona qua wild woman of the woods, Wendigo, Yeti, Sasquatch, Urine in China, Wood Boogers in the south or the Skunk Ape, and endless wild man documented new stories for the last two hundred years! The gorilla wasn't discovered until 1847 and was considered a myth. This extant fossil ape, originally from Asia where sightings still occur, migrated across the Bering land bridge along with mastodons, giant beavers, bison, and other mammals in North America. People like to joke about being a cryptozoologist but it is no different than other sciences. We examine morphology of tracks, locomotion, and hair DNA. Every time we get close it seems some vans pull up, and evidence or labs deny our findings. The Okapi, cousin of giraffe, was a legend until discovery in 1930. With human encroachment on the last edges of wilderness, we are on the cusp of huge discoveries!"

"I watch late night TV, I've heard all this before son. Answer me this, why no fossil record?" Gaucho asked.

"Humans kill an enormous amount of animals in tons of places and still only have a few fossils. Aerial conditions, ground compression, and pressurization are needed for those bones to turn to stones. Humans aren't this magical species who went from Australopithecus to homo habilis to homo erectus to Neanderthals to current homo sapiens. Animals don't want to be eaten and they know, in the wild, dead things are eaten. Also, America has crazy acidic soil. In normal nature conditions, like this here, a wolf will die within days, half picked skeleton, in weeks bones are scattered by scavengers, and come in a year nothing is left. Bears eat bears, chimpanzees raid and cannibalize their own to take over a troop. Fossil record my ass."

Gaucho nodded and kept eating.

"Just years ago we discovered the hobbit humans which were, again mythical little people, that lived alongside us. Gigantopithecus blacki, easily nine feet tall and one-thousand-pound ape. There are over twenty to forty areas worldwide with documented sightings, water sources nearby, foliage for hiding, and not just the local addict seeing shadows. It's such fucking human arrogance to think that somehow we discovered everything already. Two hundred years ago we thought we had the world on lock and look what we've made, discovered, and corrected since then?"

"How do you know all of this?" Kelso asked.

"Documentaries, monster shows, books, blogs, clips...it's all out there, if you look."

Agent Kelso hid her smile as Hershel unleashed his lectures onto Gaucho. She was a once a fangirl of the monster myths in tv shows. Obviously not the Banshee, but she was a fan of how there was a world beyond the boring predictable one in which ancient or newfound species might appear to blow everyone's minds. Even if many of the monsters were likely fictions and frauds, it was the exciting sense of discovery and protection the fueled her applying to be a Wildlife cop.

"Sure, but they can find the most rare species now, so I'm just not sold on hundreds of millions of people with GPS, phones, and now infrared cameras and we somehow missed a nine-foot bipedal primate, not to mention his caloric intake would require a very clear number of animals killed or veggies to keep him or her alive. So maybe it is just us projecting us," Gaucho added.

Hershel stopped eating and glared. Kelso's smile widened, the debate distracted her from the grueling weather. Hershel was unleashing a lifetime of Bigfoot documentary shows, but Gaucho was fed up.

"There's folklore of things beyond the cities, towns, and empires for each crew of humans. There's always this pristine wilderness, and we project a chunk of ourselves out there anthropomorphically hoping that some untethered version of ourselves is out there. Notice how, like western Gods, the Bigfoot are both wild but have some type of kinship with us in each account? Nothing wrong with that, just us teaching about ourselves. Just like most of the gods seem to always have pleasing human features, with aspirational values. Now what I do have a problem with, is missing or dead humans, blamed on mythical creatures. So what happened with your team Hershel?"

Hershel avoided their eyes.

"It's ok, we just want to help whoever is still lost out there, tell us," Kelso added.

Hershel shared his secret. A big-time financier had popped up and approached Senator Logan to film Bigfoot out here. If they caught something, this big-time financier would give them the type of funding to do never-before level global hunts. It was Hershel's idea, not Logan's, to make sure they found something.

"What does that mean, make sure they found something?" Kelso asked. Gaucho was done playing good cop.

"Fucking balls on you, lecture me, then do a 2017 version of the Patterson Gimlin film," Gaucho snorted. Gaucho remarked how the legendary 1967 film allegedly capturing a Bigfoot walking had been debunked by prankster Patterson himself.

"Seven different guys have claimed to be in a suit with muscle detail that no one had around in 1967. Legs too long and arms too long to be a male, Gimlin didn't lie!"

"Guys, enough, Hershel, continue with the story. Ok, so you all showed up here. What was the plan and what happened? We have to get moving soon."

Hershel admitted that he plotted for Senator Logan to wear a Bigfoot costume, and for Rodney, Medina, and himself to film it afar. They would take that fake and get the funds to find the real truth, justifying the sacrifice. They roamed the first day trying to find the best filming site and finally landed on one. Day two they were out filming and Senator Logan was doing his first take and all of a sudden something dragged Logan away screaming into the woods. It was so fast, so crazy, that Medina took off running like a coward. Rodney and Hershel went to look for Logan but he was gone. Rodney stayed near camp in case Logan or Medina returned while Hershel roamed the woods not finding a drop of blood or sign of Logan.

"So what did you see, Logan?"

"I didn't, I just saw him drop to his knees then dragged down a bunch of trees. He was screaming, then went quiet. I even got lost myself the first day and heard some growling so I climbed up this tree and haven't left since. I had no idea Rodney was killed by it. Bigfoot knew. He knew we were disrespecting his legacy, and we paid that ultimate price. Fuck fuck fuck!"

"It's ok, we'll find him, we're not leaving until we find your friend. On the upside, if he is still in that costume, he might be warmer than most of us," Kelso replied.

Gaucho ran through the story a few more times grilling Hershel and relayed the strange tale to SAC Gilroy by radio. The NE team hadn't found Senator Logan, so a new plan was made. NE team would regroup at south headquarters and then slowly follow up behind Gaucho, Kelso, and Hershel. Meanwhile, Gaucho wanted to keep going Northwest hoping to find Logan in some cave or rocky ravine. Gilroy and Gaucho predicted that this bear had somehow taken Logan somewhere, maybe killed him, or Logan fell and these ill-equipped Bigfoot frauds had missed an injured Logan somewhere off trail. Gaucho turned to Hershel to calm his chaos.

"Hershel, the NE team is swinging south to get supplies and more people then we are going to flood this region to find Logan. We'll also have an evac helicopter by noon to get you safely out of here. Let's check out some caves and ravines up above. What's done is done. All I want is to find the Senator."

They packed up their campsite and began treading northwest towards some rockier terrain as Mt. St. Helens summit glared at them from afar.

Chapter 28

7:00 AM SEARCH MISSION DAY TWO

Hershel was slowing them down, but it was ok since the snow made tracking nearly impossible. The storm had returned with another wave of snow and swirling fog which left radio updates not possible. At least SAC Gilroy and the teams knew of their general location. They could see the campsite and fire pit and find them if something happened.

"Ah, what's that?" Kelso asked.

Gaucho looked up from his crouched position and saw something strange. It was about twenty feet ahead, as the trees and rocks narrowed up, in the mix of snow and dirt, three giant holes.

"Those look like fucking graves! We're going to fucking die, I knew it!" Hershel yelled. Kelso kept her hand on his shoulder. To the left was a drop off that could be fatal and to the right were rocks that wouldn't help any quick movements.

"Chill out, chico, how do we know this isn't some hoax you and your crew put together?" Gaucho asked.

"Nope, nope, fuck this, those are graves man! And why are there three?"

Gaucho walked forward and noticed something had dug three fresh holes into the ground. Shallow ones but three definitive holes. Hershel wasn't off that something seemed to want to bury three unknown things. It made his nerves tense up as he saw no signs of a shovel or manmade object made these. Instead he saw traces of claws.

"Gaucho, I got something over here, to the left, we got prints. They aren't human,"

Gaucho walked to Kelso and they both examined a rather large series of padded prints with spaced pairs signaling a four-legged culprit.

"These are way too big for a mountain lion and yet also don't seem right for a bear, I mean maybe if it is like the weirdest shaped bear. Bears have been known to ravage cabins for freezer chemicals that ants have and dig into places for ants when starving. We should track these, radio it in, and see where it leads," Gaucho said.

"I'm out, fuck this!" Hershel snapped as he turned and began to run back to their campsite hours south.

"Hershel! Come back-" Kelso began to yell but it turned into a scream.

A creature massive, brown striped, and covered in snow leapt out of the woods and tackled Hershel. He was only able to release a moan before the beast had ripped his neck open, pouring blood all over the fresh snow. The beast was still mostly covered in snow so they couldn't yet identify what was attacking him. They didn't wait either.

Kelso and Gaucho began firing their weapons with several shots hitting the beast, but not impeding its feast on Hershel's face and neck. As it ripped a chunk of Hershel's chest off the snow faded and they stared at a horror they could barely classify. It had four legs, a tail, jaws like a Siberian tiger, but with the body of a bear. Even more horrifying was that its coloration matched the ground and on top of its blood-soaked mandibles which had teeth easily a foot long, lay antlers. The antlers sat right on top of its eyes so when it turned after Gaucho landed a shot by its muscular neck, he could not track its next move. Smooth and spiky hair jutted from its sides. It was a nightmarish mixture of a tiger, bear, and panther-like face under the antlers.

"Oh my god, what the hell is that? Bear-tiger thing?" Kelso gasped. She continued to shoot at it but it had jumped back under a bed of snow. They reloaded their weapons and Gaucho reached for his radio.

It was back, and despite its hulking size it moved like a car without a brake pedal. It galloped and struck Gaucho right in the arm, ripping it and exposing his bone.

"Argh. Oh. Muthafucka," Gaucho yelped and fired his rifle with his right hand. Blood hit the snow and Kelso unloaded her entire magazine at the Cascade tiger. It caught a few shots into its mane but disappeared. The radio was crushed and useless.

Kelso held her gun up but only silence responded. Gaucho continued losing concerning amounts of blood.

"Gaucho hang in there, I got you. We gotta stop your bleeding. Get somewhere for the team to fly you out of here."

She wrapped a shirt around what was left of his arm and knew that either by that monster or his blood loss he had about an hour to go before he would die, without medical care.

The sound of heavy breathing made her body fill with adrenaline and terror. She turned to see the antlers of the Cascade monster charging at them. It no longer wanted to play hide and seek and wished to finish them off.

Since she was holding Gaucho up, she had no time to go for her gun. Its jaws were locked onto her skull within the time she blinked. All she could hear was low guttural breathing and then felt a powerful blast as she held onto Gaucho. She wasn't going to let him die alone. Her last memory was opening her eyes, covered in fresh blood, as they careened off the snowy dirt trail and began to roll and fall onto the rocks far below.

Guess this is how I die. Least it wasn't the fucking Banshee.

Chapter 29

11:00 AM SEARCH MISSION DAY TWO

Kelso woke up to the sound of Gaucho coughing.

Whoa. Not dead. Not yet at least. I'll take it.

Gaucho was bruised, but his eyes were awake. She couldn't make sense of where or what had happened until she looked up. First she had to wipe the dried blood out of her eyes and painfully ran her broken fingers across the top of her scalp which was now exposed and bitten.

"Guess we're the beef jerky now, eh?" Gaucho managed a joke as he felt death coming.

"Yeah, I think he didn't like my brains and tossed us like spoiled food down into this rock ravine. I don't know how we even survived the fall. No backpack, no radio, no phones, and only my 9mm Glock left to battle a mountain tiger-bear-thing. This is great. Where did that creature even come from?"

"Yeah, my legs aren't doing so well mija, I can't move. I need to rest," Gaucho pointed to his legs that were pointing in all the wrong ways.

"Jesus Christ, you make it out of here, least you can retire now. Just will need a new left hand."

Gaucho nodded at two nearby caves. He couldn't point but nodded to Kelso that he saw a blood trail into one of them.

"Fuck. Let me prop you up against this rock here and I'll go see if it is some camper or someone with a phone. If it's the monster then I guess that makes me lunch and you dinner. I could stay here and we just wait it out, but I'd rather put a bullet into this thing rather than wait for it."

"Please, go hug this thing with a million bullets. Then come back with some Gatorade and a steak taco, please."

"Deal. Take this back up knife. If it comes, this ain't no fucking Bigfoot, it bleeds, it can die, stick it right in the eyes and you can become the monster hunter."

Agent Kelso softly patted Gaucho on the head the same way she does her grandfather and limped her way past the first cave, scanning and checking it for signs of life. Her ankle and ribs were in severe pain but she knew this was a situation in which they had to scourge for survival. She tried to lean against the cave opening and listened.

It was a massive rock structure embedded deep within a canyon, no different than Ape Canyon except in location. She hoped that some enterprising adventurers had hiked into the cave and even if the monster ate them, they left something they could use to alert rescue teams.

It was dark enough that beyond the first few feet it was unrecognizable of what lay beyond. She flashed her light but had a hard time keeping it calmly focused. There were sticks, debris, and even old bones in the first few feet of the cave. She couldn't make it very deep since her ankle and legs were badly injured from the fall. Keeping herself from fainting was a challenge. She had wrapped her head but adrenaline from the attack was decreasing, and the pain was on the uptick. She heard nothing at first and then heard a sound.

"Bello? Bellrow?" a voice yelled out. It was struggling to say hello.

Kelso replied and asked who was there. She identified herself and asked if the monster was in the cave with the person.

"Bello? Nooo, comw nowr, foreee it rerurns" a voice replied.

What the fuck language was this?

Kelso limped further and saw the source of the voice. There he was, Senator Logan, still in his bigfoot costume with substantial wounds to both of his legs.

"Senator Logan? Oh my god, I'm so glad we found you sir, I'll drag you out of here. Let's take that mask off. I can't follow a word you've said."

She propped up his body. The black and plastic fur costume reeked. She pulled off the mask and saw that his face was covered in dried blood with a broken nose and black eyes. He pointed down the cave, past them deeper into the dark, and whimpered.

Kelso swung her light past them and saw a clump of black fur and part of a skull.

"Is that like the rest of your suit or what? We don't have a lot of time to talk, I don't want to meet that thing again, especially not in its little den."

"It killed him. I can't believe it, it's there and it killed him."

"What? Who? Another hiker or?"

"Bigfoot. Go look, it dragged him in here, just like me. And it ate him, alive, poor thing. I knew they were real, and to hear it struggling and yelling, Bigfoot is dead. Fuck!"

Chapter 30

1 1:30AM SEARCH MISSION DAY TWO

Kelso didn't know if it was from the bite or the head trauma from the fall, but this wasn't registering with her draining focus. She limped a few feet closer, promising herself to not go so far she falls or is trapped, and saw the crude leftovers of the monster's meal. It had rotting chunks of muscle tissue, lungs, but she saw the skull and partial face of something that wasn't human, but wasn't too far off.

Holy shit, Hershel wasn't lying, this might be an actual Bigfoot corpse.

"Whoa, well if I die, at least I can say I saw another miracle of the mythical world, Bigfoot himself. Senator Logan, got a cell or anything on you?"

"Yeah, I have an entire satellite package inside this skin-fitting suit. I just chose to not use it to save my life."

"Lost your legs but not a sense of humor, I like it. I'm gonna drag you to my sidekick Special Agent Gaucho. You two can be besties until we are either rescued or become a feast for this Cascadian creature."

Kelso proceeded to drag Senator Logan slowly out of the cave, cautiously, onto the rocky little awning that Gaucho was propped up against. Both men looked haggard and exchanged diluted pleasantries. Kelso looked around for foliage or any type of water or food. She heard the sound of water somewhere in the distance. Under one set of rocks she saw some access to snow and figured her next moves.

"Gaucho, by the way, you were wrong, we got a dead Bigfoot in that cave. No human costume this time. Guess you owe Hershel an apology," Kelso teased.

"Guys, I'm gonna crawl or slide down those little rock caves and snatch us some snow water. I'll use one of our shirts and we can rinse it so the water drips into our mouths. Best I can do and will keep us afloat for awhile. Once I get my energy up, I'll drag you two down there so we can be further from this cave. Cool?"

Gaucho gave a thumbs up and Senator Logan was closing his eyes.

Kelso began her trek downward across two small rock caves onto a flat grassy and snow-covered embankment. Sunlight made her feel better than the shadow caves and bloodbath den. If she wasn't fighting off deaths' fingertips she would have grieved the Bigfoot killing more, since she herself had longed for the chance to see one, and know her elders' stories were true.

She began to collect the snow for the guys, eating some herself, so she could lift herself back up each rock cave back to them. The ice-cold snow felt amazing on her throat and she felt a little hope emerge for their rescue. She heard the growl.

You have to be fucking kidding me. Okay. Fine. This is it.

She pulled out her gun and saw the antler peek out from around the trees. It was bleeding, wounded, but seemed unrestrained in its glare at her.

Time to die you piece of shit.

Her gun jammed. She tried again, but nothing. The fall from the rocks had neutered her only and final chance to defeat the Cascade tiger. Her knife was back with Gaucho. She was finished. She reached for a nearby rock to hit it with as it ate her. Kelso gave it the middle finger as it began its sprint to kill her.

A giant rock slammed onto the Cascade Tiger knocking it to the side.

Three more huge rocks came thundering down from above crushing the Cascade Tiger's legs. Finally one more huge rock, nearly the size of a boulder, came down and caved its neck. It's hissing and breathing became more labored.

What the fuck is happening?

An adult female and two young Bigfoot cubs appeared from above staring at her.

Kelso was left without any ability to speak, covered in blood and on her hands and knees. They eyed Kelso as a threat for a minute then seemed to disregard her presence. They hopped down, ignored her and within minutes had dragged the Cascade tiger's carcass off into a distant cave.

The female Bigfoot turned, took one final look at Kelso, and disappeared with her cubs.

A familiar and amazing sound emerged in the distance, the whirls of a rescue helicopter. As the sun began to melt the snow around her, she turned onto her back and began to wave into the noon light, wrist dangling with broken bloody fingertips.

Chapter 31

CASE: San Juan Zoo

The sun shone bright reflecting off the waves as the water taxi careened onwards. Behind Kelso was the mainland of Washington. The gigantic blue arms of the Pacific Ocean wrapped themselves around her. She stood on the boat staring at the passing islands, Lummi, Orca, Sinclair, and finally, Matia. They were headed to the upper San Juan Islands, the mysterious Sucia Island to meet Gaucho.

It was only a week ago that Gaucho had written to Kelso asking her to meet him out here. He had described his rehabilitation and forced vacation was healing his soul and that she should come. Kelso was going to bring her girlfriend, Lucy, but she had to work this weekend. As a replacement, Kelso had convinced her sister and niece to join her. Kelso was to arrive today at Sucia Island, while her Leticia and Tia spent a day at the nearby Lummi Silver Reef Casino. Tomorrow Leticia was going to get Tia on a water taxi, get her to the island, to join Kelso and Gaucho, then she'd head back to drink at the nearby bars. Leticia passed on the offers to camp but said they could hit

Seattle with Tia after the Sucia camping. Tia, only five years old, had never really traveled much. A few times Kelso had taken her to Spokane for day trips but never over the Cascades into the islands of Northwestern Washington. Something like this was an adventure for the burgeoning little girl with a melting smile. Beyond the gorgeous island visuals Kelso held a massive smile thinking of how Tia would get to ride a boat, explore her own island, and even camp!

The captain yelled to Kelso telling her they were coming up to the Sucia Island dock. Kelso held on and stared as the bizarre island emerged. It wasn't shaped like a normal island or any of the other San Juan Islands. It had dense forests, rocky shores, and plentiful fishing areas but it was shaped like a giant upside-down horseshoe with floating strands of sandbars adjacent. Maybe like a hand with severed fingers floating next to it. It had one major island part that stretched in an arc with five other mini-islands in its Primal Bay. It was once a national park but had been bought and closed off by some tech billionaire. Kelso was intrigued that Gaucho had gotten permission to camp there, apparently he had helped the billionaire with a fishing expedition gone wrong, and gotten in his good graces.

"Hold on," the captain said. They began to head towards the Fossil Bay dock so they could moor. Within minutes Kelso hopped off the water taxi, tipped the guy, and gathered her camping gear along with two bikes. One for her and one for Tia. The one for Tia was so small she was able to tie it to her backpack and began the trek down the narrow pier. A few empty boats were also moored to the dock. Kelso turned to stare as the water taxi disappeared behind the curve of the Fossil Bay trees.

Where is Gaucho? He said he was going to meet me here.

Kelso looked around but saw no one. She walked up to the empty building that used to greet visitors for the national park. A note was nailed into one of the walls with the word 'Kelso' on the front.

Hey Kiddo, sorry running late setting things up for you and Tia. I'll be back in a bit, hang out here or take a stroll. -Gaucho

Kelso set her backpack and bikes down inside the gutted out building. It had maps all over the walls and old pamphlets. She began to read them trying to memorize camp sites and cool places for Tia. An hour passed and she fell asleep. Between the Banshee and Cascade Tiger, Kelso had been suffering night-mares finding daytime easier to sleep than nighttime. She was awoken a few hours later when she heard a familiar voice.

"Always sleeping on the job, eh?"

Kelso cheesed. She hopped up to run and hug Gaucho. His embrace was firm and clinging.

"Thank you for this, I can't wait to go swimming, get a fire going, and finally free my mind!"

Gaucho didn't reply but held a sad glare. Kelso pulled away and stared at his face.

"Aww I missed you too!" Kelso stated.

But his face wasn't full of warmth. It looked off, something wasn't right.

"I'm so sorry, I...I'm so ashamed," Gaucho said as three jeeps barreled out of the nearby woods.

Kelso, still switching gears from her nap mind frame, just kept her eyes on Gaucho.

"What is going on? What is this?" Kelso stated, voice raising. She went for her gun in her backpack.

It was too late, as six soldiers surrounded them with assault rifles pointed at her. They had dark blue camouflage uniforms.

"They have Linda, she's in a kill house. If I didn't get you here, he was going to kill her while I watched. She's the love of my life, I've...killed us all," Gaucho said. His tears fell silently on his face as he kneeled down.

"Just do it now, kill us!" Gaucho yelled at the soldiers as they pulled him up and into one of the jeeps with plastic wrist ties on his hands. They disarmed Kelso, who had her hands up, glaring at Gaucho. As they pulled Kelso towards another jeep she swung her arms out and knocked one out cold. She used his assault rifle as a bat to break the nose of another soldier releasing a blood stream down his face. She began to run towards the pier hoping to find a boat and escape.

She made it three steps before a soldier with a mohawk hit her with a tranquilizer dart. She kept running and got hit again. And again. Until she was forced onto her knees. As the soldiers walked towards her she continued to crawl on her stomach, dragging away from them. Darkness fought into her skull. Her last thoughts were what was going to happen to Tia when she arrives tomorrow?

Chapter 32

When Kelso awoke, hours later, it was dark. Outside through glass windows nighttime had set into the island. She looked around and saw she was at a dinner table, tied to the metal chair, with very bright lights around her. It was a long table stretching out ten feet. As her eyes adjusted to the contrast of indoor light she made out two other people at the table. One on the left, Gaucho, and some blonde haired middle-aged man at the head of the table opposite her.

"Good evening Agent Kelso, glad you could join us. I was about to throw in the towel. Gaucho lost his appetite. Shame? Fear? Who knows. But you, I know you might be hungry, anger can really work up a palette. Just tell me if you want a treat, I'll have one of my assistants feed you," the blond man said.

"What's wrong, I can't use a fork or knife?" Kelso replied.

"I'm afraid not. Although you did not disappoint by breaking one of my men's noses. Silvo put you down but I love how you gave them a run for their money. Let's hope you keep that up tomorrow."

"Sounds good, what do you want?" Kelso replied studying the room.

"Sorry for the manners, I am Chad Zacks," the man replied.

The name rang a bell but Kelso couldn't track. She was narrowing her angles down and saw zero armed guards. Tipping the chair might give her an advantage to take a sprint down the hallway to a weapon.

"Due to your lack of reaction I guess you don't watch the news or at least not closely."

"Enlighten me."

Chad explained how he was a quiet investor in a few industries that had taken off, allowing him to gain the type of wealth to purchase an island, even one from a U.S. state.

"Congrats, doesn't answer my question. What do you want?" Kelso repeated.

Chad slammed his hand onto the table making the plates shimmy. Kelso was startled by the break in silence.

"Vengeance. Simple and plain. You're here to die."

Kelso did not reply. Gaucho finally chimed in.

"He's the one who created the Cascade Tiger, that was his," Gaucho stated. He couldn't look at Kelso and just stared down at the table.

"Bingo. You killed my precious contribution to the world of apex predators. And now, in return, I'm going to kill both of you, and when I feel like it, any aspects of your family, friends, and existence," Chad replied.

"We're law enforcement officers, federal and state. Do you really think you will be able to murder us?" Kelso replied.

"Do you really think that two hundred million dollars in campaign funds and former FBI agents on the payroll can't make people forget? Come on rookie, the news cycle these days is horrific, mass shootings, new diseases, beheading videos. So two fallen officers who blew up during a dangerous drug trafficking sting off the island, I can sell that all day. Your families are collateral fun. I'll kill them later on so it looks less connected. Gaucho your wife I'll probably do like a car crash and, Kelso, since you put down my precious child with rocks, I'll probably throw your niece into a pit of acid."

The imagery made Kelso gasp, her anxiety began to circulate deep within her. She focused on her breathing and tried to push out thoughts by asking more questions.

"First of all, your tiger child was a mass murdering monster who killed several innocent people. Second, I didn't kill it, a group of, it sounds crazy, but-"

"Yeah yeah I heard it from Gaucho, Sasquatch magically appeared during a hoax bigfoot documentary, and somehow smashed my sacred fur baby to death. I don't believe that for a second. Nice story though, still time to die."

"For killing essentially, a methed-out mountain lion thing?"

"Volatility is what gave us the evolutionary edge. It is also what made me rich. Shaking things up is the difference between becoming a fossil and being the species that shows fossils in museums. Creating a biological creature, for spicy rogue nations? It is like having ten thousand orgasms. Nothing like it."

Chad continued lecturing about survival of the fittest, brutality of those who prevail in nature, and how humans have been the apex predator for too long. Kelso grew tired of the ramblings and cut him off mid-speech.

"Great. So you are a walking cliché, eh?" Kelso baited. Gaucho looked up and towards Kelso.

"Pardon?"

"*Jurassic Park*, *Island of Dr. Moreau*, there's more, do I need to continue?" Kelso snorted. "There's no shortage of rich assholes who are so bored with their privileges that they either hunt the poor or try to play god, so even if you kill me, it's been done before and better."

Chad grinned.

"Well, I'm more of an environmentalist. The facility you're in is run by recycled metals, solar power, and will last ten lifetimes. I finance fresh water for Africa, hospitals in Syria, and am even cornering a cure for liver cancer. Isn't that interesting?" Chad sneered at Kelso. She knew what he was implying about her grandfather before he was finished.

"Still doesn't make sense killing us or my innocent niece."

"Our species is bloated, overpopulated, and stupider than the pests we spray toxins on. We've become weak from no mortal threats. I don't see myself as a god or some dinosaur theme park guy, no no, I'm an equalizer. Predator drones destroy houses full of kids to save the greater good of civilization daily, few people shed tears. Settlers battled natives, plague, food shortages, and wild animals to lay the groundwork for the most prolific nation in modern history. Do you know how many innocent animals die per second so that your shampoo, lipstick, and eyeliner you are wearing are acceptable for your use, for a few hours before wiping it off? I'm talking carcasses of generations of apes, cats, dogs, and little innocent kittens. Misery is part of the experience. At least you, this piece of shit Gaucho, and your families will die for something worthy. A resharpening of our species as they battle new challenges. If anything, you should thank me for offering to kill you, I'm giving meaning to your final seconds on this planet. And maybe you are right, I won't kill your niece, I'll just let her grow up, on the reservation, and let her flame out at age 16 from a fentanyl overdose. Who knows, depends on what I feel."

Kelso was done and it showed on her face.

"You going to pull the trigger or what's the process here, can we get things moving? I'd rather you just put a bullet in me than listen to any more of your hot garbage philosophies."

Chad nodded at Kelso and she began to hear footsteps behind her.

"Too pedestrian, what am I some developing country dictator making snuff videos? Come on! Have some class Kelso! No, you will get to meet my other children tomorrow. Out on Patos

Island, and when they are done with you, I'll stop by and make a necklace out of your bones."

"Patos Island?"

"Yeah, this island is too high profile and still close to the passerby ships and tourists. Patos, I bought just last year, and while it is small, the dense forest and solitude allows for accidents to go unnoticed. I even paid off satellites and provide a false visual so if my children peek out from the tree canopy no one will notice. Drug traffickers are usually the best protein, their childish attempts to move drugs through or on my island are met with tasty ferocious snacks for my kids. You two might provide them some real hunt options, nothing makes a meal tastier than truly having to hunt for it. I'd suggest you both try that out some time, but too late."

"You have an island full of more Cascade Tigers?"

"No, there was only one of those, hence your death sentence. But I do have other guys and gals who want to say hi to you. Probably detach your head while you are still alive, it's really pretty cool. There's some cameras out there so hopefully I can watch you die. If not, so be it, fitting end for what you did out there at Mt. St. Helens. This will be the last time you see me. Just know when you die that you are walking in the shoes of every extinct animal that ever took its first step against the new king on the block. I hope you get to meet all of them before you die! Bon Appetit! It's time!"

Kelso had no time to respond or react as she felt the needle pierce her neck. Darkness sprang back into her mind as she fell into a deep sleep.

Chapter 33

SHE AWOKE TO DIMMING daylight and the sound of a boat slowing down. At first she thought she was arriving at Sucia and everything had been a nightmare. Staring up at Gaucho, handcuffed, with four armed soldiers, clarified her situation. On the other side of the boat were three other, eastern European men, also handcuffed. One nodded at her.

"Welcome back, Kelso," Gaucho whispered.

"Where are we? Who are those dudes?" Kelso asked.

"Albanian drug traffickers. Balkan crew. Zacks caught them on this island, formerly Patos now revamped as Zacks animal habitat, 209 acres of mainly thick forest, some caves, and thins out to the west into the lighthouse. Although something tells me that Zacks and whatever creatures in here has shifted what used to be a quaint little park."

"Shut up!" a soldier replied. He blasted Gaucho with a hit across his head. Gaucho groaned.

Kelso was still seething that Gaucho set her up. Now her niece might be in harm's way, but her focus was on doing whatever it took before the next twenty-four hours, when Tia was scheduled to take her ferry over to Sucia Island. The beautiful Cascades stared back at them from behind the boat as the water foamed around each thrust of the ship. Sea lions and their babies swam alongside them with no concept of the merchants of death aboard. Kelso took a long look across the southern horizon and saw the distant San Juan Islands some full of families, tourists, and a world of normalcy that she longed for. A weekend of fishing, camping, and roasting marshmallows was the original concept, now it was becoming breakfast for some madman's pet monsters.

This shit is getting old. I need to put in a transfer where I just give out tickets for illegal fishing or chase vandals defacing shorebird nests.

Minutes later the armed soldiers yelled commands and the three Albanian drug traffickers, Gaucho, and Kelso were hauled off the boat.

One of the soldiers had a bruised face which she recognized as the one whose nose she had broken. He glared at her. She looked around, took in the island, Zack Island, which she had never been to nor really known much about. A very small island in the most northwestern fingertip of the San Juan Islands. Also a former national park, with a hiking trail where you could make it around the entire island within an hour or so.

A soldier dialed up a satellite phone and Chad's voice blared out of the speaker.

"Welcome to my San Juan Island Zoo. I want to thank you again for your service to my children as they continue to train. They get so hungry and you have no idea how rough it is to get enough elks, deer, and horses here to keep them happy. You all won't provide that much caloric intake but the hunt will really make their week, so we all thank you. I hope you all make it a long time. Most last a few hours, but one time a survivalist made it into nighttime but then he became a snack. No rules except to survive, any way you can, for as long as you can. Oh you can swim off the island, but with my four security patrol boats, stationed in each corner, you will just be put down to let the ocean chew on your corpse. Plus, then my children don't get to meet you, so where's the fun in that?

With my three children on the island, we are taking bets who gets who first. Kelso and Gaucho don't let me down. Don't feel sad either, maybe I'll bring your niece here. Gaucho your wife seemed bored, why not bring her here? So sooner or later you'll all be together on the island, most likely inside the digestive tract or waste system of my children. It's fitting for what you did to my Cascade tiger. Enough chat, time to experience the lower rungs of the animal kingdom once again.

It is an honor to let my children eat you, be blessed!"

The soldiers made them each kneel as they cut each plastic zip tie cuff off, an AR-15 pointed for cover, as the other soldiers stood watch. They then backed away slowly getting back onto the boat and started the engine, turning and keeping the rifle pointed at them.

"Stay close to me, we are not going to move with them," Gaucho whispered to Kelso.

"If my niece sets foot onto this island, I'll dig your body up and re-murder you, understand?"

"As if I had a choice."

"Let's focus on getting off this island and then you can cry me a river, deal?"

Gaucho nodded. The Albanian men were chatting amongst themselves. There was an older one with gray hair and two younger men in their twenties. One had blue eyes and the other had deep brown eyes with a Joseph Stalin moustache. Gaucho and Kelso introduced themselves and all five slowly walked from the shores against the thickening forest east entry point. An old state park trail path emerged between suffocating ferns and lush green trees.

"We go south, least someone might hear our screams," Gaucho offered. The Albanian crew agreed and Kelso stayed silent.

The sounds of birds and ocean currents gave a thin veil of calm. Kelso had seen what Zacks was capable of, at Mt. St. Helens, and she wasn't looking forward to any sequel here.

"Hey, before we go naked into a fucking forest of monsters, how about we get some weapons?"

"You read my mind," Gaucho replied.

They paused and broke off into a small circle to collect sticks, rocks, and began to sharpen their island weaponry for whatever came next. Their spears were not as good as their firearms, still housed at Zacks Sucia Island headquarters, but gave a sliver of confidence to battle the island's pets.

"Really, this is a small island, I mean you can make it around in like one or one and a half hours," Gaucho said.

"What you are saying is that we are going to meet our buddies soon. If so, then what is the best way to spring out of this death-trap. Any ideas?" Kelso asked.

"There's a mini-island right off the southwestern tip of this one, might not have anything on it, could be an option."

"That or we return to the east entry so we can protect my niece and your wife, tomorrow night. We never know, some tourist could stumble across that area and we escape. All it takes is one explorer who slinks past Zacks boats. Or some fellow drug traffickers like our buddies here."

The blue-eyed Albanian man laughed and replied, "No shipments for another week, maybe longer if they think DEA got us, sorry."

"Great, nothing signals hope like when even the criminal underworld is taking a breather."

Chapter 34

NEIGH. NEIGH.

All five of the prisoners turned to see a bizarre sight. Two horses and a deer were cowering by a huddle of trees on the path left of them. Dark storm clouds beckoned in the sky to the west.

The three Albanian men began to argue with an older one taking off towards one of the horses.

"Hey! Follow the signals, we should hang tight," Gaucho barked at the elder Albanian man.

"Fuck that, I'm taking this to the stash," the Albanian man replied without turning around.

The horse backed up, but the man approached hands out and petting its mane.

"What stash?" Kelso asked.

"Oh nothing, he's old and senile, pay no attention," the brown-eyed man replied.

The elder Albanian had begun to stroke the horse and tried to mount it.

"Bud, without a saddle or reins, that could be a rough ride, this isn't a western movie," Gaucho scoffed.

PRRRRRRRRRRRRRR.

"What the fuck is that?" Kelso asked.

Within a split second a giant bird, with the height of an elephant but with the speed of a panther, sprinted out of the woods. It looked like an eight-foot cross of an eagle and an ostrich. Its body was small with wings too small for flying, but its two legs, thin and long, gave way to razor sharp claws at the bottom which were galloping at the elder Albanian man and the horse. The deer and other horse took off running into the invisible forest paths. At the top of this gigantic bird was an eagle's head with a beak that stretched out several feet in a curved sharp downward talon shape. It was as if a parrot had been given the body of a velociraptor with a razor blade sledgehammer for a beak.

No one but the horse was able to move, due to the bird's speed and horrific appearance, the Albanian man put his hands up.

Crunch.

The bird's first downward swoop of its beak crushed the Albanian man's skull. The remainder of his head crumbled down and off his body like a rock. His body dropped as its feet gripped onto the ground allowing the bird to begin to bring its beak down and down again. Each blow downward caused more blood and fluids to spray all over the area. In a matter of ten seconds, it had jack hammered the elder Albanian man into fleshy rubble.

It was now picking apart his intestines and stomach, chewing chunks of it.

"Hey fuck you!" the brown-eyed Albanian man ran towards the bird trying to jam his spear into its head. He got about three steps towards his goal before the bird had hopped off the elder's corpse and disappeared into the woods.

He began to cheer to himself, meanwhile Gaucho and Kelso pulled the blue-eyed Albanian man off the trail and onto the ground, inside a nearby downed tree. Of the three, the elder was dead, the blued-eyed man was petrified silent, and the brown-eyed man wouldn't stop yelling.

"What are you all doing? Come out here, it is scared of us! Let's go!"

During the last syllable of his words the bird had leapt out of a different part of the trail tackling the brown-eyed man. This time it used its talons to tear him apart as he screamed for help.

Kelso and Gaucho held down the blue-eyed man who whimpered.

"No, don't you dare, we are letting this thing be until we have better weapons. Stay down I'm sorry," Gaucho said.

Inside Kelso's mind she imagined her niece and fought off tears, taking a deep quiet breath. Adrenaline shot through her bloodstream as she listened to the man slowly being eaten alive.

Ten minutes later the bird dragged both corpses away, one at a time. When thirty minutes had passed with no further sounds they emerged from the downed tree.

"Well, that was great, two people dead, and a psycho ostrich eagle thing. One 'child' down, I can't wait to see what the other two creatures are, sign me up," Kelso said.

"Those my cousins man. They dead. I can't believe. I thought Chad guy full of shit. We caught all the time. Never problem. Bribes. Shootouts. Not bird monsters."

"Sounds like a promising career path, I'm sorry for your loss but we have to keep moving," Gaucho barked.

"Ok, but what was that?" the last remaining blue-eyed Albanian man asked.

"Something I don't want to meet again prior to escaping," Kelso quipped.

"Terror bird," Gaucho replied.

"What?" Kelso asked.

"Yeah, they actually used to exist. Maybe not exactly like that, but they found old bones of those things way back. Alpha predator of South America. Used to hunt mastodons and Jurassic giant horses. Used their beaks for lack of being able to shake side to side like the lions do. Saw a special on TV, also there was this hilarious movie on them," Gaucho replied.

"Let's get moving. We are heading north and hanging tight against the shore. Those things can't sneak up on us if they don't have the cover of trees," Kelso stated while picking up her pace.

"Agreed, but first, we need to have a chat as we walk with our amigo," Gaucho replied putting a spear to the blue-eyed man's ribs. "One that includes the details of what is in that stash and where it is, comprende?"

The blue-eyed Albanian man replied, "I'm Albanian. Not Mexican. Name is Chako. From Kosovo. Use real name if we speak. Otherwise fuck off fast. I will kill bird with hands."

"So be it Chako, I have a little girl coming this way in now twenty-three hours, let's get to know each other," Kelso replied eyeing him up as they walked.

Chako, Gaucho, and Kelso made their way north as the sun began to fade in the afternoon's bleak stare. Under Gaucho's lead and Kelso's back guard watch, they stuck to the northern shoreline. Climbing over the brown and gray rocks intermingled with ocean waves made it slow but safer passage. It was all they could do to avoid further interactions with the Terror Bird.

Kelso and Gaucho, along with Chako's silent consent, agreed to navigate the northern shoreline of the island. In the booming distance lay other islands, Canada, and far-fetched dreams of rescue. The Pacific Ocean battered itself against the rocky shoreline. Foamy ocean water billowed beneath them as they struggled to stay off of the forest tree line, trail, and only using the rocky edges of the island.

"This is hell, I'd prefer the Cascades over hopping rock to rock," Kelso remarked.

"Yes, this not good man. Why don't we hop into trees?" Chako replied.

"Unless you want to meet your cousins at the gates of heaven, I'd suggest hanging tight against these rocks, no Terror Bird is going to feed here, much less be able to balance. Safest path," Gaucho replied.

"Dude, only twenty-five ah maybe thirty minutes. Cross island. Done it before one time. Old park trail. We going the slow way," Chako stated.

"Chako, maybe you weren't a dinner guest like me and my lady friend here, but Chad made it clear he had three happy critters to meet and eat us. We've met one huge one, it's still loose, hunkering down to possibly sleep, since most birds aren't night predators, so I'm not about to (a) wake that bitch up or (b) meet the other two critters in thick forest, with light fading," Kelso said. Her face signaled zero negotiation power for Chako.

"As much as I'd like to haul ass to that lighthouse, I'd rather be on the edge coastline instead. We need to set up a camp site soon. Given it's the start of spring, we have some rain coming our way. Would be nice to catch some drinking water. We'll need it for tomorrow's morning sprint," Gaucho replied.

Chako cussed and mumbled in Albanian.

Chapter 35

One hour later the three hunted survivors were finishing their makeshift camp.

"For Americans, not too shabby, I'm impressed," Chako said as he bit into crab.

Gaucho and Chako had agreed on an outer rock area for their camp. Kelso wasn't thrilled at the trees being right against it, but it had a little rock cave shaped like the letter C, that allowed them to build a small fire using forest materials and a knife Gaucho reveled he stole from Chad. Kelso had snagged some shellfish off the water, not the greatest amount but worth some minor protein. Guacho had also repurposed some abandoned plastic bottle trash into a makeshift water funnel. He would load up the ocean water on one side, heat the bottle up, and then catch the condensation in another bottle. This primitive desalination was not yielding much water, but luckily some nearby rocks held fresh rainwater that allowed them to take turns drinking from another empty twenty-ounce plastic container.

Kelso was still hung up on the knife.

"So you had the knife hours ago when we were dropped off and didn't use it?"

"You mean you wanted me to use a steak knife to defeat an apex predator bird that can kill us with one hit?"

"Yep. Where did you even get it? Didn't they search you?"

"Only before the dinner. Before you woke up, I started crying and weeping and fell out of my chair."

Kelso didn't reply.

"Look, I am sorry you are involved but they had guns on my wife. The moment we put down that mountain monster, somehow, Chad was going to either murder you or get you here. Least I made sure we would be together."

Kelso stared out at the ocean as Gaucho talked. She processed his words. It still was betrayal to her, and her niece was the unacceptable collateral damage.

"Now we have a knife. Next up guns, right Chako?"

Chako smiled as he continued to tighten the strands on his tree bed. Despite repeated lectures from Gaucho and Kelso, Chako picked sleeping in a high tree bed.

"You two get eaten by some shark tonight. I wouldn't sleep in that cave. Fire draw attention. I'll be hanging out way up there, higher than that bird thing. If we survive the night, then yes lighthouse, west shore, there's a big cave. We stashed bag of guns and drugs. Chad's men not see it, because hidden."

"What type of guns?" Kelso asked.

"Not blow up a boat. Two MP5s. Two Glocks. Enough to kill bird monster," Chako responded.

"If it sits still that is, buddy, that thing moves at about thirty miles per hour, that's like shooting a Corvette with a jackhammer. What we need is to put down that bird or lure that security boat to the shore. Take it and get to the other islands. Lopez, San Juan, Orcas, doesn't matter somewhere with phones, civilians, and no fucking lab creatures," Gaucho stated staring at Kelso.

"I'm getting a boat and meeting my niece at the Sucia Island main dock. You two can do what you want," Kelso retorted.

Leaves rustled in the forest behind them causing a panicked silence. Chako flirted with hopping down into Kelso and Gaucho's cave set up.

"Last chance Chako, join us, I created some leaves and used nearby tree branches, we have a legit rock bed here. Even a branch that keeps us from hopefully falling the hell out of the cave at night into the ocean."

The rustling passed as the rain began. Fatigue, limited food and water, with their nerves taxed by not knowing when the bird would return left them eroded.

"Nah. I'm good. Tomorrow, you can have one of the Glocks but we are taking the MP5s and we getting to another island. I call my uncle's boss and within hours we can have one of our submarines. Tons o' guns. Enough men. Kill anything that walks. You should join us Kelza."

"It's Kelso. And that won't stop my niece from arriving tomorrow. I have to save her. Either of you make it, alert the feds, coast guard, DEA, every federal asset nearby. We have no idea who is on Chad's payroll."

"Also monitoring those calls. No federal. We kill bird then disappear," Chako said. He climbed back up the hill to the trees and slowly crawled up the tree.

Due to the rain he was already struggling but made it up to his tree bed, made of leaves, branches, and his own t-shirt as a tie to force him to hug the tree. Sleep was unlikely for all of them but they tried.

Chako looked down below and could see the shadows of the flames of the fire flickering out as the rain picked up. It felt good on him as he leaned into the tree and tried to relax his legs and arms to sleep.

Within twenty minutes Kelso and Gaucho were asleep, intermittently interrupted by waves and weird noises in the forest. They slept crouched against the rock with their body heat helping each other.

In the distance one of Chad's security boats sailed into the area. It had tracked their fire and the two security guards watched them with binoculars but didn't engage. Chad's orders were to let the zoo operate as nature intended.

Chapter 36

EARLY SUNLIGHT AND A desire to keep moving awoke Gaucho and Kelso.

"How'd you sleep, Kelso?"

"Got maybe one hour or two tops. Chako was right, there's a reason I've never set up a tent on a rock, in the fucking ocean."

"True but we are alive. So onward we go. Let's wake up Chako and drink some water. My plastic containers are probably full, we should drink them, fill up from that rock hole, and can use that for the rest of the day. You can go weeks without food but without water you are down in like two to three days."

Kelso stretched out, her back was killing her from sleeping on the rock. The leaves provided little comfort beyond having a wet blanket on her. She looked around and saw beautiful Mt. Baker towering in the skyline.

"The sick irony," Kelso said.

"What?" Guacho replied.

"It is a gorgeous day, look at the Cascades, far enough you can almost see mainland. Yet we are being stalked by an actual dinosaur. What a world."

"Once we get the guns, we'll be the ones stalking Chad and his crew. I won't let your niece get hurt, I promise you Alex."

For the first time in days, Kelso smiled. Her eyes met Gaucho's.

"Chako, buddy! Rise and shine! Come get some grub and water and let's roll!"

Chako did not look good. He grumbled to let him sleep some more. He complained that he had to pee on himself to keep warm and lost circulation in his joints due to being tied to the tree all night.

"Buddy, we gotta roll, sleep tonight, in a hotel, protected by your lovely criminal cartel family. Right now we gotta go. It's quiet, I don't see a bird here, let's go tree hugger. Slide down we'll make sure you don't fall bub."

"You've been waiting to use that line haven't you?" Kelso chuckled.

"Ever since he climbed up there like an activist battling a bulldozer."

Kelso laughed harder. Chako untied himself and wiggled his legs and arms to get the blood flowing. He saw a water seal surface right behind Kelso and Gaucho's case. He pointed as they turned to stare. It was a shared moment that paused the terror of their island prison.

"Cute little guy, my cousin once ate-" Chako's sentenced was crushed mid-flow.

RIIIIIIGHHTT.

The human-like sound made them all snap their heads towards the trees beside Chako.

No one spoke. They all were scanning the nearby ground. No terror bird. No soldiers. Nothing.

"Chako was that you? Not funny man, that's creepy as fuck!" Kelso yelled.

RIIIGHT.

This time the sound was right next to Chako. Kelso's eyes bounced up and what once was thought to be a dead tree with a weird branch was moving. The actual branch was moving as if it was alive.

"Oh my god!" Kelso shrieked.

It was no tree branch but was a massive half sloth half human beast. It hung about five feet tall with arms stretching three feet wide with three razor sharp talons on each fingertip. It had a human torso with a rib cage, muscular chest, and a partially human face but with two sets of eyes besides a crushed nose. It's mouth was human but held oversized mandible fangs. It had a primal voice box that was repeating the same sounds that almost sounded like a man whispering "right".

"Chako, slide down, now!" Gaucho yelled pulling out his knife.

It was too late.

RIIIIIIGHT.

As Chako pushed downwards to escape the sloth man swung its three-foot arm, now a scythe, so fast that Chako's arm sliced clean off causing him to fall down onto the ground. As blood began to pour out of the hole that once held Chako's arm, Kelso and Gaucho approached Chako, makeshift weapons drawn.

"Kelso, we aren't gonna hold this fucker off with a steak knife and a wood cut tree spike. He just cut Chako's fucking arm off like a great white shark snacking. Pull him back, we gotta stop his bleeding. On three reach down and pull and I'll cover you."

The sloth man reached back to its mouth and with a long purple tongue, began to lick the blood off of its talons. It tilted its head downwards as Kelso bounced into gear yanking the whimpering Chako back off the grass and dirt onto the ocean rocks.

RIIGHT.

"Why does it keep fucking saying right?" Kelso yelled.

"Maybe it's a parrot, and it mimics what it hears humans say. I didn't create it how the fuck should I know?" Guacho responded.

Chako continued to moan in pain. Kelso ripped off part of her shirt to create pressure to stop the bleeding. She pleaded with Chako to not fall asleep and stay with them.

"We need to run," Kelso stated.

"How are we going to run with Chako bleeding out and a two-hundred-and-twenty-pound dead weight on us with that thing chasing us?" Gaucho asked.

"Aren't sloths fucking slow? Like that's their thing, to hang out and not move. What the fuck?" Kelso's voice was raising as she masked her terror.

"Has anything on this island abided by any rules of nature? God knows what animals and weird traits Chad's team gave this thing. It obviously has the arms of a goddamn sword with the verbal skills of an infant. Let's just try to lure it onto the water, its feet don't look superb for swimming."

Sloth man made some clicking and whistling noises. Kelso realized now all night long it had been slowly moving into position to have them for breakfast, the noises that kept her up now had their origins before her. It swung from branch to branch like a monkey. It was swinging lower and lower until it swung onto the last tree branch and landed onto the ground.

They backed further back onto the rock cave, behind them was only the unflinching ocean.

"If it gets too close and you can't club it, we're hopping into the ocean, I'll drown that fucker," Gaucho barked.

RIIIIIGHT. RIIIGHT.

"I'm not dying to something that talks like a stoned surfer," Kelso said.

As the sloth man began to walk closer to them, ten feet separated them. Gaucho noticed it limped. Its legs were so thin that its upper body weight, perfect for climbing and swinging, made it awkward for it to walk, much less run.

Right as Kelso was about to joke about its chicken legs it reached back and quickly swung its three-foot arms out striking the ground like a thunderbolt. The ground shook near them as dirt flung upwards. It began to pull itself closer to them by using its arms like an ice axe on a mountain.

"I don't like this, Chako goes in now," Kelso yelled. She pushed Chako into the water as she began to slowly back off the rock cave. The sloth man was flicking its purple tongue as it reached back to strike its arms now within mere feet of them. Gaucho readied his knife.

"Whatever happens just keep swimming, I'm going to try to cut off his hands, without them he's useless," Gaucho commanded. Kelso climbed around Gaucho with her wood stake ready to help pin the sloth hand into the ground.

"Not letting you die alone old man, let's declaw this thing," Kelso said.

Sloth man pulled itself within four feet of them as Kelso and Gaucho readied themselves for a single and only chance at disarming it. The sloth man reached back. The forest shook behind it. A high-pitched squeal emerged. Sloth man turned.

BARRRRRRRRRRRRRR.

The terror bird sprinted out of the woods headed right for the sloth man, Gaucho, and Kelso.

"Jump!" Kelso yelled.

Gaucho and Kelso leapt off the rock cave into the ocean and began to pull Chako away from the rock cave right as the Terror

Bird was hit by the sloth man's talon. It toppled over, small face opened up by the razor-sharp slap, and hopped up ramming it heads into the sloth's right arm, severing it.

RIIIIIIIIIIIIIIIIIIIIIIIIIIIIIIIIIIIIIIIIIIIIIIIGHT.

They continued to swim westward away from the rock cave but near rocks watching the battle.

As the sloth man's left arm bled and dangled off tendons, it used its right arm to swing and hit the Terror Bird in the face cutting its eye. Between moans and primal screams, the terror bird began to go in for the kill, pinning the sloth man against the rocks. It used its feet to pin the sloth by its arms to the ground. The Terror Bird was bleeding from its eye, hanging loose from one of its sockets, but was raising and lowering its fatal beak onto the sloth like a drunk man hammering an ant with a sledgehammer on concrete.

Gaucho and Kelso stayed long enough to hear the sloth man stop talking and moving. The Terror Bird continued to bash it out of either revenge or due to a lack of depth perception with now only one working eyeball. They managed to swim far enough away until they could only see the top of the Terror Bird as it drug the carcass of the sloth man into the woods for a late brunch.

"We are not making good time, remember I only have until five o'clock and then my niece arrives at the main Sucia Island center. Chako might need to be secured in one of these caves and we return for him. Chako that ok with you?" Kelso asked.

"No, don't leave me behind!" Chako moaned.

"Fine, but you need to start swimming, it is the only way we can get you to medical help man, work with me," Kelso held onto Chako guiding him in the water.

They continued to swim using the rocks and waves as a floating mechanism. It was not fast but no one wanted to set foot back into the forest after what they had just witnessed. Five minutes later, right as Kelso was going to renew her desire to let Chako sit it out in a cave, the lighthouse emerged.

"Thank god!" Kelso exclaimed.

"That's it for the island. So place Chako over there on those rocks. Let's grab those guns and get moving," Gaucho said.

Kelso and Gaucho pulled Chako onto some rocks, far enough out so that he wouldn't be forest food, but with enough room to not fall into the ocean for now.

Kelso and Gaucho carefully stared as the island now narrowed out into the western shore. It was the end of the forest and about a hundred feet of four feet tall ocean grass, no trees, and then a rustic pretty old red lighthouse. Built in 1893, automated in the 1970s, and finally restored in 2008, the light house used to be operated by the Coast Guard until Chad purchased it. Given the abnormal creatures that walked the island it was a welcome sense of normalcy. To the west of the lighthouse, only a few miles out, was the international US Canadian border.

"Long as there's no snake or grass beast these next few steps we are golden. Hell, we could try to wait out for help in the lighthouse or see if there's radio equipment inside."

"Time is ticking, it's what, roughly noon? We have four hours to get the guns, escape, and grab my niece. Let's not overthink this and just sprint. Weapons ready?"

Gaucho clutched his knife as Kelso held her wooden stake. They began to sprint gambling to outrun anything that should arise. Chako watched, clutching a rock.

Chapter 37

KELSO SPRINTED ACROSS THE grassland in nearly thirty seconds, hitting and leaning against the white paint of the lighthouse walls. Gaucho was a little bit slower, but saw nothing as well. He smiled and turned to give the thumbs up to Chako. Chako was crawling and wading through the water off the rock and had begun to walk slowly from the shore towards them. Gaucho and Kelso's eyes darted to the forest, but nothing emerged, even as Chako's slow stride made them anxious for a last second animal attack.

Nothing.

Kelso helped Chako onto the ground. Gaucho volunteered to clear the lighthouse and check for a radio or any rescue options. He opened the lighthouse door as Kelso sat down herself.

"Beautiful view, right?" Chako said.

"Yeah, it's the fingertip of America, gorgeous. My grandfather used to tell me if maybe the Europeans had approached America from this side maybe they'd been nicer," Kelso said.

"Funny man," Chako replied.

"Yeah, I miss him already," Kelso stated.

"Fucking thing took my arm," Chako said as his mood swung. His blood loss and exhaustion was setting into lethal phases. Adrenaline had receded to gruesome pain bursts.

Gaucho reappeared. Lighthouse was clear, no radio, no equipment beyond the light, and yet no monsters either. More of Chad's cameras so he was still watching them.

"Great. Still death show for rich American. Promise three monsters, we got two," Chako said between labored breaths.

"On the positive side, we didn't cover the south side of this island. After Terror Bird and Sloth Man I have zero interest in discovering the third species, even as a Wildlife officer," Kelso replied patting Chako on the back.

"Goddamn Chako you look like dried shit. Let's get these guns and I have a plan. Let's move off screen more near that rock cave. Chako, we'll get you patched up bud," Gaucho said.

They moved to the southwest side of the lighthouse which was only a few feet from the cave with the gun stash. Gaucho outlined his plan. Kelso would go into the cave with the knife, Gaucho watching her back, retrieve the guns. From the lighthouse digital clock it was 1pm so they still had four hours before Kelso's niece arrived at the Sucia headquarters island. They could start a fire and use the lighthouse as a beacon to lure a rescue ship. Kelso also argued for them swimming to the nearby Little Patos Island, it was a small satellite mini-island right next to Patos Island, separated by half of a mile. No one was thrilled to swim even five hundred feet with Chad's security patrols in the water with a quick ability to catch and kill them, so she relented to Gaucho's plan of the lighthouse fire here on main island.

"Ah, what about Chad's security patrol boat? He'll just come and redirect them."

"Good, I saw one off the north shore hanging around. We want any boat to come out here whether civilian or Chad's. Even a firefight is loud enough that passing commercial ships or leisure boats will call it in. So even if Chad is watching above, near the forest and lighthouse, we'll piss off his crew enough to get an opening."

"But I sense a catch coming?"

"Yeah, we don't want Chad to know we have guns until it is too late. So we have to keep them in the bag or concealed on us. Easy for the Glocks maybe harder for the MP5s but if Chad sees them he'll know we can take out his patrol boat."

"Ok, whatever needs to be done let's do it now. The ride between Bellingham and Sucia HQ is like what?"

"About 20 nautical miles give or take."

"That means my niece will be boarding within the hour. Meaning I can't make it to Bellingham but I can make it back to HQ dock to save her before she reaches Zack's main command center. We can also use the communication equipment on the security boat for alerting people."

Chako put up a fight wanting to be dropped off at Orcas Island about five nautical miles south so he could alert his own crew but was defeated by Gaucho and Kelso. They promised to take him to medical help or a side rescue boat, but only if her niece is saved first. Kelso's glare provided the veto power as she grabbed the knife and hopped down the rock cave.

Chapter 38

THE OCEAN WAVES THROBBED around her as she began to walk in the dark cave. Sunlight helped with the first half of the cave, which was just rock and moss. Fear hit her and it made her gulp, forcing away bad thoughts of the prior cases, Banshee, Cascade Tiger, or Trinity Terror Serpent. It got stronger as she crept into the final corner of the cave where with limited sunlight, she could see the outline of a large green duffel bag.

Here goes, please let nothing jump out at me.

She took a deep breath and reached out and grabbed the bag, pulling it towards her body. It was so heavy it almost tipped her over into the water. The last thing she wanted was a twisted ankle. She crept backwards out to the edge of the cave and unzipped the bag. Inside were the two Glocks and two MP5s that Chako promised. No drugs left, just remnants of cocaine, the wrapped containers all shredded. There was, however, a flashlight and it even worked. Kelso noticed holes all over outside of the bag, like someone had stabbed it with a knife. It was also covered in red paint, but soon after leaning further out into the sunlight she saw it wasn't paint. And that trepidation returned down her spine. It was blood and covered the left half of the bag. Dried but still blood. She looked around and saw nothing. She turned on the flashlight and saw no threat from the surrounding cave walls. Then it caught her eye.

More dried blood splatter patterns on the furthest cave corner, left of where the bag was originally placed. She pulled out a Glock, readied it, and used the flashlight on top.

Whoa. There's our third creature.

In the lower left-hand corner was a corpse, or the remainder of one with only shoulders and a head. The body was missing, but the blood trail showed something had died a violent death. It had stab marks across its shoulders and head. Its face was of a huge orangutan but with the jaws of a piranha. It had white eyeballs and white tufts of hair still hung from its shoulder chunks and skull. It looked like one of those Halloween yard décor where you stuff just the head of a zombie onto the ground. It was definitely dead and smelled like it had been killed a while ago, maybe days if not a week or more.

"Kelso, you clear?" Gaucho was yelling down into the cave.

"Yep, coming!"

Gaucho helped Kelso up but they perched on a lower rock, outside of the visibility of the lighthouse and Rick's forest cameras, they hoped. Kelso told him about the ape monster corpse and gave him a Glock to conceal in his waistband. They took the MP5s and began to try to fit them under their shirts and into their pants without seeming too bulky. Without straps it was a struggle.

"We look ridiculous. I used to do this for my grandkids at Christmas or Birthdays, hiding toys under my shirt until they noticed and then revealed it," Gaucho said.

"Won't hold for long but we just need to start that fire now and get any boat, ship, anything to stop by and get us off this island. Least we are only down to one monster, the Terror Bird. Ape thing down there dead, sloth man dead, I'll take it!"

"Yep. Already got the fire going with Chako helping or trying. That grass is great for burning, hell maybe the fire will piss off someone over there on Saturna Island or elsewhere and report us for trying to start a wildfire," Gaucho said.

"We could also try swimming to Little Patos Island, it's like a short swim and maybe less critters," Kelso replied.

"Yeah, we could do that as well. Chako couldn't make that swim though so maybe we keep him here as a decoy."

They kept the green duffel bag, holes and all, as an imperfect backpack. Kelso and Gaucho resurfaced up a few more feet to the lighthouse high ground. The fire was beginning to burn tall and Chako was tossing more and more sticks into it. They whispered to him that they had the guns and are all set.

"Cocaine?" Chako asked.

"Gone," Kelso replied.

"Figures. Who took it?"

"Don't know, don't care, but my guess is the third monster, a weird monster ape with like razor teeth was taste testing it. Guess you cut it too much with other things, getting greedy like all dealers, eh?" Kelso said raising her eyebrows at Chako.

Chako laughed, shrugging. He pointed that there are several holes all over the ground in the tall white grass in front of the lighthouse.

That's weird, maybe the Ape Monster's style was to poke holes in anything to check it out.

"So, no more monsters, like new?" Chako asked.

"Guess not. Check it out, Chad's security patrol is already heading our way, see him from the north. Remember no guns, just hide against the light house so they can't snipe us off," Gaucho reminded them.

"Where my gun?" Chako asked.

"No Chako, you can have that wooden stake, we need the guns," Gaucho snapped.

Chako cussed mumbling something about shady Americans. They crouched down watching the security patrol boat get closer. It was manned by two men, as far as they could see, one piloting the boat and the other armed with a semi-automatic rifle on the deck.

Ten feet away, out past the cave that held the guns, behind them something was crawling out of the far south rock cave. It was all white except for its spike legs, which were midnight black. It had a human sized body but where the arms and legs should have been, they were replaced, with two-foot spikes along with spikes on its chest and back, crawling like a four-legged spider. Its head was human-like with a large cranium, white, bald, without eyes or any real face, just a massive white skull with a circular suction mouth, adorned with five rows of teeth inside it. It made no sound as it began to crawl from the rock ledge onto the ground with soft spike steps.

Gaucho, Kelso, and Chako's eyes were glued to the security patrol boat who now had stopped some distance away from shore. Both security guards had stood out on the deck of the ship and stared back at the three survivors.

"Something's not right," Kelso said.

"No kidding, they should be barreling at us, this fire isn't getting smaller. I see like three ships in the horizon I'm sure this is getting reported in by now. Why are they both just staring at us?"

"We should shoot them. Now. They lined up," Chako said.

"These are MP5s and Glocks, not sniper rifles. The water, boat, and wind, we'd waste our ammo, expose our positions, and then ten of Chad's patrol boats would just come and slaughter us. Any other great ideas?" Gaucho replied.

The two patrol security guards then waved at them, smiling. One even gave the thumbs up.

Before they could react to the waving, Kelso felt a sting shoot through her side.

"Argh. Ohhhh," Kelso groaned. Turning to watch as the spider creature leaned down and took a small bite out of her scalp. Its leg had cut through her side and she was unable to move away as it nibbled on her skullcap.

"Fuck!" Gaucho yelled as he swung his knife at its skull stabbing into it. It began to release its grasp on Kelso's head and retracted its leg grip on her. She fell down and began to fumble her way to the Glock firearm hidden under her waistband, but it had fallen down onto the ground five feet away since the creature had pinned her.

Gaucho kept stabbing its head as the spider creature scampered away. Chako had dipped his wooden stake into the fire and turned it into a torch swinging it at the creature. Down below, some thirty feet out, one of the security guards was clapping while the other watched in silence.

After a swing by Chako, the spider creature jumped into the air striking both Gaucho and Chako in the abdomen with its spike legs. Gaucho was able to rip away, even though he screamed in pain. Chako became pinned by all four of the spider spikes. It was now releasing the layers of jaws to chew on his eyes, nose, and mouth within seconds. His torch arm grew limp as the torch fell onto the ground. He didn't even get to utter any last words as the spider creature gobbled up his tongue, teeth, and chewed on his skull.

"I'm so sorry buddy," Gaucho cried out as he watched Chako be fed to the spider creature. He reached into his waistband and saw Kelso clearing her gun and aiming it. They began to fire as the spider creature squealed. They unloaded the only magazine they had in their Glock 19s. At fifteen rounds a piece, over thirty rounds blasted into the spider creature causing it to turn and fall down with the rapid-fire hits to the abdomen. Its legs still kept moving and its teeth chattered. It began to crawl again with a limp.

"I'm not wasting all of our ammo on this thing if it's still alive. Chako's dead, we gotta roll!" Kelso yelled.

"Little Patos Island now, before the security boat can get here!" Gaucho commanded.

The wounded pair began running off the high grass and leapt off the rocks into the shallow ocean water. The water felt refreshing but with their wounds they were struggling to swim against the current. The short half mile water jog was becoming a challenge. Adrenaline, terror, and panic helped them keep swimming. With the blood from Kelso's head and Gaucho's side they'd soon become a magnet for sharks. They were halfway to the Little Patos island when they heard the motor get closer.

"Get the fuck back on the island, little piggies. You know better!"

Gaucho and Kelso looked up as they saw the security guard pointing a rifle at them. Both of them put their hands up. The other one was angling the boat.

"Now get up here, we can't have sharks eating you up, Chad can't use that for his sales studies. I'll even give you a drink of water before we deport you back to the island."

The security guard backed up to let Gaucho get on board but without helping him. Gaucho groaned revealing something under his blood-soaked shirt.

"What the fuck is that?" the security guard yelled at Gaucho. Kelso was still in the water beyond the guard's visual focus.

The MP5 roared to life from the water with a spray of bullets hitting the security guard in the head. He had no time to react beyond falling down as the other security guard reached for his rifle on the control panel.

"No, no, no. Don't do that!" Gaucho yelled as he pulled out his MP5. Kelso had hers aimed at the guard's head.

"Ok ok ok, this is my first week on the job. Chill the fuck out," the guard replied. He moved away from the gun. Gaucho helped Kelso onto the boat. Gaucho moved in and took the gun as Kelso made the guard get on his knees with his arms up.

"The game has changed. New rules. Sit there and listen the fuck up."

Gaucho powered up the boat and began the course for the headquarters.

Chapter 39

"FIRST THING WE NEED to know, is how does Chad watch, like does he know we are on here now?"

The security guard explained that they were watching the entire time. Each kill would be confirmed by radio in addition to any footage Chad had from his trail cams and lighthouse surveillance.

"I'm going to need you to confirm that we are dead. You can accredit it to the spider creature. Tell him that you got injured forcing us back onto the island, it killed us, harmed you, so you are coming back for medical treatment. Got it?"

The guard radioed it in as Gaucho blasted the engines. He took a wide route to avoid the headquarter patrol boats since there would be no cover in such a small patrol boat. Chad's voice on the radio made both of their heads turn towards the guard.

"Yeah yeah, we'll get you patched up. Did that bitch kill my spider?" Chad asked.

Kelso's eyebrows arched and she shook her head at the guard.

"No sir. It is injured but seems alive. Yes, both the girl and the old man are dead. Spider finished them off in the cave area. Yes sir, that's why you couldn't see it."

"Hmm, we got another one of those being born this month. We'll have to replace it but this is good data. I'll stop by the dock when you arrive, we'll need a corpse clean up team to ensure nothing is left out there. That lighthouse area is too exposed to outsiders. And guess who is going back out to do that?"

"Yes sir."

The guard took his hand off the radio. Kelso raised her gun at him.

"So, we have ten minutes to chat, tell me what psychopath would take such a job?" Kelso asked.

"I am a vet, I have a family, and it pays a lot. I have three kids with different women, child support is killing me."

"That's a terrible excuse, I'm a veteran myself. Son, you could have been a cop, correctional officer, and you chose to watch people be eaten alive?" Gaucho said.

"I'm working a job. Don't lecture me on how to provide for my family. You don't know me. This job, until a day ago, was just patrolling boats. Your buddy, the Albanian? He was a drug trafficker, god knows how many people he capped while moving drugs into my kids neighborhoods. You all just killed Lonzo who was a retired cop."

"Oh he's retired permanently now. He seemed like a really nice guy as he was marching me to my death. Can't imagine how great he was," Gaucho retorted.

Kelso seethed as she gripped the MP5 still aimed at the security guard.

"I have a five-year-old niece coming to Sucia master island, tell me, you family-of-three motherfucker, were you planning on feeding her...to...the...fucking...spider creature? Followed by Gaucho's wife?"

"Kelso, he's not armed. Don't do it," Gaucho warned.

"Hey I didn't know anything about kids. Lonzo told me most of the subjects put on the islands were drug cartel members and drug addicts. Never heard a word about kids man. Chill the fuck out."

Kelso clenched her teeth but didn't pull the trigger. She pointed it at the ground, staring at some scuba gear and oxygen tanks in the corner of the crammed boat. Fictional memories of what the trip could have been like with her and her niece snorkeling underwater near shore flowed across her mind.

"Where are we? This isn't the right path."

Chapter 40

"I KNOW, I HAD to make sure we didn't hit any of the patrol boats."

"No I get that, but it's still, wait is that Matia Island right there?"

Kelso turned to look at Gaucho. His face masked his thoughts.

"Gaucho, what the fuck?" Kelso yelled.

The security guard saw them glaring at each other, and used it to grab the radio, and leapt off the boat cascading into the water behind them.

"No!" Kelso screamed.

"Fuck. Guess this is it," Gaucho replied.

"Code mercury! Code mercury, SE quadrant two hostiles, patrol boat. Active fatal sweep."

"Gaucho, how could you? I should have fucking shot him, we're dead now!" Kelso said. He didn't respond.

The security guard was yelling into the radio in the distance. Within minutes he became a blip on their watery horizon.

Gaucho didn't let up on the gas until he saw the mooring buoy on the western side of Matia Island. It was an island immediately southeast of the Sucia Island headquarters. Much smaller, but without any creatures as it was still a state park.

"There you go kiddo, your ticket home."

He saw a white boat moored to the buoy with no one inside. Unsurprisingly, they left their key in the turn switch. Typical tourists exploring the Matia Island by kayak. He shut off the boat. Kelso was confused and panic was still coursing through her bloodstream as she saw it was 4:00 P.M.

"This is my apology, for everything and involving that wonderful little girl in this hellscape."

Kelso realized what was happening and shot him a glance.

"No. Come on Gaucho, come with me, we can make it," Kelso pleaded.

Gaucho leaned over and hugged Kelso, kissing the top of her bloody head. He whispered into her ear, "Tell my wife I love her, nothing was worth anything without her."

"Come on, Gaucho, we got this," Kelso repeated. Gaucho shook his head.

"We both know that's not true, Chad will hunt down our families, his boats are already doing whatever code mercury means, only one way out. I'm going to take this boat and ram it right up his ass at his dock. See those scuba oxygen tanks, I'm going to try to blow that bitch up, catch him on his own dock area. It's the right way to go out, with Chad gone you'll be safe, now don't argue. They won't be looking for this white boat. Just find that water taxi with your niece on it and get somewhere safe. I've had my time on this planet, you are just getting started."

Kelso was still hugging him. People in the distance were watching from the shore confused.

"Told you, kiddo, I'd make it up to you. Time for me to return to the Pampas, my homeland. I miss Argentina anyways."

He helped Kelso onto the white boat and with a final wink he powered the patrol boat and turned away sailing towards the Sucia HQ. Other patrol boats were appearing from the various bays of that island. Kelso turned the key and unmoored the boat, taking one long look at Gaucho torpedoing back at Rick's headquarters.

The boat owners were now kayaking back towards their boat yelling at Kelso. She silenced them with a swift upwards tug of her MP5. She turned the boat and powered it towards the closest island near the Bellingham port where the water taxi might be.

She scanned at least four wrong boats that weren't water taxis whose owners just glared at her as she got too close to their boats. Finally she saw the same water taxi company that had brought her out to the island twenty-four hours ago. She honked and pulled up to it. The captain started to scream at her until she pointed at the MP5 that she kept pointed down. It was an unstable union as she hopped on board. The blood had dried from her head.

"Auntie? Auntie Lexie?" a little voice shouted out.

"Tia! Baby where you at?" Kelso asked. The little girl appeared from behind the Captain in a life jacket smiling. Kelso hugged her.

"Oh my god, your head? You're bleeding!!! Where is Mr. Gaucho?" Tia exclaimed.

Kelso laughed, "Auntie slipped and fell on a rock, I'm ok baby, we're ok. I'm sorry but the island is closed, so that's why I'm here. Mr. Gaucho is ah, he couldn't make it, he got sick."

"Sick like grandpa, like the cancer?"

"Something like that. He needs to rest, he's back home baby."

"Where's mommy?" Kelso asked looking around for her sister.

"She said she met someone, she will meet us tomorrow at the hotel room."

"Of course she did," Kelso muttered.

Kelso tapped her MP5 again and told the water taxi pilot to turn the boat around and get them back to Bellingham now, and to do it quietly. She told Tia the gun was just a toy. Kelso still didn't know who to trust until she got to her back up work cell phone in the parking lot trunk. ASAC Stevenson would know who to activate to get the right people out there.

Kelso gripped Tia tightly, running her fingers through her hair.

A few minutes later, a massive explosion roared in the distance. It created a medium fireball with smoke billowing into the air. The water taxi pilot glared at Kelso who returned a steely glance back at him. He radioed his position and kept the water taxi going.

"Whoa! Fireworks? Explosion?" Tia asked staring at the fireball in the growing distance.

"The island, it's under construction," Kelso replied.

"Well that sucks, if we can't do to the island, can we at least go to the Space Needle?" Tia asked.

Kelso replied yes and began to cloak her tears, a slow, deep and muffled cry emanated beyond her control. The anguish of the last twenty-four hours poured out of her eyes. She continued to hold her now-confused niece with one arm and the MP5 firmly gripped in the other.

Chapter 41

Intermission: Lost in Seattle (One Month Later)

"I think I've died and gone to heaven! I never want to leave!"

"You haven't even seen the other club we're hitting, Fried Oyster. It will blow your mind!"

Lucy Stone was shouting at the group of four girls around her, dancing in the Emerald Gaze, one of Seattle's top dance clubs. The dance floor was packed as lasers and two dueling DJs kept the three hundred people moving. Moving out onto the dance floor, along the huge second floor level were balconies and green lights, in the center, behind the DJs, were two ascending staircases. The owners had flipped a bankrupt theater into a popular magnet of the Emerald City night life. The decadent ceilings gave way to a variety lighting options that made other clubs dwarf in comparison. The capacity was always pulsating over the fire code but without an accident yet. Upstairs, there were three different themed bar areas, Ocean Dreams, Tasty Tundra, and Hipster

Heartland. Each bar had their own unique drink combinations as an on-the-nose nod to their patrons.

Agent Kelso sat sandwiched between loud drunk couples at the Tasty Tundra. She was not in the mood to dance and sipped her Antarctica Vodka Tonic while staring at the dance floor. She tried to wipe away the image of Gaucho but failed, giving into her third vodka tonic. Lucy looked up and tried to wave but didn't see Kelso staring back at her. She excused herself from the group and hit the stairs.

"Alex!" Lucy said. She smelled of perfumes and sweat.

"Hey there, you look like you're having fun," Kelso offered. She forced a smile.

Lucy grabbed her arm and Agent Kelso stayed put, resisting. A drunken frown emerged from Lucy as she leaned into Kelso's ear.

"What is your problem? Come dance with me, this is the greatest!"

Kelso looked away at the reflecting glass. There were enough lasers to feel like she was about to have a seizure. Someone spilled a drink by her feet, it was the sixth time.

"We didn't come to Seattle to party, Lucy, we came here to attend Gaucho's funeral and my disciplinary hearing."

"We did his funeral, I'm sorry, but don't sweat that silly disciplinary hearing, you'll be fine, girl. Let loose and destress! Might help with your answers!"

"Did his funeral? What does that even mean? My career, my badge, what happens if I get fired?"

Three girls came up to Lucy pulling her back to the dance floor. Lucy mouthed 'sorry' to Kelso as she writhed her way back to the dance floor. Kelso chewed on her lip, it was a nervous tic, and returned to her drink.

"Tough night?" a man asked her as he sat down next to her.

"Listen, I don't mean to be rude, but I'm taken and tired. All roads lead to no, so while I'd love you to buy me another vodka tonic, your efforts are better spent elsewhere."

He laughed and bought her a vodka tonic.

"A lifetime ago, I did a few things overseas for our lovely nation. One of my training officers, his thing was, situational clarity. Heard of it?"

Agent Kelso shook her head and ignored him over the pulsating beats.

Least his pickup line is creative, even if he is barking up the wrong tree. *Nothing new.*

"Situational awareness situational clarity, same thing?"

"More like inbred cousin. Situational awareness is being aware of your surroundings for security threats, vigilance on safety. Situational clarity is order out of chaos. In special operations, while there was a plan, really one has to be ready to gain traction amid a black hole of violence. So let's say the target or asset goes sideways. Where can you gain some leverage on the opposition? IED just went off and you no longer have a leg or arm, can you still make it to cover for a rescue? Someone just blew up the plane engine, time to jump out, do you have a parachute and even if you do, amid enemy fire, where are you going to land?"

Agent Kelso was nodded.

"Lovely story, thanks for the drink. I'm going to regroup with my crew. I hope you gain some situational clarity tonight. I'd go lighter with some of those violent examples, some women aren't turned on by the alpha male stuff anymore. I liked it though."

The man got up and tossed a hundred-dollar bill onto the counter for the bartender.

"Find your situational clarity Agent Kelso, someone is throwing you out of a plane."

Agent Kelso snapped her head back towards the man.

"How do you know my name? Who are you?"

"Gaucho was a friend. From a prior life. Saw you at the funeral. This is me paying Gaucho back for all that he did for me. Chad Zacks is alive, recovering in hiding, and is leveraging all of his wealth and connections to lead to your termination, but also a federal indictment of you for terrorism, murder, with an icing of other fed crimes."

Kelso was speechless as she processed his words. It eroded the faint and distant hope she hosted for her surviving the San Juan Zoo incident. Lucy and her group were making their way up the stairs towards them giggling. The man stood up, buttoning his blazer, he stared into Kelso's eyes.

"Figure out if you have a parachute somewhere, in your life, and where you will land amid enemy fire. If I can help I'll be in touch. Oh, and I don't need to remind you that we never met."

He walked away as Lucy made her way, stumbling, into Agent Kelso.

"Time to bounce! Rusted Taint has a special on body shots!"

Lucy was already hammered but there was no slowing her down. Agent Kelso feigned support and made her way out with the pack of five. Outside two girls began to vape and one friend wanted to go home.

"I'll help you home, I'm heading to the hotel myself." Agent Kelso said.

"What? Why? Come on, don't look so serious. I want to dance with you and paaaaarty!"

"Not my scene and not my night," Kelso muttered. Her eyes painted a storm headed at Lucy if she persisted.

"Not your scene? We are surrounded by clubs where we can be ourselves. You can't hold my hand in some parts where I live, without whispers, cussing, and people cursing that we are gross. In a goddamn grocery store!"

Four girls cheered, two guys walking by chimed in with a 'hell yeah'. Two girls were texting while another complained that they need to get walking now. Lucy told them to give them just a minute as she stepped closer to Agent Kelso. Kelso was smiling as she issued a seething rebuttal to Lucy's taunts.

"I don't need a lecture on where I grew up. I am who I am, I don't hold back. Anyone has a problem with that, then too bad. The clubs and the people around us are amazing, no doubt, but just isn't my scene. Period. I'm just a small-town girl. Anyways some guy just told me-" Kelso was cut off by Lucy as she pulled away.

"Well, I hope you get it together girl, since I applied to like five different police agencies here and have an interview with one next week! Seattle! We can move here, start a new life, and this can be our every weekend! You can move to the west side federal offices. It's perfect!"

Agent Kelso felt tears creep into her eyes but fought them off. The culmination of Gaucho, the mysterious man's forecast of hell tomorrow, and now romantic betrayal was tilting her world.

"Wait what? You applied to fucking jobs out here and didn't tell me? When did you plan on telling me?"

"Oh don't trip baby girl, she found you guys a place to stay, with Monica my cousin. Until you know, you get on your feet here in the big city!" a girl chimed into the conversation.

"What? What am I supposed to do with Silas? Tia? Cancer treatments in Wenatchee?"

"Girl, that's just barns and livestock, you too cute to be stuck out there like some windmill waiting for the rain. Move them over here too!" another girl in the party group chimed in. Kelso rolled her eyes.

"Thank you, can you please give us a minute?" Kelso signaled at the girl.

Agent Kelso glared at Lucy who rolled her eyes in matching attitude.

"Look, I like love you, but we don't have a future where I live, its small, everyone knows my business. They have Thai food here! I need this!" Lucy whined at Kelso. A girl patted her on the back consoling her as Kelso began to be glared at by the group of drunk girls.

"You are just saying random phrases. What are you talking about? This is how you operate when you love someone? You know, I've been feeling bad about Silas and Tia, what the fuck?"

"Stop with the cancer stuff, he's like, in remission. He has Aunt Susan and Tia has Leticia. Stop fronting, you are just scared to leave and you don't love me. Bianca was right, you are not down for being part of all this? Seattle is my future, I want you in it, I have a plan. So you can either be part of my future or not. I wanted all this to be a new start, for us, together."

"Why would you do this to me, now of all times?" Kelso asked masking her pain.

"I'll be home later. Don't wait up. You are such a grandma!"

"Grandma!!!!" two of the girls laughed and pointed at Agent Kelso.

Lucy's eyes watered as she turned away to join the girls on the sidewalk to the next club. She knew her words were heartless and the alcohol was powering through in bad ways.

Kelso turned to the quiet girl who only said 'oh my, I'm so sorry' as Kelso helped her to a nearby shared drive vehicle. She looked down at her phone hoping for an apologetic text from Lucy but nothing. Just emails offering deals on flights to Cancun and a reminder that her car is up for service.

Agent Kelso decided to skip the ride and walk in the rainy and glittering streets of Seattle back to her hotel room. She drifted to what tomorrow will be like as she's thrown into the rotors of corruption. A car drove by splashing water all over her outfit and she just replied by releasing slow painful laughter.

Say what you want about Wenatchee but least we don't have all these fucking hills.

Large batches of people walked by Kelso but she had not felt more alone in her life.

Chapter 42

CASE: LEVIATHAN

THE HARSH DARK BLUE Puget Sound water flowed alongside Lt. Michael Loy as he jogged against the morning sunrise. Elliot Bay, home to some of the top tourist traps of Seattle, was his preferred morning jogging course. Despite the endless construction on the Alaskan Way viaduct, it was his preferred way to start the day. Amid the delivery trucks, early riser traffic, buses, and seagulls, it was his city symphony. He had begun his jog at the Seattle pier some mile or so north and had made his way down past the Seattle Aquarium heading to do his lap at the Great Wheel.

A car horn honked as he blasted across a crosswalk and smelled the putrid but familiar scent of fish and water garbage. Lt. Loy pointed at the 'walk' sign and gave a sarcastic thumbs up sign to the rookie driver. Onward he sprinted hitting the Miner's Landing, a den of shops and eateries for tourists and couples. A worker recognized Lt. Loy and waved.

"Why don't you just toss those old bagels into my mouth, man?"

"Because I like keeping my job. Your outfit is so 90s."

"Anytime you want to take me shopping, let me know."

Lt. Loy snickered at the dig in his matching pin stripe sweat suit. His knit hat kept falling down over his eyebrows which annoyed him. Being one of the few Chinese-Jewish heritage cops, subject to endless ribbing by coworkers, gave him a sharp wit. This along with his background in working vice crimes had led to his quick rise in the ranks of the Seattle Police Department. As he hit his late thirties he was sorting out his future options while keeping his mom off his back about slowing down his career for a family.

He kept jogging past the bakery and dug into his stamina to make it to the end of the pier where he'd loop around the Great Wheel and head back up his route. He still had one hour until his shift started but he often cut it way too close.

Seattle's Great Wheel was a late addition to the city, opening in 2012, to dominate the west coast claim to Ferris wheels in both height and swag. It was over the water and the cars bellowed over the Emerald City skyline. Even if expensive, it was a view worth experiencing. Lt. Loy had used it on so many dates the operators had come to know his face and would give a knowing smile. It did not open for another four hours so it provided a decent empty landmark to circle in his morning journeys. A lady was walking her dog ahead of him near the end of the pier. A Yorkie terrier who was not obeying her commands. Its barking was getting louder.

That's odd, he thought. Up ahead he saw a white sheet draped over one of the Great Wheel cars. The sheet was just flapping over and over against the car. It was about forty feet up.

Two people ran past him, almost knocking him down. They ran so fast a delivery truck almost careened into them.

"Hey douches watch where you are going, fucking assholes!"

As Lt. Loy neared, he kept looking up at the white sheet. The woman twenty feet ahead had begun to gasp. Lt. Loy jogged faster to try to help her if it was a heart attack. He slowed down, put his hands on her back, and asked if she was ok. Her dog began to try to bite him.

She couldn't speak. She just kept pointing up at the Great Wheel, in the direction of the sheet.

Lt. Loy looked up, now much closer, to the sheet. Behind him, a group of teens were holding their phones up. His eyes strained to get a better look when a wind gust hit, making the dog pause, and the sheet rip off the cart. It blew downwards catching itself onto a nearby bench. He told the older lady he would be right back and walked over to the bench to catch the sheet before it blew away.

It was more gray than white and had large gashes in it, as if someone had cut violent holes in it. The wind gust came again and now the smell hit him. He recognized that scent. Also, now he could make out a distinct body-like shape to it, like a Halloween costume, a bad one, with parts ripped out.

Fuck. The smell hit again and made him choke down a dry heave. He used a winer glove to hold onto it so it wouldn't blow away. He had worked enough murder cases to know what he had in his hands, but he also had never seen anything quite like this. He pulled out his phone, yelling at the growing crowd to keep back. Also, for someone to help the lady.

"Yeah, Lt. Loy here Seattle PD, I need units here now. We got a dead body. Crowd forming and also send me EMS unit, got a possible cardiac event. Mid 70s, gray hair, responsive but should be checked out."

"You don't see it, do you?" the lady yelled at him.

"Ah, I got my hand on it ma'am, I see it, this is now a crime scene. EMS is on its way, I'm going to secure this body...sack...thing and will stay with you until units arrive. I got you."

"No! Look up, you don't see it!"

Lt. Loy shielded his eyes and followed her finger's direction upwards, up past the car that once held the corpse sheet and saw an object dangling, by a string or rope, on a car's exterior window. As he stepped to the right allowing the sun's shine to be blocked, he saw why she was gasping.

A severed head dangled, banging loudly against the empty Ferris wheel cart.

Oh shit.

Without eyes, the head's face was frozen, mouth screaming in perpetual agony at Lt. Loy, the pier crowd below, and the

Seattle skyline. Sirens bellowed drowning out the lady's barking dog as the Space Needle, towering from several miles away, cast a shadow on the morning.

Chapter 43

ACROSS TOWN, AGENT KELSO was running late to her investigative meeting with the Washington D.C. law enforcement inquiry. Her anxiety had made her not only spend most of the morning in the bathroom, but also second guess even her outfit. Normally she couldn't give two shits about what she wore, preferring sweaters, jeans, and boots to dresses and heels. Now she was sprinting across the gruesome hills of downtown Seattle to get to the 45 Queen Anne Street building.

Minutes later she arrived to Room 568, knocked, and entered.

"Agent Kelso welcome, please sit down."

Kelso sat down and scanned the room. It was a massive banquet hall styled room with a long table and several chairs alongside, but only on one side. Two men and two women sat behind the long table. In front of her was one single chair, for her to sit down and stare at all four.

Typical interview technique. They aren't slick.

"Do I get introductions before we start?" Kelso asked.

A man in a blue suit thinly smiled and nodded.

"I'm Tyron from Department of Justice Office of Inspector General (OIG). With me is Emily who is also an investigator on this case. We work administrative cases in which the FBI representatives, are the focal point. Carly and Janelle, down the way are from Department of Homeland Security, since there were some national security aspects of this inquiry. I'll be doing most of the asking of the questions, subject to them chiming in, ready?"

"National security?" Kelso asked.

"We'll get there. So let's first make it clear this is an administrative inquiry, meaning you are not being compelled to answer anything and we are looking into strictly if any federal policies were violated. We are not asking you to waive your constitutional rights against criminal self-incrimination. Whatever information is gathered from this inquiry will be shared with the U.S. Attorneys' Office and they will determine what happens."

"So if I say I don't want to speak, then?"

"Then we simply take note of that, and finish out our investigation without your input. Action will be taken, based on other witness statements, and the U.S. Attorneys' Office will still inherit our case file for their usage."

"Ah, so if I don't talk I get stuff pinned on me, but if I do talk then I get build my own grave and probably still get stuff pinned on me. Love it."

Across the next four hours Kelso was grilled about everything she had done in the last year. From the small routine U.S. Fish and Wildlife cases to her special deputized FBI Unique Investigations Work. The first few hours the tone was very relaxed and informational, but quickly the tenor of the questions had changed.

"So, after that Trinity incident, in Walla Walla, you know multiple people died, right?"

"Are you telling us that a, what was it, Banshee monster ghost, killed Barron Morris and several gunmen? That's your statement, under the penalty of perjury?"

"Per your prior statement you are admitting you committed bank robbery at the Walla Walla National Bank? We'll get to the part with the leprechauns or banshee thing, but you know that you have admitted to committing a felony during the course of a federal operation?"

"Agent Kelso, are you aware that no such creature that you describe was recovered near Mt. St. Helens?"

The questions were relentless from all sides.

"Bigfoot? Are you telling the Department of Justice that a fictional bipedal primate that has yet to ever be subjected to the rigors of a scientific existence, magically popped up and killed an otherwise-also non-existent tiger beast, in the Cascade mountains?"

"Did you say a baby Bigfoot? So, it was like the three little bears?"

"We searched the San Juan Islands you spoke of, and we found no such animals. No sloth man, no Terror Birds, and surely no man-spider or any other mutant creature."

Kelso had arched her eyebrows and tensed up her face with each barrage of questions.

"I've told the truth, these things happened. I know it sounds crazy, I think I'm crazy sometimes, but they happened, it's all in my reports."

Tyron shook his head.

"Wrong. I must tell you there isn't a single word of corroboration of what you've testified to in your official FBI reports. I've looked at the A-19s, we pulled them from the database, what do you think we are staring at?"

Kelso's face dropped. They handed her a stack of case reports. She flipped through them. All of them were missing any references to a Banshee, Cascade Tiger, or the various monsters on San Juan Islands.

"These reports...they are missing, someone must have changed them."

"ASAC Stevenson, whom we already spoke to, testified these are the reports and his signature is at the bottom. So unless you have some copies that we can see, verified by the chain of command, these are the reports we are relying upon."

Kelso's posture drooped, for the first time, and she felt herself sinking beneath every floor of the skyscraper. The doom was setting into her. Why did Stevenson change my reports?

"None of the Stevenson County Deputies saw your magical Sasquatch buddies, Deputy Stone refused to talk with us as did Professor Pendleton, and these Albanian traffickers, as you admitted, are presumed dead without forensic proof of their existence."

Kelso was finished.

"Guess what we did find proof of? That you and Agent Gaucho trespassed, terrorized, destroyed massive amounts of property. Per Mr. Zacks account, Agent Gaucho then took a boat and crashed it, killing seven men on Sucia Island. In cold blood."

"It was only through excessive grace and teamwork with Mr. Zacks that we were able to keep the press and local citizens out of the story and danger. No Jurassic Park birds, no demon banshees, the real world, Ms. Kelso, with real world consequences."

"Chad Zacks kidnapped us and tried to kill us."

"We've heard that fable already. Let's add accessory to murder, if you want to stick to that statement, Ms. Kelso."

Tyron was angry and blurted out, "Look at the damn reports, you caught a snake, a flood occurred in Walla Walla leading to drowning deaths, you located Senator Logan, but Hershel was killed, and your alleged vacation at the San Juan Islands led to the death and destruction of seven humans and millions of dollars. Yet you want to sit here and babble on about demons and monsters? This is real life, wake up. No one is giving you an award anytime soon."

"You're the ones asleep. How do you not see? Gaucho lost his arm to the Cascade Tiger. Me, Stone and Professor Pendleton watched men be dragged into the river, everyone in Walla Walla knows of the Banshee, ask the college students Marc and Lisa! Chad Zacks is behind all of us, he can't be commanding the U.S. Department of Justice, come on!"

"Thank you, Ms. Kelso. Based on your responses today you are now suspended from duty pending further investigation. We'll take your badge, firearm, and know that the U.S. Attorney's Office will be in touch. You are to speak to no one about this, and the OIG will let you know the outcome of this investigation after we speak to some more witnesses."

Agent Kelso got up and walked to the desk, placing her badge and holstered firearm onto the table.

"You know, I put my life on the line for all of this...Gaucho is dead. My niece almost got slaughtered. I don't sleep much anymore. I wish I could lie and not tell the truth."

"Right, more about boogeymen, please spare us-"

Everyone's phones began to vibrate on the table. An FBI agent ran into the room and whispered into Tyron's ear. They immediately turned on a TV screen in the corner. Kelso was confused at what was happening.

On the TV screen the local Seattle news team was covering, as was every other news channel, the Space Needle.

"I'm sorry sir but field office wanted eyes on this, sorry ma'am," the FBI agent stated.

The camera lens zoomed in and the news reporter stated that for the last hour there had been a standoff with five people who had climbed up on top of the Space Needle and were refusing to come down. One of the people, a middle-aged woman in a purple dress, addressed the cameras.

"He has come and we rejoice! It used to be dark but now he shows us, there is a kingdom below that we all need to show!"

Agent Kelso and the investigative team watched silent.

The other four people were holding hands, singing, all in purple outfits as police and others yelled from the Space Needle restaurant below. Police and news helicopters swarmed the air space around the Needle. It was breaking world news and was only a few blocks from where Kelso was standing.

"He comes for you...he comes for me...he doesn't stop for the G-O-D!"

The Space Needle cult people all began to sing their strange song. In the middle of their song, the female leader put her hand up and turned to the helicopters waving.

"It begins now! Are you ready? He needs to eat, so we feed him the world!"

All five people looked at each other, smiled, and turned and began to sprint downwards off the slope of the top of the Space Needle.

In slow motion, it seemed, everyone watched as all five people leapt off the Space Needle careening downwards onto the screaming Seattle city streets.

"Shit let's go. Kelso, we'll be in touch!" Tyron yelled as he got onto his phone. Everyone else filed out of the room behind him as they texted on their phones.

Kelso stayed in the empty room, staring at the news coverage, mouth open, caught between the horror on the screen and in her life. Already unverified and panicked reports were coming in about another group of similar-dressed people, on top of various buildings across Seattle. This morning's grisly discovery of a severed head with a corpse of only human skin on the Great Wheel was leaked. Tweets and interviews showed the hysteria was beginning to rumble across the Emerald City.

The timer on the room's light clicked off leaving Kelso standing in the dark, vacant eyes staring beyond the TV and into the abyss of her future.

Chapter 44

DETECTIVE ELIZABETH MARANO WAS sitting in her cubicle at Hill Crest Police Department when she got a call alert.

"Marano, you got one, missing dog, out on Humana Drive."

"You've got to be fucking kidding me, tell them to contact shelters. This is a police department. As much as I love my fur babies, I'm not animal control."

Sixty seconds passed and Marano heard Shift Lt. Trosper's voice.

"Marano, my patrol guys are tied up, please handle the dog call."

"You know I'm a detective, right? Like I solve investigations? Like murder, bank robbery. As the only woman, detective at that, I feel like your 'patrol dudes' can handle this smoking hot case."

His showed zero inflection for her sarcasm.

"Elizabeth, this guy is blowing up dispatch. He won't stop calling, and you know that there hasn't been a murder here in literally eighteen years. There's only eleven officers, two detectives, me and the chief. You're the only one in investigations, patrol is handling a multi-car crash, and so that leaves you."

"You are lucky I just happen to love dogs. So I'll do it, but I want my objections noted."

"Our bank, Anton National, was on the front page for number one girl scout cookie sales. Out of our 4,000 calls a year we had zero cartel prosecutions. But guess what we did get? An award for outstanding community policing. This resident is on the edge of our zone, so the last thing we want is for Lake Park PD to snatch this case up, then the complaints, city council, funding, annexation, and before you know it we go from having two detectives...to one."

"I'm guessing I'm not the last detective standing in your little story?"

"Bingo. Answer the call, find the dog, and save the day."

"Gotcha, but Trosper, if a murder comes in while I'm finding some retiree's dog, I want that case!"

"Got it. When someone reports the chief was seen murdering a bottle of tums from eating a chili dog, you'll be the number one big city homicide detective working that scene."

Detective Marano shuffled out of her cubicle. Tall, with long dark hair, dressed in black slacks and a gray suit coat, Det. Marano was on a mission for clarity. She shook her head at the non-emergency receptionist in the front lobby.

"You know you could have just transferred the call to any of the four shelters nearby, right? Like there's nothing criminal, in any way, about a missing dog?"

The blonde just fake smiled back at Marano. As she left she grabbed a piece of candy from her stash under her keyboard.

Ten minutes later Detective Marano was nodding as the elderly man rattled off Chumbo's daily routine. She felt bad for him, you could tell the dog was his only remaining friend, but after the fourth time of him detailing Chumbo's preferred brand of dog toys, her eyes darted outside to the waters of Lake Washington.

"Excuse me sir, may we step outside? Maybe I can get a look at where Chumbo might have wandered off to? Is that ok?"

Detective Marano helped the elderly man up and onto his own balcony. Lake Washington was full of people sailing their boats as the sun began to set across the water. It was the second largest natural lake in Washington and an immense blue brother to the Puget Sound. Seattle was hugged on the left by the Puget Sound and Lake Washington on the right. It's length stretched from several cities northwest of Seattle all the way down across Mercer Island and into the deepest fingertip of King County in Renton and almost the Seattle-Tacoma Airport. Endless homes surrounded it along with Stauer State Park.

"Mr. Gisler, let me knock on some doors and we'll see what shakes out, ok?"

"I'm sorry, Chumbo is a sensitive fella. After Lana passed...there were some dark days, and Chumbo would bark at squirrels, chase the waves, and he got me through. If I didn't have my hip surgery, I'd chase down every lead for you!"

Detective Marano's stare softened. She felt bad for him and regretted making a big deal about taking this call. Mr. Gisler was a sweetheart, and this is better than shaking down some teenagers who have been drinking.

I'll never admit to Lt. Trosper that he was right.

"What about Stauer State Park, think he ventured into the woods? Do you walk him there?"

"Maybe, but I don't go there much, ever since...you know...the weirdos moved in."

"Ah, not a fan of Attis College?"

"Not my scene, I preferred the prior school."

Attis College replaced a previous notable alternative medicine college which had recently moved downstate to a new campus setting. The culture shift was immediate from the prior neuropathic and open campus to this shadowy new institute. Attis College was a mysterious new entity whose courses, mission, purpose, and student body remained a mystery. Even the website had become infamous for just being a blinking white dot. When pressed, it posed a series of questions about the illusions of existence. Large concrete walls had been installed blocking the former open and free campus aligning the beautiful Lake Washington waterfront. If Chumbo had headed there least it would be a nice way to break the ice and meet the new Attis College President and peer inside their secretive campus.

She hugged Mr. Gisler and headed down the street to start knocking on riverfront houses with a picture of the missing adorable black and white border collie.

Chapter 45

"This food tastes like rat vomit," Kelso said. Her face exploded in a sneer as she chewed on the gray hospital chicken chunks.

"I've tasted rat vomit, in the Vietnam war, it was better."

Alex Kelso was arguing with Silas as they sat in his hospital room at the Seattle Cancer Center. Outside, 24 floors below, Seattle was abuzz with the ongoing madness of the Great Wheel carcass along with the suicide space needle investigation. From their room, in the dark, they were watching old action movies.

"I got a banana, it's old and brown, want it?" Kelso pulled one from her purse.

"Sounds like my liver, I'll take it, thanks."

Kelso passed her grandfather the almost-banana-bread ready banana. She shifted in the chair that seemed custom fit to be the most uncomfortable chair in the world.

"Do you think they design these to dissuade people from visiting?"

"I asked them to put little pieces of glass in yours."

Kelso snickered and rubbed her grandpa's shoulder. As he ate, without turning to look at her, he asked the obvious.

"We know my prognosis, three to six months. Six if I keep bombarding myself with toxins or a batch of weeks if I roll out into death standing tall. How is your fate Alex?"

"Pop pop, that isn't funny. We are getting you a second opinion, just because the first doc says something doesn't make it testament."

"Unless you give me a second lymphatic system, it probably is. We knew this time would come. I'm fine joining the elders, just not spending my final weeks barfing. Stop avoiding the question, how did the administrative meeting go?"

Kelso looked down at the floor. She pushed away tears knowing he would scold her for crying over his terminal condition. Chewing on her bottom lip she recounted how she was ambushed with what seemed like a frame job.

"Wait, so none of the details of the Banshee, Cascade Tiger, or those San Juan mutant things...your reports weren't there?"

"Nope, ASAC Stevenson apparently edited them. I spoke with him this morning and he told me it was for my own good. He didn't know this was coming and sensed higher-ups weren't feeling the monster hunting stories, so he edited them to protect me and ease any oversight inquiries. And so my investigative statement sounded like I was on shrooms. Worse yet, it only makes what happened to Gaucho and his attack on Chad's base, look more terroristic when you discount my account. They threatened federal indictment."

"Who do you have to blame?"

Kelso turned, head tilted.

"I also survived active duty amid the swamp of the Vietnam War and tribal police politics. Whenever the feds come knocking, everyone finds a chair. I'm just trying to find you one."

"Well it's just weird, like just one hour ago, this guy, the one I told you about from the Seattle club, friend of Gaucho's, stopped me. Here, at the hospital, outside and told me I have to pin it on Gaucho or else U.S. Attorneys are coming for me as accessory to murder with additional terrorism-based charges. This is Gaucho's own buddy, crazy right?"

"So what will it be?"

"Prison, if need be. I won't lie and I won't do that to Gaucho, he saved my life. Fuck the feds."

"You are a fed."

"You know what I mean."

"Look I love what you are standing for, but in fed prison you do eighty five percent of your time. That could be a long haul. Gaucho is dead, what's the point of not taking the deal?"

"Truth. Honor. I still wake up screaming some nights, stupid ass nuclear monster, other nights the Banshee. I sign that sheet attesting it never happened and Gaucho is a psychopath, and it was all for nothing. Probably is all for nothing anyways."

Silas turned and stared at her, his stern face broke off into a growing smile.

"Well good, I was just making sure you knew what you were doing. Proud of you. Most take the deal to save their badge and freedom. What they don't realize, is usually, this is the first step across a line, which becomes a road, later a freeway, into an escalating maze of decay whereby the time you retire you cannot shake the filth of a career spent burying the truth."

"I'm worried about you, and Tia. If I'm in prison who will take care of you two?"

"We'll be fine. My hourglass is broken and Tia will be ok, your sister will surprise you. She has the wild streak but she's still full of love, don't count her out. I'm sorry you ended up in this predicament. Honestly they'll probably drop most of the charges and just slaughter your career. That Chad guy must be pretty connected? Heard his crew won that bid to build that new bridge across Lake Washington, amid tribal protests, he has the world in his pocket, it seems."

"I'd like to put a bullet in his cranial pocket."

"Ah, yes, please say that at your federal sentencing hearing. It will go over great."

They both laughed as the door opened. Susan and Fr. Harrison walked in.

"I'm so sorry, Silas I got your chicken tenders here. Eat them fast before the nurses see. They were all out of ranch, but I got you blue cheese. Sorry, it is wild outside."

Kelso hugged Fr. Harrison and Susan.

"It's ok we were just finishing this lovely purse banana, what's up? That Space Needle suicide group thing heating up?"

"You guys didn't hear, did you?"

"Hear what?"

"Turn to channel 2."

Silas flipped to the local news channel as breaking news tickers, talking heads, and moving boxes danced across the screen.

SIX VANS FOUND ACROSS SEATTLE.

FOUR POLICE OFFICERS HAVE FAINTED AT THE SCENE.

OVER TWO HUNDRED HUMAN CARCASSES FOUND INSIDE THE VANS. ALL WITH INTERNAL ORGANS AND BONES REMOVED.

WORK OF SATAN? INTERNATIONAL TERRORISM? RAPTURE?

NINE HOMELESS SHELTERS REPORT MISSING RESIDENTS, NUMBERING IN THE POSSIBLE THOUSANDS.

MOBILE MORGUES HAVE RESPONDED ASSISTING OVERWHELMED LOCAL FEDERAL AND STATE FORENSIC TEAMS. THE PRESIDENT IS SET TO ARRIVE TOMORROW TO HELP MARSHAL ALL AVAILABLE RESOURCES AS TERROR GRIPS SEATTLE.

Susan turned the news off. Silence deafened the room.

"So then, is it buddy cop movie or retired ninja becomes a dog groomer?" Susan asked.

Everyone voted for retired ninja becomes a dog groomer. Kelso eyed the window as she saw police helicopters circling the crime scenes pregnant across the Seattle skyline.

Chapter 46

LT. LOY HAD NOT slept in days and it was showing.

"Coffee. Black. Find me the fucking tags on those vans now!"

"Sir, you really should sleep, it's been seriously two days. Tags came back all from different rental places, different signatures, no common source. We're running the names, most are from out of state, not local Washingtonians."

"Fucking bizarre. No wonder the feds are on this terrorism war path. Just doesn't seem like that type of op. What about the IDs on the five dead from the Space Needle, any hits?"

"The condition of the bodies weren't the best, so we're still working on it. There's some tips from the cell phone footage before they jumped. Might hear back on those as they clear them out from the loonies to the legit."

"Ok. Well we need something, literally America is watching us, people are panicking, and I have the actual U.S. president stopping by tomorrow. His chief of staff hinted we need at least three positive progress points for a press conference. If I don't have that? Guess what will happen? Toss my career into those vans as well. Feds are taking this over so maybe it is a cartel symbolic gesture. Just the most gruesome one I've ever seen. Dumb for business."

"Lieutenant, line three! Got a Sgt. who only wants to talk to you, got something hot. They think it's another van, this time, with the driver in tow. Pick up!"

Lt. Loy waved over his team, shut his door, and put the speakerphone on.

"Lt. Loy here, go ahead."

"Lt. Sir, I think you need to get your team out here. I'm on the 520 Evergreen Floating Bridge halfway westbound. We got a van here, with...bodies...and the driver. She tried to cut her own throat but we were able to stop her in time. Lots of blood loss but she'll likely pull through."

Lt. Loy waved at three guys to haul ass and get there. They took off sprinting grabbing more men.

"Thank you, Sgt. Molstone. Has she made any statements? Ran her license? Name?"

"Well, that's the thing. She has no tongue, she had cut it out, so she won't be able to make any statements. Name, Veronica Fent, Virginia license, dob 4/9/1990, came back clear no warrants but figured with your feds in tow, run her name and see what hits you get. Media just arrived."

The line cut out.

"I'm mobile, hitting that bridge and you tell me the moment you find out anything about her last Washington contact. Address. Yelp review. Social media gym post. Find it and tell me. We are seconds away from both the media and feds taking this from us, if we can nail her, then we can put this to bed."

One hour later as Lt. Loy was finally making progress towards the bridge he got a call from his team.

"Lt. you're gonna wanna keep driving and not stop on the bridge. I've already dispatched a S.W.A.T. team, ready on-scene within next thirty minutes. Veronica's addresses all checked out for Virginia-only, but yours truly snagged the Rosetta stone."

"For god sakes, get to the fucking point. Anytime you want to tell me the ending and save our jobs, would be nice!"

Lt. Loy gunned his car as his siren pushed cars out of the way.

"I'm on the bridge, tell me right now."

"Her last social media post, a year ago, was telling everyone that the illusory life and empty existence was over and she was heading to be reborn. To connect with the ultimate. And she signed it with some bizarre ancient symbols. I did some digging, they are also the signs for Attis College. It's apparently some new school over in the Hill Crest Lake Park area. Where Stauer state park is?"

"Got it. On it. SWAT and back up meeting me there?"

"Exterior guest parking lot is set up, out of the tree line view from the campus admin buildings. Feds will be updated just a few minutes later so we get the jump, as you requested. One more thing."

"Yes?"

"King County deputy just texted me that one of those jumpers guess where she just up and left to attend?"

"No fucking way, Attis College?"

"Boom. Same as the identification last address of two bodies from jumpers at the Space Needle."

"Christ. What the fuck is going on at Attis College?"

"Whatever it is, be careful. They're counting the dead sir, from the carcasses, and they are up to four hundred and ninety. They're emptying part of the local med school to store the bodies for forensics. It's insane."

"Hmm, could be a biological agent, sarin gas, anthrax, or something new. Alert our chemical agent teams and the federal partners. I'm fine with the CDC, I just don't want the fucking FBI taking four decades to storm this campus. Ask State Patrol to toss us some of their surplus gas masks for accidents. ETA ten minutes."

"Copy that, Lt. you stay frosty, there's something horrible out there."

Chapter 47

Detective Marano was sweating amid the heavy forest trail.

316 acre state park, how will I ever find Chumbo?

She had already worked the neighborhood by Mr. Giesler and had begun to work the trails in the north side of the large state park. It was mainly a wooded area with trails, state park administration building, formerly a seminary, and Attis College. The state park building and Attis College campus were diagonally set, so after clearing the darkened state park building, Detective Marano began her short trek five minutes to the campus. She had run into a number of joggers and people walking dogs, but no Chumbo.

The front gates of Attis College were a menacing mix of concrete and steel. No guard, no way of entry beyond a finger pad. She pressed it, a red light emitted, and a computerized voice repeated "the infinite has not set upon you, eyes of tomorrow denied" three times.

"Hello? Hill Crest PD? Are you freakin serious?"

Detective Marano was talking to herself as the massive ten foot walls and gate failed to respond.

"Fine. I'll just walk around the trails. First time I've seen a campus that locks its door."

Detective Marano walked around the side of the left wall and saw a giant hole about twenty feet ahead in the concrete security wall. She walked up to it and stared at how something like a car, truck, or wrecking ball had careened through the wall. It wasn't fresh and she could see weathering on the broken chunks of concrete and wall debris. Out of the still darkness she heard a barking and peering into the five foot wide hole she saw a girl in a purple dress running.

The girl had a strange bag in her hands, which was moving as she ran.

Chumbo!

"Hey, stop it, right there! Hill Crest PD!!!"

The girl kicked off her sandals and launched into a full sprint past the parking lot.

Detective Marano gave chase. They ran through the parking lot into campus housing with a garden full of statues of faces with a hand over their mouths for silence. As they exited the bizarre garden a massive sculpture of a Greek god eating a school bus stood in their way. The girl with the purple dress darted around the end of the school bus and the god's fist. Chumbo kept yelping as the girl had tied his legs together in a crude hog-tied ready-for-bbq way.

"Put the dog down!"

Detective Marano's warnings went without response. She radioed in for back-up and that caused her to lose the girl behind a short six-foot brick wall. The main campus building, a towering five story brick fortress, stood in front of her with a large black metal door. The door was open.

"I know I'm gonna regret this. Chumbo you better thank me."

She ran past the black metal door, clearing her corners and turning on her flashlight. It was pitch black inside the nighttime campus building hallways. Only the glow from the emergency exit signs illuminated the stretched into oblivion-sized hallways. The hallways looked normal enough with classroom doors. Detective Marano continued checking each locked door, putting her flashlight against the windows scanning for signs of life. Four down, fifteen to go.

The patter sounds of footsteps made her turn off her light and crouch down. It was only a few feet away around the corner.

Yelp.

Chumbo cried out and Detective Marano jumped and hit the purple dress girl as she was running away. Chumbo tumbled to the ground while the women crashed into a glass case on the wall. Detective Marano quickly wrapped her arms around the thrashing girl and got her into a controlled position on the ground.

"Chill out! You are being detained until you tell me what is going on here. Stop resisting!"

Detective Marano was able to secure handcuffs onto the girl. She took a deep breath and checked on Chumbo.

"It's ok little fella. It's ok. Let me untie you here."

Chumbo was limping as the girl had hurt one of his legs while tying him up. Detective Marano cradled Chumbo, petting him as he licked her, whimpering. Rage funneled its way throughout Detective Marano as she radioed in her position. Back up was about two minutes out.

"He's hungry. We have to feed him. He has to be fed! Master said it's...the only way."

The girl in the purple dress was cut from the glass case shards and mumbling as she bled.

"Take the dog. We can't be late for the feeding. I tried. I tried. The jogger got away from me but at least take the dog. For the feeding?"

Detective Marano then noticed the long blood stain from near where they sat all the way down the hallway to a staircase descending into the lower school's basement level.

"Hey shut up, listen, what is that blood stain about?"

"The feeding. I've tried to tell you, but you can still help out, go. Feed them!"

"Who? Were you about to feed this goddamn dog to someone? What type of school is this?"

Just then two patrol officers ran into the hallway. Detective Marano kissed Chumbo and asked one of the officers to take the dog to the nearby animal hospital to treat its leg. Meanwhile she asked the other one to read the girl her rights and arrest her for resisting arrest, theft, and animal abuse.

"After you get her secured, come follow up in the basement. I'm heading there now. I want to check out this bloodstain path."

"Are you sure?"

"Yeah, just get her to the car and double back. I don't want any other dogs hurt. She wasn't armed so I'll be ok. Lake Park PD is around the corner, since the College is technically their half of the park. We also alerted State Patrol since they get the forest. It's a family affair so within minutes it will be a party."

Detective Marano turned her flashlight back on and followed the bloodstain to the stairs. She peered down and saw nothing. Quiet and undisturbed. The blood stain grew thicker as the stairs descended and began to widen until it was almost covering the entire basement floor. She stopped at the last stair and looked around the hallways. Same darkness with glow proceeding from emergency exits. Four black doors appeared on each side of the hallways. The blood stain pattern began to not just widen but splatter all over the walls, floor, and even parts of the ceiling. It was all in the direction of a door at the end of the basement hallway.

As Detective Marano made her way towards the door, a logo or symbol affixed to the door reflected back at her. It was a giant white circle with an hourglass inside. It was so large that the logo stretched from the top of the door to the bottom. The quantity and pattern of the bloodstains took an extreme form around this hourglass-in-circle door. Something was clearly dragged from this hallway into that door.

"Hill Crest PD, open that door!" Detective Marano commanded.

After waiting five seconds, Detective Marano pushed the door open slowly. Before she could see anything the smell hit her.

Putrid rot. Levels like nothing she had encountered on any crime scene in fifteen years. She began to dry heave and cough. She struggled to adjust her gaze. It was a towering room that was built like an underground lecture hall, gutted, and repurposed as a temple. The ceiling had to be at least one hundred feet up, staircase descending downward until it hit a platform where a giant ten foot hourglass wrapped inside a circle sat. Along the walls of this temple room were dimmed blue lights and some type of hanging plants. At least thirty hanging plants adorned the edges of the temple walls as Detective Marano made her way down the steps. As she got closer to the massive hourglass statute, she saw it was illuminated by torches hanging on each side. The blood stains were everywhere, but it was too dark to figure out a pattern or origin. The rotting smell was growing to the point where Detective Marano kept coughing. As she entered the final bottom level of this lecture hall-turned-temple, where usually the professor would have stood, the hourglass totem was covered in bloody handprints.

It was then that she swung her light towards one of the hanging plants and realized that they weren't plants at all. Her light caught the foot and thighs of one of the hanging things and she flipped it up and saw its hollowed-out face. They were human pelts, hanging by ropes, thirty of them, dangling against the daunting blue lights of the temple walls.

"They weren't ready, but I am."

A voice rung out from behind the hourglass as Detective Marano spun and aimed her gun.

"That gun won't stop what has already begun."

Detective Marano, amid the human corpse fumes and her own shock, struggled to form words.

"Hill...Crest...PD...freeze! Hands up. Oh. My. God."

A figure with a skeleton mask emerged, dressed in one of the human pelts.

"I said, hands fucking up!"

"Welcome to the Extinction. I am the Leviathan."

Detective Marano charged forward and pressed the figure against the hourglass. He put up no resistance. She attempted to find her back up cuffs but ended up grabbing zip ties as back up. Lt. Loy barreled through the door followed by at least thirty officers who all began to cough as they digested the temple room, hanging corpses, and the figure Detective Marano was attempting to cuff. She had just gotten the cuffs on him when Lt. Loy stepped up to the platform.

"Lt. Loy, Seattle PD and task force commander. We appreciate your help and I'll let your superiors know of your outstanding assistance in apprehending this suspect."

"This is my arrest, Hill Crest PD, this isn't even Seattle city limits."

"Ma'am."

"Detective. Marano."

"Detective, Seattle PD and FBI supersede, and we have crimes of both Seattle origins as well as a possible threat to metropolitan and domestic security, stand down. Scene is ours. We'll be in touch."

Detective Marano sighed but released her grip of the figure. He was smiling through his skeleton mask. As the SWAT teams and various law enforcement waves filled the room, someone had discovered a mass pit of even more human pelts dug in a corner. In the back of the room, thirty feet behind the hourglass where Detective Marano was perched, a giant industrial sliding door opened exposing the night air and light into the temple. It revealed how the temple could be accessed by the door Marano had used or by ramp from the hourglass up into the back part of Attis College campus, leading into the woods.

"Bingo we fucking got him!" a SWAT officer yelled.

As Detective Marano made her way out of the swarming law enforcement teams, forensics, and now media news helicopters, she radioed for a status on Chumbo. She gave a quick run-down of what had happened to a federal agent and was given a ride to the animal hospital. When Chumbo saw her he began wagging his tail, sedated and limping, but otherwise happy. Chumbo rubbed against her as she fought off shock processing what she just experienced.

Chapter 48

"WHAT'S YOUR NAME?"

"You already know. Why waste time? The killings won't stop."

"Neil Bates is your name. 23 years old, former high school valedictorian, and Ivy League drop out."

"But now...I've given you a page in history."

"Pardon me?"

"Yes."

"I don't follow?"

"History. Lt. Loy, this case, my arrest, decades from now books, films, remakes, and documentaries will only begin to touch upon this very conversation we are having."

"Because?"

"Because I am the deadliest serial killer that has walked this planet, across two hundred thousand years of existence, 6,000 years of civilization, I stand before you. As the omega. And you get to be the guy now. You are welcome."

It had been more than an hour since cuffing him and getting him into this room. Lt. Loy showed no reaction as he stared into Neil's eyes. FBI Special Agent Collins shifted in his chair. The interrogation room had towering bright ceiling lights, bland brown table, three chairs, and a camera to allow people to watch the interrogation. Gone were the special viewing windows and metal bar to secure suspects. Next door was even a new friendly assault victim interrogation room full of books, and a cathartic theme for confessional interrogations.

"So how did you end up at Attis College? Here in Washington? Aren't you from Ohio?"

Lt. Loy was leading the interview while the FBI agent chimed in from time to time.

"I had a cousin who lived in Ohio, he was happy to get out too," Agent Collins offered.

Neil yawned.

"This conversation bores me. You want to know why I did it, let's get to it."

"So oblige us then, what did you do?"

Neil smiled, "I liberated them. Gave them a connection to the movement. The Extinction Group. It's the entire purpose behind Attis College."

"Ok, so you killed them?"

"Murder is easy, the how and why is what sets the gang banger from the noblemen like Kemper, Dahmer, and Bundy. Although now, they pale in comparison to the testament that I've provided you. Go ahead tell me, besides maybe September 11th have you ever bared witness to anything more life-altering?

Ridgway, Kublinski, and even Jack the Ripper are footnotes to me now."

Both Lt. Loy and the FBI agent were unimpressed. Neil continued his monologue.

"I was worried about H.H. Holmes. You know, his murder count was three figures too, 20 or so confessed and rumored to have killed over two hundred in his little death mazes. Given how many I've liberated and more to come, every serial killer is an apostrophe to the sentence of my existence."

"Good job, so how many people have you killed Neil?" Lt. Loy asked.

Neil blinked a few times, attempting to count in his mind.

"550 I'd say. But fellas, I gotta tell you, after you get past like 100-150 it is seriously hard to keep track. It's just a blur. I'm comfortable with 550 but could really be 700."

Lt. Loy nodded while Agent Collins stayed silent.

"That's something else, so let's start with how. You said it matters, so tell us, how did you even pull that off?" Lt. Loy asked.

"It wasn't like overnight. I mean Hitler had to tweak the gas chambers, Stalin the purges, and even Genghis Khan fumbled a few times. With such limited resources and staff, I think I did pretty good, don't you?"

Neil proceeded to describe how he always felt special growing up, beyond the mortal existence. He had stumbled across the Extinction Group's books on how existence is a prison and their goal is to liberate people from their suffering, thereby unlocking the doors to cosmic eternity. Every religion has been either in tribute or fear of this ultimate truth. Attis College, recently sold by a former homeopathic institute, was set up by dark web financiers to fulfill human's destiny to self-destruct, thereby unlocking the next galactic chapter of history.

Once Neil had arrived, he found it to be full of fifty misled youth fumbling their way through witchcraft and alchemy textbooks. It was only once he discovered a lost ancient tome called the Abbadon Prophecies, a batch of ancient spells, that he found his purpose. After killing a stray animal and repeating the Abbadon words, he felt the Extinction Deity, the Leviathan, enter him. It is also how he got that symbol seared into his forehead.

"I was going to ask, what is that?"

"Leviathan's antimony. A circle with a cross anointed. The contradiction of existence and the truth of your impending self-destruction, clarified through death, antimony."

"You do that yourself or?"

Neil shifted in his seat, the first time he looked fazed for the past hours.

"Yes, and you'd find it on the others, if their fall from the Space Needle hadn't removed their faces. But sacrifices must be made."

"When did you kill your first victim?"

"One week ago. I became Leviathan only two weeks ago, I wasted some days denying my own greatness, but then after I took that first jogger. Consumed him, and hung his flesh pelt for tribute, I knew as my followers saw, the Extinction was upon us."

FBI Agent Collins began to ask detail after detail as Neil avoided answering specifics. Lt. Loy felt his phone vibrate and ignored it. Neil's close shaved black hair, soft brown eyes, and five o'clock shadow facial hair all did not match with what his team had found in the temple. His arrogance alone would have turned off several victims, so the story had holes.

"It's been hours, Neil. All you've told us is there are 500 victims to your greatness. How and who did you pick for your victims, I want names and I want the method. Especially if you want that history chapter on you to be thick, not a thin one. All of the greats had very crafty methodologies, what's yours?"

"True. Well I'll tell you, Seattle's homeless problem was about to be solved, if you get my drift."

"Outside of a jogger, are you saying you killed over 500 homeless people?"

"Civilization has already decided they were disposable, so I obliged. In reality, City of Seattle should issue me a tax rebate or something for all the work I just did for the city. Many begged for my lethal mercy, they knew it was better than the years spent begging, trading sex for food like a prison of existence, and the shame they felt. Their tears were tasty."

Neil took a sip of the water from the bottle provided by the interrogators.

"We'd lure them in, either by promise of food, shelter, or drugs and then off to the temple. It wasn't hard, cut them open, eat their souls, toss the carcass into the pit. The best part is you don't know who is next, do you? I'm not done. My physical is here but I am beyond the physical now. I am the end of times, Tibetan book of the dead, book of revelations, darkest of Dante's nightmares, you have no idea."

"Neil, I'm sorry bud, but I don't follow. It takes an immense amount of time to stab, cut open, ingest organs, blood, bone, and then move carcasses around. There's no human way to do that across 500 people in only 7 days. So was it a group of you or?"

"You saw the Great Wheel, Space Needle awakening, and now the vans full of liberated souls. You'll find more. The real question is, have you made yourself ready for your own extinction?"

"Is that a threat, or?"

"It's a promise," Neil stated as he tapped his forehead.

"Neil, we're gonna take a break and be back in ten minutes, want a snack?"

"In short time, Special...Agent Collins and Lt. Loy, you both will witness my full arrival. Same fate as those pelts haunting your crime labs and deepest fears. And like them, I will crack open your flesh prisons, rip out your insides, and I will have your souls. And then...you will see the truth of the Extinction Group. Leviathan is here."

Lt. Loy thanked Neil for that touching promise as he and Agent Collins exited the interrogation room. After the door shut and they were walking down the hallway to the task force debriefing room, Lt. Loy pulled Agent Collins aside.

"The kid is a creep, but I don't believe he killed 500 people in a week."

"Right, malignant narcissism aside, he has to have co-conspirators."

"We can hit the players here in Seattle but you all, as feds, got the money and the wiretaps. Can you help us track down who financed Attis College and get search warrants for them?"

"No problem, I'll get my team on it."

"Probably some death cult, like Jonestown or Heaven's Gate but maybe not. Maybe it is some type of kill squad. Maybe ten to thirty deep, could be all over King County for all we know. One thing is for sure, no single person killed 550 goddamn people in seven days, but let's keep drilling away at the Mount Rushmore of Serial Killers in there. Ego on this bastard."

As Lt. Loy rounded a corner someone told him that three more vans were recovered near Discovery Park in northwest Seattle. Drivers dead, self-inflicted gunshot wounds to the head, both with similar marks as Neil.

Lt. Loy sighed and walked into the task force room to debrief everyone.

Chapter 49

CHUMBO COULDN'T CONTAIN HIMSELF. He exploded, with a slight limp, out of Detective Marano's arms off into Mr. Gisler's embrace. The reunion helped lighten the mood Detective Marano had been in since encountering the horrific Attis College scene.

"Oh my little Chumbo, I missed you boy! Look, I have your favorite treats and toys."

Mr. Gisler helped carry the dog into his home. He waved Detective Marano in as well.

"Vet says he's going to be fine, just a tender leg that will go away in a few weeks or so. Here's some pain meds and lotion you can rub on it."

"Detective, I can't thank you enough."

"You can call me Elizabeth, please, and you are welcome. I'm just glad we caught them in time."

"Oh heavens, I don't want to even think of what those weirdos were going to do to my little Chumbo. I told you that Attis College was trouble!"

"You called that one. Shit."

Mr. Gisler poured out some food and freshened up Chumbo's water. Detective Marano turned to leave.

"Oh wait, Detective...sorry, Elizabeth. Can I beg of you for one last favor?"

"Sure. What's up?"

"I'm sorry, they're here and I don't want to be rude, but they'd like your help."

"Ah...ok?"

The doorbell rung and in walked three men and one elderly lady. Detective Marano greeted them and they all sat down on the living room couches. Behind them the sun was setting, perforating the sky into colors of purple, red, and streaks of otherworldly colors. Edward Hopper's Sun in an Empty Room hung next to the window.

"Sorry, Mr. Gisler didn't explain, but I'm happy to help. How may I help you folks out?"

"Well you did such a great job saving Gisler's Chumbo, we'd just like to know if you could help with this wild animal. It is keeping us up at night. Setting off night lights, cameras, and scares my grandkids when they visit. I called animal control but they haven't done much. It seems to always dodge camera footage, but we have some drawings. Can you please help us out?"

Detective Marano fought off a smile. *This is gold for Lt. Trosper. I'm now going to be the full-time wildlife animal control cop for Hill Crest PD. Great. Probably bear, mountain lion, or some pet alligator that outgrew its fun factor. I'm still going to call animal control, they just won't know.*

"Sure. I'd love to try to help animal control and get rid of it. Show it to me."

The elderly lady was first. She passed over a piece of paper that had lots of red on it, horns, and an indiscernible shape. But it looked sort of like a bull standing on its back legs.

Weird, but ok. Maybe a larger estate with farm animals and one got loose?

Another neighbor, next to her, handed her a more detailed drawing.

Detective Marano stared at the crinkled paper and stopped breathing for a moment.

"This...is what is hanging...outside of your house?" Det. Marano asked.

"Yep. At night mostly, I never see it daytime. Usually it is moving along the tree lines. Pretty annoying. Howls and yells. Animal control needs to do their dang job!"

The final two men handed over their drawings as the table full of red things stared back at Detective Marano.

"Ah I see trees, how tall is this animal thing?"

"That's the strangest thing, given the distance we've seen it. Hard to tell, but maybe six foot or seven. I figured it was some type of bear, maybe suffering from rabies or mange."

As the neighbors talked and Mr. Gisler nodded, Detective Marano's mind was leaping in various directions. They continued talking about how it runs when they turn on the lights. How they have seen it for over a month and they think it has something to do with Mrs. Gepperson, who went missing twenty days ago, despite a missing person's report filed.

"Why do you think this has to do with a missing person?"

"She saw it many times, told us that she was going to camp out and tell it to get away. She did that and poof, haven't seen her since. Her kids say she just went for a walk and got lost, but they've been waiting on her to croak for the estate money. Call Titlow PD, they have it on file."

Detective Marano took one final look at the drawings. What stared back at her was the thing of extreme nightmares. If it exists, it was something far more disturbing than even Attis College's cult creeps. The creature depicted in the drawings was huge, with two horns adorning each side of its skull, roughly the shape of a human skull. A semi-human face but with gold eyes, a mouth that seemed to be ripped open to the sides, exposing reptile like rows of teeth. The creature's body was sort of striped or ribbed with bones across its abdomen, arms, and legs. There was a hole in its stomach area and looked like three football players pushed into one muscular massive body. Its' hands seemed clawed or possibly some type of long nails.

It looks like a goddamn nightmare. I can't write a police report on this.

"Ok, I'm going to borrow and copy these drawings, I'll return them. And let me see what I can do. No promises, but I'm so sorry you are dealing with this. Let me make some calls. In the meantime, for god sakes, lock your doors, windows, and keep those security cameras on. I don't know what this is, but it doesn't seem friendly. You see it, you call us, ok?"

Everyone nodded as Detective Marano stood up, hugged Mr. Gisler, and left.

Three embarrassing calls to animal control, Fish and Wildlife, and even a zoologist led to a dead end. More laughter than leads. One final call, to a U.S. Fish and Wildlife office in Spokane, did generate one thread to explore. The federal agent informed Detective Marano of some weird animal cases that a special agent had assisted on, but she's currently on administrative suspension. Detective Marano asked for the number and thanked the agent.

Alex Kelso. That name rings a bell.

She checked the internet and realized she had read several stories about Special Agent Kelso and the nuclear serpent in the Tri Cities, Bigfoot scandal, and murmurs about San Juan Island explosions but no clear details.

Worth a shot, all she can do is turn me down. Detective Marano typed the number into her phone and took a long shot at finding help for Mr. Gisler and his haunted neighborhood.

Chapter 50

"OK, YOU HAVE FIVE minutes. I've had bill collectors with less persistence than you. When my grandpa, Silas, finishes his final chemo session I need to be there to help him," Kelso stated to Det. Marano.

"Got it. And again, thank you for agreeing to meet me. I can't really do this over the phone and I'm tired of being laughed at because this doesn't seem like a joke."

The ambulances screamed around them, leaving and arriving, the symphony of suffering. Stressed out family members and overworked hospital staff moved in packets at almost a cyclical pace. Kelso eyed Det. Marano warily, trying to gauge if this was a trap or legit.

Detective Marano handed over the drawings, looking around to ensure no one else saw them. She was embarrassed to even possess them. It felt like a ticking time bomb for someone to find and ridicule her career into further oblivion.

Kelso took in each drawing, moving on to the next one, until she got to the end. She looked up dispassionately handing them back to Det. Marano.

"Sorry, can't help. Doesn't look like any animal local to that area but probably just a prank. I worked a case at a military base where they kept seeing a goat man, I spent days there. Unlike those TV shows, zero spooky words, shadows, and the goat man ended up likely being Elk distorted by lighting. Or sleep-deprived soldiers biting onto the mythical hazing that new staff get when first arriving at base. I doubt a seven-foot demon is walking around Lake Washington. Call a priest if the people are worried, problem solved."

"Well it's not that simple, someone has gone missing and I think this thing might have been involved. I hope not, but please just come along with me to look around?"

"I've got enough problems without chasing this thing, which is probably a joke or these elderly residents taking compromised meds. Or those Attis College cult members, isn't this just north of that place? Probably them playing dress up with Halloween Satan costumes."

Susan and Fr. Harrison had arrived behind them to visit Silas.

"Sorry, I'm heading up, was just finishing up with Det. Marano here."

"About what?" Susan asked.

"Oh nothing, just some pranksters in a costume scaring elderly folks."

"Not exactly," Det. Marano's patience was thinning.

"Look, if I were betting just ask the lead officer on that cult case," Kelso replied.

"That was me. Until I got pushed out for Lt. Loy's fanboys."

Susan shot a glance at Kelso.

"Yeah. I was working a missing dog case, laughingstock of the station, ended up encountering a woman trying to feed a dog to some psycho. Took him down in his cult den, in the basement of the Attis College, bodies and all. And poof, magically I got pushed off the case."

"I'm sorry," Susan said. Kelso was silent, staring at Det. Marano.

"Guess that's how it goes, right? Still a boys' club. Same shit as when I got promoted to Sgt., long story. Took twice as long to make detective and I mysteriously get the snicker and smile type cases. Murder? Drug trafficking? Nope, missing dog. But I don't care about any of that, I'll work a goddamn missing dog case if it helps someone's suffering. And right now, I have five people who are terrified to sleep, walk, and look out their window. And one person missing, possibly dead or off somewhere needing help. I'm a burb cop, I can work a drug case or even abuse but I don't know anything about wildlife. Not a hunter, fisher, and I haven't a clue how to find, track, or at least prove it is safe there."

Susan was staring at the drawings, her mouth dropped.

"Many people are seeing this?" Susan asked. She turned the drawings to the priest. His eyes widened and then narrowed as he focused on each one.

"Someone is a book of Revelations fan."

Agent Kelso took the drawings back and handed them again to Det. Marano. She shook her head at Fr. Harrison.

Kelso had heard enough. She was done.

"Well not only does my grandpa have cancer but apparently my career does too. And both are terminal, so I don't know what you want me to do. I'm staring at federal indictments, for crimes like I'm some terrorist who beheads people on videos to increase recruits. I doubt anything I'd do would help you, mere association with me might get you fired. Not to mention getting me further in trouble for working while suspended."

Det. Marano tried to protest, but Kelso cut her off, her tone rising.

"Look, I'm sorry you got pushed off the cult case and believe me I can relate. But I can't help you, I'm officially suspended pending federal indictment. Right now I'm here in Seattle for my family and that's it. I wish you nothing but the best and I hope you nail the case, I do. Thanks for stopping by."

Det. Marano sighed.

"Ok. I hope your grandpa beats his cancer. And that you beat your job cancer too. If you change your mind shoot me a call. Didn't mean to bother you. Take care and nice to meet you all."

Det. Marano walked away as Susan made a face at Kelso.

"Alex, that wasn't right. And you know it," Susan stated.

Kelso put up a protest about Silas and caring for him but was easily defeated by Susan pointing out that she had taken a week off work to be here. Fr. Harrison had coverage at his parish so he could stay even longer.

"Marano just wants help. You aren't officially doing anything. Remember, you don't even have a badge or a gun. That poor woman is off fighting in the dark, not just this animal thing but also her own career, like yours. Help her. If it lasts longer than a few days then sure, tell her you have to get back here, but it's right across the bridge. It's not like she wants you to fly to Utah to hunt a wolverine."

"Wolverines don't live in Utah."

"Twenty-five years and still with such a smart mouth eh? Put it to use, help her."

"Alex, you know how you'll feel if you see the news. And-" Fr. Harrison said.

"Don't say it Tommy."

"It must be said, Alex. You know if anyone else dies in that area, while it's not your fault, you will spend a decade carrying that burden on top of everyone else's and a million things you aren't responsible for, it's just you. So even if you won't do it for the Detective, do it selfishly, for yourself. Also, so I don't have to hear you complain over and over."

Kelso pursed her lips. She tried to continue her protest on helping Det. Marano.

Three hours later, she succumbed to defeat. Susan, Fr. Harrison, and Silas all teamed up on her until she caved. Plus, she couldn't deny she was bored, restless, and listening to the beeps from Silas' vitals had made her feel like she was lost in a dream.

Sucking in her breath, amid her teeth, she dialed Det. Marano's number.

Three days to help. Catch douchebag in demon costume. Come back, take care of Silas, get fired, and possibly go to federal prison for crimes she didn't commit. Sounds great.

Chapter 51

"What the hell happened?" Agent Kelso muttered.

Det. Marano was already blasting out of her SUV leaving Kelso to speak to herself.

The dynamic duo had just began to work the north side of the woods adjoining Mr. Gisler's home and area where sightings had occurred. Kelso had advised canvassing for track signs and any wildlife patterns that could help nail down what people were seeing. Hours later they hadn't encountered much more than hikers, joggers, and evidence that teenagers were smashing beer bottles in the northern forest above Attis College. They had left, deciding to drive around the south Hopper area situated northeast of Seattle but sitting on the furthest edges of Lake Washington. It was just the upper northeast end of the lake, where a seaplane terminal, marina stocked with boats, used and abandoned industrial docks, and a golf course sat against a highway.

For over forty minutes Kelso had queried about any hidden caves or natural habitats in the area that might be able to host something like in the drawings. Det Marano kept repeating how built-up Lake Washington was with almost every inch, stacked with a residential home with a dock. There were only a few places where nature was king.

As they rounded the corner of Inglewood Golf Club, by the clubhouse, they stumbled across the grisly scene that led to Det. Marano barely parking as she sprinted out of her vehicle. Agent Kelso moved in slow motion feeling the uncomfortable stench of her prior trauma resurfacing.

Bodies were strewn everywhere. Some pelts with no insides remaining as the skin billowed against the night breeze. Others were still partially intact with organs, limbs without a body, and a few heads just thrown across the asphalt.

"Not again, no, no, no," Det. Marano muttered as she radioed for help. She canvassed this parking lot area going from corpse to pelt, searching for signs of life. Blood caked the area.

Agent Kelso bent down and touched a pelt, she rapidly retracted her hand. *What the fuck*! She shook off the creep factor and treated it like an animal carcass. She searched for signs of distress, cutting, bite marks, or kill points.

"Kelso, look at the bus, that's where it attacked!" Det. Marano pointed twenty feet away. Next to the clubhouse, one of those mini-sized buses was parked. The windows ripped out, side caved in, with a massive tear opening it up. It looked like how people tear into a bag of chips. The bus's engine was still running but there was no one behind the wheel. Streak of red blood stained the side ripped open. A pair of torsos and human pelts were nestled underneath the tires as exhaust kept pushing out.

Sirens called out in the distance, still minutes away, but the echo refracted off the waters behind the golf course.

"I'm not finding any survivors, is this like what you found at the school? With the cult guy?" Kelso asked. She was walking with Det. Marano towards the bus, regretting she had no service weapon.

"Sort of. This seems a bit sloppier but I don't know anymore. Any ideas from these pelt things? Are these actual humans or an elaborate ruse?"

"Definitely human. Not a ruse. I could see residue of fluids, blood, and even their hair still intact in parts not ripped out. It is like a vacuum took hold of them in center mass, and proceeded to suck all the bone, organs, blood, and inner stuff but left the skin somewhat intact. I've never seen anything like this with humans, except maybe like when we find dead bodies underwater and sea life has fed on corpses," Kelso responded.

"What about bear? Wolf? Bull bear thing, as they drew it?" Marano asked.

"There's zero bite marks really. I see tears, near the face or center mass wherever the vacuum or whatever connected, some trauma to limbs or the leftover limbs themselves. It seems inconsistent with any bear, wolf, or attack I'm aware of on land. Even if it were some deranged bear it wouldn't have the stomach capacity for, roughly twenty humans that we see here. I don't know of any biological creature that can eat twenty humans this quick. I mean, the motor is still running, this probably was within the last ten minutes."

"Help...help...me."

They ran to the sound of the voice, emanating from behind the bus. It was from a man who had no bottom torso left and was bleeding out fast. He was African American, in his 60s, gray hair, glasses, and soaked in fleeting pain. Det. Marano held his hand, cradled his head, and told him help was seconds away.

"Please. Can't feel my legs. Happened so fast."

Agent Kelso looked around for his legs but saw nothing but scrape marks on the asphalt. Sirens neared, fire, medic, and police.

"Sir, can you hear me? I'm so sorry, stay with us. We got you. Sir, what did this?"

"Mary."

"Mary?" Det. Marano threw a look at Kelso.

"Mary who, sir? Was this an animal? Bear or family of bears?" Kelso asked.

"Marry. On."

"Don't worry sir, we'll make sure we call your wife, she'll be there. Was this an animal?"

"No. Listen, it's getting darker, ah, ah, Marry On. It killed my wife. She screamed so much."

"It's ok sir, just stay with us. I can see the ambulance now," Kelso replied staring at the whimpering man.

Det. Marano yelled for them to get over there to help him.

The man groaned, tried to lean up, even with only one arm.

"Demon. Red. Big like a truck. Repeated name. Marry. On. He ate us."

He began to release silent tears.

"Came out of nowhere...ripped open bus...opened its jaws and ate us. Our insides. Oh Bonnie, no!"

The medics stepped in and began to try to save his evaporating life.

Det. Marano let go of his hand as it had gone limp. Agent Kelso had walked away towards the waterfront next to the golf course. Det. Marano was talking with a patrol officer and joined Kelso.

"See why I need you? The guy said a fucking demon ate them. True or not, this ain't no dog attack, My god. Poor guy, what in the actual fuck?" Det. Marano said.

Agent Kelso was bent down again, at the end of the dock, staring across the water towards the industrial buildings. Blue and red lights reflected off the waters from the distant response teams.

"Whatever it is, attacked, fed, and took off from here. Notice the trail left, ends here. We might have something that can travel on water and land, can't be alligator, but something is hunting here on Lake Washington."

"What about Marry On? Think it was just brain neurons firing from massive trauma and blood loss, or think it's something?"

"Doubt it is anything, the man was terrified. But I know someone who we can run it by. Think you can get us a short flight to Walla Walla?"

"Why?"

"An old friend. Professor Pendleton. Maybe this is just a really apex predatory land-water animal. But...if it isn't, and it is something that is more, ah, extra then he will know. I'll explain more on the flight."

They left just beating the news choppers and spotlights.

Chapter 52

THE FORTY-MINUTE FLIGHT WAS bumpy, but quicker than if they had done the four-hour drive from Seattle to Walla Walla.

"So you're telling me a Banshee demon killed that entire crew?"

Kelso glared at Det. Marano to keep her voice low, as they maneuvered through the extra small Walla Walla regional airport. It only had two waiting areas, a diminished rental car area, and sat on the corner of the sleepy but welcoming wine country town.

"There's cases where I've encountered new biological entities, like the San Juan or St. Helens situation, and then there's what happened here. It had no biological dimension to it beyond its ability to inflict pain and murder on anything it felt had violated the curse."

"Dude that's insane, you need to tell more people, that is bad ass," Det. Marano said.

"Yes, it is so amazing I'm suspended, federal criminally investigated, and my partner was killed to save me and my niece from a rich fucker's nightmare zoo. And there's no proof that any of this has happened, reports altered, evidence disappeared, so yeah I'm a real bad ass."

"You got my vote," Det. Marano quipped.

They sped from the airport towards the university. Kelso had texted Professor Pendleton and set up a meeting at his office. She was lucky he was in town, he traveled often to his mythology conferences.

"But hey, please let me play lead, I don't know how comfortable he feels talking about the Banshee. Ok?"

"No problem, is he cute? I got a thing for people who aren't cops."

"Marano, we're working a mass murder, not doing a double date."

"Whatever, and it couldn't be a double date, you don't have a date."

"Thanks, remind me further."

Five minutes later they were sitting in Professor Pendleton's office. He wore a navy suit with white shirt, orange pocket square, and was asking how Kelso was doing.

"Seen better days. But since the clock is ticking I was hoping for your help."

"Oh my, I'm sorry. I had wanted to tell you, but only in person."

Professor Pendleton looked around the room, lamps, corners of the ceiling, and eyed his desk phone. Det. Marano tossed Kelso a puzzled look.

"Sorry, pays to be cautious. I was served with a subpoena yesterday. They approached me in the hallway after a class. At first I thought they wanted an autograph on 'Festival of the Banshee', but sadly it was just a subpoena."

"You wrote a book...about the Banshee?" Kelso asked.

"Fictional. My Athena, I kept my word, but I don't really want to commit perjury in a federal interview. So soon, I might have to share, but Alex, you saved us all, don't sweat it."

"Is she in the book?" Det. Marano asked.

"Oh yes, she is the heroine, but I moved the story to Ireland and made it more of a cult thing than what we experienced. It is selling pretty good. Alex, please take a copy. I hope my book didn't cause your trouble. I'm sorry."

"Nah, wasn't you. Federal government is a moody employer, subject to the passions of politics over truth," Kelso replied. She stared at the cover of a demonic face she didn't recognize with people in a circle chanting.

"We have to head back soon, so I'm gonna jump in here. In my jurisdiction, Lake Washington area, I have a demon loose, can you help us with that?" Det. Marano asked.

His eyes lit up.

"I have been watching the news coverage, absurdly gruesome things being alleged. Vans of human corpses, insides gone? A detained young man who is head of this death cult? The head on the great wheel and group suicide off the Needle? What does this have to do with a demon?"

"Unofficially, we are worried there is either an animal loose or as some are depicting, there is some type of more Banshee-like creature in play. Red, tall as a stop sign, killed twenty people hours ago, and I hope we are wrong, but figured worth asking you."

"Does Marry On mean anything to you?"

Professor Pendleton leaned back in his chair. He closed his eyes for an awkward passage of seconds until he opened them hopping up.

"Alex, can you close and lock that door please. I have something that might help."

Det. Marano watched as Kelso locked the door, and the Professor pulled off the Dante's Inferno canvas that had been staring at them. Det. Marano got up and helped him pull it off the wall.

"Ah, what is happening?"

"Marano, I've given up on stopping him when he's nerding out."

Professor Pendleton set the painting down. Behind where it hung, a small little bump appeared in the drywall. He pressed it and the wall opened up revealing a small safe.

"This is why, despite the promotions and offers to move me down the hall to a larger office, I've stayed. This isn't exactly university approved nor do I want anyone finding out about it ladies. If you would."

"Dude I'm not campus PD, I'm working a mass murder, you are good."

Professor Pendleton pulled out a single medium sized book bound in crimson red. It had ancient writing all over the cover. He walked back to his desk and took a deep breath.

"Ladies, do you know what this is?"

"No, but you're going to tell us and I'm guessing it isn't legal."

He laughed. Det. Marano had a creeped out look on her face.

"Perfectly legal but highly dangerous. Worse than a silo of missiles. This ladies, is the Literata de Daemonica. It is an actual encyclopedia of demons. Accumulated from Catholic priests, forbidden or stored works, and of course field work."

"Field work?"

"Exorcisms, possessions, historical accounts and such. I'm not saying it would be admissible in court but I can tell you that it is so sacred that this is the only copy in the United States. There's one in Russia, and of course the original in Vatican."

"Prof, it's rare, got it. Marry On?"

"Alex, always in a rush, but you just better hope Mayrion isn't running around in Seattle. If so, the Banshee is an ant in comparison."

Det. Marano mouthed Mayrion to herself. That makes more sense. Sort of.

"Do tell."

Professor Pendleton turned to the page dedicated to Mayrion.

"We're talking about a commander of the Void, in hell. After being invoked by spells, he usually commands armies and is thought of as one of the top lieutenants in the underworld."

"There's military ranks in hell?"

"There's a hierarchy and this guy is near the top. Worse, he's usually invoked inside of hell. Like demons call him up to take on causes to make strikes at God's plans."

"What does this have to do with the pelts?"

"Says here he also goes by the Mauler of Souls. There's no pictures of him but he seems to have a way to devour souls and seems like a heavy middleman. It's not Satan himself but Banshee, Sasquatch, and even your best Hollywood movie won't come close to this guy. He's the real deal."

"Ok so how'd you kill the Banshee? Let's get that going. Exorcism or crosses dipped in holy water?" Det. Marano asked.

"Banshee isn't dead. It just, kind of pauses until the curse is enacted again. It is everlasting just not on this realm, until called into existence by humans violating spiritual codes."

"Some of us...still see it every so often," Kelso admitted. She looked away outside as students walked in the quad texting and smiling. An innocence that won't return to her.

"Well fuck, what are we supposed to do with General Mayrion, then? Why is he here? I'm not going to let him run around killing innocent people in my city. What does your magical book say about that?"

"Not that kind of book. Just a collection of profiles on dark spirits."

"Fucking convenient. Well this has been fun," Det. Marano got up.

Kelso apologized for Marano's crudeness and asked the Professor to keep digging.

"Alex be careful. This isn't what we dealt with here in Walla Walla, like not even close. It's like comparing a crossbow to a nuclear missile. I'll keep digging. I know a priest who dabbles in this landscape. So that we leave on good news, Det. Marano, it might not be Mayrion."

"A man's dying declaration was that the thing that eradicated his wife and killed him declared itself Mayrion."

"These are demons, if that's even what this is up in Lake Washington. Demons aren't exactly the most reliable things to grace this realm. They often trade in lies and deceptions to get possession of people, homes, and areas. A ton of exorcisms have captured lower ranking demons calling themselves all types of things, even declaring themselves Satan but they were just small timers. A few rounds of exorcism and poof, off they went back into the darkness. I hope that's what this is."

"If not, then we need to know how to put it down. And fast, Professor, if it is what is behind hundreds dead bodies in Seattle and counting...we need a plan. Counting on you."

Professor Pendleton nodded as he put the painting back over the safe.

Kelso and Marano got into their car and Kelso drove them to a neighborhood on the west side of Walla Walla.

"Ah isn't the airport on the other side of the city?"

"Yep."

"And sorry, I know that was your friend, but he was pissing me off with his lectures without any solutions. Smart but not my type. Although I did like his little safe I bet there was porn in there too."

Kelso ignored Marano's ramblings as she stared at 4556 Humet Lane. It was an unassuming yellow house with a white door. Bushes, flower garden, and a police cruiser parked in the driveway. She wanted to knock on the door, go inside, and see how Lucy was doing but couldn't get the courage to move. Text messages sent without reply, emails, and even trying her Seattle apartment but no Lucy. She wondered if the door was really shut or if it was just a rough patch.

"Also, what priest writes a goddamn encyclopedia of demons? I don't want to meet that guy, bet he has great stories though. I once dated a guy whose sister became a reverend. She claimed to battle demons by dousing stuff in holy water. Maybe we should dip our bullets in holy water, well you don't have a gun, but I do. I have a crucifix at home but I got it at like a flea market, doubt it's like gonna compel people by the power of Christ type stuff, you know?"

Det. Marano's cell phone interrupted her own monologue. It was her Lieutenant, asking where she was and ordering her to respond to a repeated burglary up by the Hopper Seaplane Terminal. She told him she would connect with them tonight smoothly not disclosing she was far away in Walla Walla as they spoke.

"Kelso we gotta roll, brass is on my ass. While I'm looking into why some tweaker is stealing plane engines for scrap, you can take my personal vehicle and check out Gisler's neighborhood, cool?"

Kelso put the rental car into drive and said goodbye to Lucy again, in her head.

Chapter 53

MARANO STOOD TAKING NOTES on her notepad as the Hopper Terminal manager spoke. Agent Kelso hung back about five feet away, giving them some space to chat.

"So nothing was stolen?"

"Well, not exactly. I mean they broke the goddamn door and ripped holes in the wall."

"Ok...so we're talking more destruction of property, not burglary?"

"Well they broke open the terminal. Without a new door now these seaplanes can be stolen at night."

"Is that really easy to do?"

The manager was becoming irritated.

"If you have the equipment or know how to use it, sure. These planes aren't cheap, now with the wall and door damaged, it's on me if anyone's planes are stolen. Is that your partner?"

"Hello sir, I'm special forces, wall damage division," Kelso chimed in.

"Oh it's stand-up comedy time?" the manager snapped back at Kelso.

"No no sir. Let's go inside and show me what happened. I'll take some pics and we'll write a report. Follow up if we can tag any leads," Det. Marano said.

The three of them were outside the Hopper Air Terminal. The Hopper Air Terminal was a large depot of seaplanes, docks, and hanger with repair areas inside. It was a large factory sized warehouse that was shuttered and dark. On the left was the asphalt cement factory and to the right was the enchanting Northeast Seattle marina. The boats were anchored but drifting as the Lake Washington water flowed under them.

"Explain to me, why are we doing this at night?"

"One, you haven't answered my call for twenty four hours and two, they aren't coming at 11:00 a.m. in the morning."

They walked past two vans in the parking lot and Kelso listened to the traffic behind them. While there was an industrial yard across the water from the terminal that seemed quiet, the marina and cement factory could get busy at times.

"Kind of ballsy to do that with so many possible witnesses?" Kelso asked.

"Exactly." The manager unlocked the gate as they walked, "I think they might be acting like they are my staff so no one asks questions. Still, how did they blast through my door?"

Det. Marano let Kelso chat with the manager as she started to look at access points. Water at end of seaplane terminal dock, one seaplane is currently docked there. Marina boats. Cement factory had a flimsy fence separating their properties. No breaches beyond one area that was caved in from some rock.

"Sir, has that cement factory fence been like that for long, or is it new?

"Nah, that's been like that for years. I keep telling them to fix it but they are slower than two dead turtles fucking. I'd fix it, but fuck them."

"Wait. How do two dead tur-" Kelso replied. Marano waved her hand to keep focused.

"Ok so if the cement factory is open that's one way they might be coming. Is that seaplane one of yours or a repair job?"

"No. That's strange."

They rounded the corner where the repair and hanger hub terminal door was located. The manager pointed out the massive hole. It looked like someone had exploded out a chunk of the door. Steel was ripped and charred around it.

As they walked into the terminal, the manager shouted at a group of five men.

"Lenny, what are you doing here? Who are these guys?"

Before Marano could reach for her service weapon a man behind them put a gun on them. Kelso rubbed her hip area recalling how she no longer had any service weapon.

"Over there, on your knees," the gunman shouted.

The crowd of men encircled Marano, Kelso, and the terminal manager.

"Lenny, you promised us privacy. I don't like voyeurs unless I'm paying for them."

A man in a tan suit, in his late 50s, with silver hair, spoke with a Mexican accent.

"And the police? Lenny, you an undercover?"

"No sir, I'm sorry this is my boss, he is cool."

The gunman shot Lenny in the head before he could finish his sentence. His body fell as Marano began to cuss.

Chapter 54

Det. Marano was untethered with her words at the band of criminals.

"You can't kill a fucking cop, even if you are cartel, which I'm assuming you are, you don't want that heat. She's a fed. You want a cop and a fed murder charge on you? Think of your operations."

The men gathered them against a metal wall of the terminal. Around them sat six seaplanes in various stages of repair and one ready to go. The lights were half-lit giving a glooming hard-to-focus visual to the moment.

"And so the best thing you can do, is to take off, I'll give you a head start, hit Canada. You know you will be killed for bringing that level of..."

As Det. Marano was talking they executed the terminal manager. Blood leaked out of the bullet holes as he slumped over.

The gunman pushed Kelso and Det. Marano onto their knees. Det. Marano's jabbering trailed off but she appeared to refuse to accept the situation.

"Even if you kill us, one, I'd like to tell you that tan suits are not in anymore, so after I'm dead please get yourself to a better mall. Next, who flies away in a seaplane? Is this a James Bond film from the 70s? Dude, you need to hire me as a consultant. I can fix so many problems with your org. Call your boss, he'll vouch for me. Seriously, look at that guy over there, he has a mullet, where are you recruiting from, a teenage 1980s after school special about cocaine?"

The man in the tan suit chuckled, as did all of the men except the gunman behind them.

"I do like this one, she's mouthy, but...sorry we're fully staffed. Pleasure meeting you."

While Det. Marano was mouthing off Kelso had slowly arched her back and leaned more upwards. She knew there would be no negotiations for safety.

When he puts the gun to my head slam it backwards. Marano better have an ankle holster. Tia and Silas I love you, hope you never see these crime scene photos. We need to dive behind that work bench area for cover. Fuck fuck fuck.

"Hey douchebag just do me first," Kelso yelled. It startled everyone who hadn't heard her speak yet. The gunman obliged and stepped from Det. Marano's back to Kelso's. A loud clanging sound was behind them.

Everyone paused and looked as the terminal door was being closed. But it wasn't by the two cartel henchmen, the man in the tan suit, or the gunman. Kelso tried to speak but choked on her words. The smell of burnt ash pervaded the air. Heavy breathing emerged with a voice that was deeper than any human octave anyone had heard.

"FEED OR SERVE."

"What the holy fuck is that?" a cartel operative asked.

Chapter 55

A CARTEL HENCHMAN MUMBLED a prayer.

Standing twenty feet away, at the terminal door, was something that made Det. Marano yelp. Kelso began to pull on her to get them away as the gunman turned his aim at it. All eyes of the terminal were on the new guest, standing 6'8" tall, skin the color of dried blood, with an exoskeleton of human bones all over his chest, arms, and legs resembling a bone armor. It had a human head with two glowing gold eyes, human-like nose, with two giant horns protruding off of the top of its skull. Its mouth was huge, wider than most of its face, giving it an alligator-like smile with rows of sharp teeth and a serpentine tongue.

"Come on!" Kelso whispered louder as she dragged Marano away. The cartel did not notice their escape, as the demon began to walk towards the tan man with his cartel group.

"Hey, get fucked!" the gunman yelled as he shot his silenced gun at the demon. The bullets hit, ripping holes into its body, but no blood emerged. The demon walked with a sense of calm as the gunman unloaded his magazine into it, and proceeded to rip his entire arm off with one swipe of its clawed hand. The gunman tried to scream but the demon, with a simple second swipe, knocked his entire head off his body. The head rolled clumsily across the cement floor like a deflated basketball.

"Move! Now!" Kelso yelled dragging the starstruck Det. Marano deeper away from the slaughter scene unfolding. The tan man took off running in another direction, leaving the two henchmen before the demon. One took off behind it for the hole in the hangar door, the other remained kneeling praying. The demon gave chase to the fleeing henchman.

As Kelso scanned the terminal, she saw no doors or exist options in their northwest corner of the hangar. She heard the death screams of the fleeing henchman. She noticed a fire exit door blocked by a heavy work bench with repair tools on it.

"Marano, come help me push that out of the way, we'll blast out those doors and try for your vehicle."

The tan suit man had made a loud noise as he tried hiding inside a trash can on the hangar floor. The demon easily located him in seconds and grabbed the trash can and squished it, crushing the tan suit cartel leader inside.

Kelso used the loud execution to push the work bench inches, but still not enough.

"Marano, just a little more and I can kick the metal bar to get us out. Focus on the bench."

As they pushed the bench, Det. Marano was able to see the last henchmen's fate. He was still praying, repeating his words as he wept. The demon circled him and repeated its words.

"FEED OR SERVE."

The henchman didn't reply so the demon filled in the blank.

"FEED ME."

Det. Marano watched in utter disbelief as the demon's chest area opened up, like a mouth, so instead of a stomach it had a glowing red hole with teeth. The stomach mouth reached out and locked its jaws onto the henchmen's head and proceeded to liquify and suck out all of his insides. His bones, blood, organs, and even eyeballs melted out and were vacuumed up into the demon's glowing stomach within sixty seconds.

"Oh god." Det. Marano began to wince at the sight of the demon's feeding pattern. "The pelts, this is how...its him...he's eating them...oh god."

Kelso had kicked the fire door and grabbed Det. Marano as she screamed. The demon was sprinting their way. Kelso pulled Det. Marano through the door and they kept running. Marano's vehicle was too far and the demon could probably rip it open like a T-rex anyway.

"Kelso, cement fence hole, right there!"

As they turned to the fence hole they heard behind them, the crunch, clash, and sound of the demon ripping apart the terminal wall. Kelso didn't turn around as they galloped and dove through the cement fence wall with no time to see beyond the side.

Det. Marano saw a red arm breach through one of the terminal walls, as the fire door was kicked out, allowing the demon to take one final look at them as they fell down a massive two story tall rock pile.

"Is it coming?" Kelso yelled.

"No clue. Let's head for that ladder, it can't fit on it. I want to get up high."

"So it can trap and eat us? That sounds brilliant."

"It's built like a dump truck. Its weight alone would crush the ladder. He can't make it up to the top. Trust me."

A night watchmen yelled out from the cement factory guard house as they kept running. Det. Marano yelled something about watching for a demon but the guard ignored her words as the ravings of an insane woman.

They barreled to the metal ladder and began climbing. With each rung they ascended, they could sense the demon nipping at their ankles. Within a few minutes they had reached the top, five stories high, and had only a small control panel and a rock chute by them. Beneath them was the darkened cement factory and night guard still yelling and pointing at them. Sirens emerged in the distance as Kelso took a long breath.

"I don't see him, do you?" Agent Kelso asked.

"Nope, nothing. Why didn't he chase us?"

"Probably wanted to finish his cartel sampler platter meal in there."

"Gross. You didn't see it feed. It sucks our insides out. I've never seen anything like that in my life."

"Camel spiders. Wasps, I think. Nothing that big."

"Thanks Fish and Wildlife, I wasn't asking like in real life. That's a fucking demon. Where does something like that come from?"

"I don't know, but we're gonna find out. And fast, that thing can be the end of the human race."

"And I thought the guy with the god-awful suit was a problem."

Kelso saw Marano's hands shaking and put her arm around her.

Chapter 56

KELSO WAS SITTING IN a hospital waiting area staring at the news updates.

FBI arrests twenty-two people in Seattle Slaughter case. Murder. Conspiracy to commit murder. Terrorism.

Local Panda bear dies from eating donut thrown inside its enclosure.

Chad Zacks refused to answer questions on new drilling at the bridge worksite. Worker deaths and environmental impact reports falsified. Activists build a wall protesting one of his many Seattle condos.

No further vans with pelts discovered. President and mayor thank brave around-the-clock work of the FBI agents working the active case. Homeless shelter manager Ton Jordan stated this happened since no one cares about the homeless, this has to change.

She looked out the window away from the carnage of the news. The sky was gray and looming.

Kelso's phone began vibrating. It was Professor Pendleton.

"Hey Gaia Earth Goddess," he said.

"Please tell me you have something, the cops are fumbling. It isn't that kid they have in custody," Kelso replied.

"I have something but you won't like it and I'm worried, if what they say is true. Don't go alone, for many reasons both earthly and non-earthly, ok?"

A nurse came in to tell her Silas' meeting with his doctor is now. Kelso nodded that she is on her way.

"I got a cancer update with my grandpa's team, make it quick. Spare me the theatrics."

"Upstate. You know that famous Sedro Woolley mental asylum site?"

"Yep. About ninety minutes north of Seattle, a shuttered asylum sitting on a thousand acres where primitive things happened, patients died, and supposedly haunted. I've been there, while visiting a friend. Trails, stunning views of the Cascade mountains, and of course picnic areas. Am I supposed to invite the demon up to play a mean game of frisbee golf?"

Professor Pendleton didn't laugh. Kelso kept walking down the hallway of the hospital as whitecoats and nurses rotated rooms.

"That's what the public knows, but I have a friend in the archaeology department, and they stumbled across something big and horrifying. A similar thing popped up on digs in Canada. About a mile north of the edge of Sedro Woolley asylum lays the ruins of an old elementary school."

"Ok, and?"

"Well I'm trying to be sensitive about this, but on a current dig they are encountering children's skulls and fossilized body parts. Apparently, it was a private religious orphanage, not part of the Sedro state system, but set up when they were moving some tribes around so they made the adults move to the reservation boundaries while demanding their children become "civilized" at these schools. But, from the condition of the bones, it seems like, well, no way to put this gently, they are finding enormous amounts of children's bones in the dig."

"Fuck. Who does that?"

Silas looked up and smiled amid tubes and ports. His eyes cut through the lie of his smile, Kelso could tell he was tired deep inside. She motioned to the doctor and nurse to give her just one minute to wrap up the call.

"How does this solve our problem?"

"Under the school's first floor is a cave or sort-of-basement. Rare and kind of strange for this region where soil and bedrock patterns don't allow for basements, but they have a primitive one. From what my friend says, on the dig site, it is more like a large meeting room. It has an underground burning oven, tools, and apparently is where they disposed of the sick and dying children. But on the furthest corners of it, they discovered that it has several markings, bizarre ones. I got that call and linked up with an ancient spiritism specialist and the writings on the corner wall indicate, prior to the school, this was a massive magnet for tribal leaders and troubled people. Tribes would send people to this site to interact with some type of ancient wisdom to solve problems. Some would return with power in hand, others would never survive the journey to this wisdom. No names or further info, just something is down there that used to help troubled generations. Either way, short of calling up a priest and asking for an exorcism, this might be something to explore."

A long pause emerged. Kelso sensed something else was being held back.

"Pendleton, out with it, I know you."

"Kelso, the dig has been suspended pending investigation."

"Investigation for what?"

"Accidents. A few deaths under strange circumstances. And bites."

"Bites?"

"Yeah, two workers had to go to the hospital since something took a bite out of them. Like a tiger or shark. Early investigation showed nothing and no one down there but the walls, rotting pillars, and broken brick. My friend refused to go back. They're pulling another archaeologist to help lead the team. Several tribal writings reference otherworldly weapons and solutions, worth a shot Alex, you'll need anything to take on Mayrion."

"Got it. I'll handle it and will bring a friend. If you had seen what I have recently, you'd be far less scared of a basement that takes little bites than a demon who deskins you for food. Mayrion does terrify me. I agree, if there are any answers there, it's a risk worth taking."

Kelso texted Det. Marano as she walked back into the hospital room with Silas and his team.

Time for a field trip. We can only hope it might have some answers for us about big red.

Det. Marano fired a text right back.

Sold. Chief thinks I need an asylum after I refused to edit my report about the demon.

Kelso replied with a smiley and the details on meeting her later that night. She slid her phone into her pocket and took a deep breath to hear Silas' progress update. The doctor's face seemed as promising as an executioner's smile.

Chapter 57

FOUR HOURS LATER, KELSO and Det. Marano pulled up to the decaying school site. It was hard to even see in the dark, luckily Professor Pendleton had given them exact GPS directions via his friend. It looked like an old colonial schoolhouse. Single one room building, wood with windows adorning each side, short bell attached to the triangular roof, with a chimney. A broken wood staircase lay in pieces in front. The front door had been removed with yellow police tape wrapped around the entryway. Around it stood a circle of dead grass and dying trees whose branches seemed to lean over in worship of the little schoolhouse.

"Dude, this is way more trippy than that shuttered Sedro asylum. Those idiots who built this didn't think ah, hey, let's build this on a sacred tribal site? That wouldn't be super disrespectful? Also, did they watch any horror movies, my god!"

"Marano, there wasn't electricity, much less horror films back then, and from what Pendleton mentioned, only the tribal world knew about the sacred aspects of the cave underneath. To the settler and colonial world they figured let's build around it, use it for storage of dried goods and things. I can't tell you how many times developers gloss over an area that held sacred value to tribes. We can talk colonialism later, for now, let's just get in and out. I want to be back for Silas' next treatment, I don't know how much time I have left."

"Sorry girl. I got a few bars on my cell so least we got that if something pops off."

They exited the SUV and took one visual sweep before entry. Deafening silence.

"I like the police tape, it's a nice touch against the two centuries old schoolhouse motif."

Kelso carefully peeled the tape off so that they could reset it after looking around. Using their flashlights they entered the schoolhouse and began their search. Despite the passage of time, the wooden walls were intact, as were most of the windows. In the center of the open wooden room was a giant black metal wood stove. A few wood pews were collapsed against the wall. A chalkboard shattered across the floor.

"Looks legit," Det. Marano stated.

"Yep. The basement entry is apparently in that corner if you pull up on that rope. Let's head down."

Both of them pulled on the rope as it was a heavy basement entry door. Outside it began to rain.

Det. Marano took one look down at the small curving wooden steps descending into deeper darkness.

"If I see anything move down there I'm shooting. Got it? Demon, ghost hunter, or archaeologist working overtime, I'm at least firing a warning shot immediately. This is so fucking creepy. It better all be a goddamn hoax."

Kelso nodded and they put the flashlights on top of their firearms as they slowly descended down the stairs twisting to a solid muddy basement floor. As they spun around to decipher the darkness their light revealed a massive room the size of a basketball court. Their light barely reached the other corners of the expansive basement room. While the floor was hardpacked mud the walls were a mix of stone and brick. Giant metal poles were installed every four feet from modern school operators and the archaeology crew ensuring they wouldn't be caved in during their dig. In the far corner they saw some of the writings. They walked towards there. It was freezing cold as the rain upstairs and outside made the earth groan.

Let Me Out.

You Can't Hide.

I taste like the dreams of children.

"This isn't helping with my nerves. Stupid ass teens are creeping me out with their graffiti," Det. Marano said. Even her coping mechanisms were failing in the hands of this site.

"I don't think these are teens, check that out, Professor Pendleton stated the area would have that symbol. Look there, I think this is it."

They shined their lights onto the wall where no less than a thousand depictions of the same symbols were carved into the brick walls. It was shaped like the letter E with an extra line but tilted on its side, with a line across the top.

"Ok what next? How do we meet this wisdom or do we just start talking?"

"He told me to use a phrase and see what happens."

"Oh great, nothing ever goes wrong when someone does an ancient chant. Awesome."

Kelso ignored Det. Marano's sarcasm and began to repeat the five words that the Professor told her to chant. It was a mix of words that she could barely pronounce much less say properly. She felt stupid doing it and each chant had to end with a name, Elim. It was one of the many names the wisdom had gone by that translated to rough English form.

Nothing happened and there was no response beyond the rain billowing way above them upstairs. Kelso repeated her chants while Det. Marano kept exploring. She hit the other corner of the room, finding the burning pit.

Det. Marano was looking at the pit that had been dusted and preserved by the archaeology team.

"Whoa, there's the burning oven. Oh no, my god. Those poor kids, fucking monsters."

"Depends," a raspy voice blurted out at Det. Marano and Kelso. Det. Marano shrieked, whipping her flashlight and gun in the direction of the voice. Nothing. Fear prevented her from firing off her promised warning shot.

"Demons. Angels. Screams. Laughter. Always depends."

The voice had hovered in another direction as both women tried to track down the source.

"Show yourself!" Kelso shouted. "We came here for answers."

"So be it, explorers, you have arrived."

As those words were hissed at them, a very thin figure appeared from behind one pillar. It had no face beyond a white mask with a strange thin mouth, no eyes, nose, ears, or other facial features. Adorned on top of the white mask was a giant hat similar to the ones Catholic Bishops wore, but this one was made of veins pulsating to the top. It assumed a human body with a robe on, its long bony hands ended in four fingers, each one had nails as long as a baseball bat sharpened to the tip. The robe was not made of fabric but some type of flesh. It smelled of rock, wood, and a faint smell of burning metal.

"Ask me. I have eternity, but your mortal clocks tick faster."

Chapter 58

DET. MARANO COULD NOT speak for several seconds. She kept her gun pointed at it.

"Who the fuck are you?"

"Elim, the gatekeeper between worlds. You already know that, wasting time just like pointing that ridiculous device at me for comfort. There is none where you are now."

Kelso chimed in.

"So we got a demon loose, Mariyon, it's killing people. Why is it here?"

"Summoned, like you did me. Millenia ago, people had problems, and sometimes you regret what you wish for. His existence in hell is legendary, he is a conqueror of worlds."

"Great, how do we kill him?" Det. Marano blurted out.

"Wrong question. You can't kill what isn't alive. Demons aren't like you little fleshy primates running around so fragile for the eating. Mariyon isn't the worst thing to face."

Det. Marano sucked her teeth in, those last words sent shivers through her body.

"Stop playing games, how do we stop it or send it back to hell?" Kelso asked.

"Better question. It was already contained, many centuries ago they built a sacred box to entrap it for all of time, dumped at the bottom of your waters. Your metal machines ripped it apart while you were trying to build your floating roads over water for those silly rectangles with wheels."

"Cars. He can't even say fucking cars. This guy is all riddles and shit. Patience is thinning with this douchebag," Det. Marano chimed. The creature did not respond or look at her.

"So we can just build a new box, and put it in there, and boom Mayrion done?" Kelso asked ignoring Det. Marano's insulting banter at Elim.

"No way to make new box, shamans long dead. There is just one last way to expel him from your dimension back home. You have to behead him with the Talon of Tears, set it on fire, and repeat a special chant. Then no more Mariyon, on earth."

"Fuck me, let me guess, the Talon of Tears is some toenail of a mythical bird that's in like Egypt?" Det. Marano asked.

"No, it resides here. Over there the walls don't connect, a series of tunnels exist. It rests down at the end of the tunnels."

"What is the Talon of Tears?" Kelso asked.

"Ceremonial device, sharp, helped with human sacrifices in ancient times. In more recent times it gave false hope."

"Meaning?"

"The children of this site were marched down here and given a choice. Either they walk into the oven to die, or they could have a few minutes to go hide in the tunnels. What happened next would be a hunt, with the Talon of Tears, and eventually they'd get found. No one escaped, but mortals always cling for a few more minutes before death, right?" Elim replied. His empty glare was devoid of empathy, compassion, or any form of context for the darkness he just spoke about.

Det. Marano gasped unleashing a litany of profanities. Kelso imagined the terror of the children in those final moments. She got herself back together and took a deep breath.

"Ok, what aren't you telling us?" Kelso asked. The creature tilted its head a little in almost a nod.

"Wise question. Always a price for things, especially of this nature. If you obtain the Talon then we will chat again about the price. Until then, see you in time."

The creature evaporated into the darkness around them.

"What the hell man?" Det. Marano said.

"Let's proceed very slowly and with extreme caution. There may be some traps or something that kills people when they try to get it."

"Ah like in those adventure movies where you grab the golden skull and like a massive rock or batch of poison-tipped arrows blast you?" Det. Marano huffed.

"Exactly. We aren't separating and we aren't moving but at a caterpillar pace."

"Got it. Let's do this!" Det. Marano replied.

As directed, they made their way to the corner of the room and stepped through the four-foot gap. They stared at a very dark hallway lit only by mining lights that the archaeology team set up during their dig. Shovels and other digging equipment lay in the hallway. Huge stone pillars paced the two hundred foot hallway. The pauses in the wall numbered roughly a dozen. The stone roof was black as if it was burned. It was freezing cold.

"Where the hell were the kids supposed to hide?" Det. Marano asked.

They stepped into the first hallway and both turned to the right. It ended about ten feet away into a giant dirt pile against some brick walling. They turned back across the way to see the left passage hallway which led to a similar ten-foot end, but with a small hole inside the brick, about the size of a box or small child.

Kelso let out a deep sigh.

"Guess that's my answer, you run and hide in the dirt or curl up in brick waiting to die. My god man, we are the worst species ever. I'm hugging Chumbo when I get back. I'll take a missing dog over this any day," Det. Marano kept talking to herself as they kept walking.

They made their way across the next four hallways each one mirroring the first set. On the fifth hallway, Kelso noticed there was a small hole in the brick, about the size for a small animal to fit into, but not Kelso or Det. Marano.

A muffled set of voices began to resonate. It was the sound of giggles muffled behind mountains of rock. Det. Marano and Kelso looked at each other, both turning to see nothing behind them nor ahead.

"Fuck. Time to move faster than lightning, this feels wrong," Kelso said.

Quickly they began to move faster as they cleared the hallways leading to the final twelfth and final one. The giggles were getting louder amid the darkness, their sound distorted like when a record is played too slow or backwards. It was children's laughter but hidden behind the walls. They both pressed their backs against the end of the stone hallway.

"The giggles are a nice touch, as if this place wasn't depressing enough. Did we miss something? I saw just dirt, stone, and brick. I didn't see any ceremonial knife, you?" Kelso asked.

"Nope, and this tunnel ends here. Maybe passageway five, that small rabbit hole. Whoa, wait, take a look at that, it looks like a hole in the wall. See over there, the brick is broken and it's just big enough for a child to crawl under. My bet is on that."

"So got two candidates, fifth passageway and this twelfth one. Let's clear this hole and return to passage five, one of them has to have-"

"Hands up, right fucking now!"

Kelso and Det. Marano turned pointing their guns at the light. Someone had light on them so they couldn't make out anything.

"Last time, hands up!"

Kelso counted now four lights on them, adjoined by a black military dressed security team. She lowered her gun and put her free hand up. Det. Marano followed suit.

"Least it's not that timekeeper creep."

"I wouldn't be so overjoyed, I feel this isn't Sedro PD checking on a complaint."

One soldier held up a phone towards them, as a voice cackled out.

"Heyyyy Kelso, you remember me? What you up to here, buddy? Playing ghost hunters?"

Kelso cussed under her breath.

"Who is that?" Det. Marano asked, lights still blinding her.

"Chad. Zacks. And I doubt he's here to help us."

Chapter 59

Minutes later the soldiers had them sit down in the eighth tunnel, kneeling as one soldier kept the phone on them.

"How do they even have signal down here? I'm jealous," Det. Marano asked.

"Chad owns so many tech companies he probably has satellites," Kelso replied.

"And spaceships, heading to the moon with a crew in six months. Hey, who are you? We haven't met!" Zacks broke into the conversation.

"Detective Marano, Crest Hill PD. Think you can cut us loose? We got shit to do, I don't know why Kelso dumped you in high school, but don't think this is the time for that shit," Det. Marano said.

Chad laughed on the phone. Two soldiers walked back to the end of the hallway to the twelfth passageway and looked around. Seeing nothing they leaned against the end of the hallway pointing their rifles at the ground. One soldier remained with his rifle pointed at the women kneeling in the dirt while the other held the phone steady for Chad to see and speak. All had ski masks over their faces.

"Hey Detective, love that sense of humor."

"Fuck," Kelso muttered. Her eyes darted around them. She homed in on a brick two feet away from them.

"Kelso here killed my newest product up in Mt. St. Helens. I invited her to meet my pets and she killed some of those, and had her coworker, Gaucho, real asshole type go all suicide bomber on me. Burned part of my face, lost most of my right arm, and killed some staff. Yet I am more alive than ever. Revenge just really gets my adrenaline going. Right, Kelso?"

Zacks began to explain that he had been tracking them for several days. He was going to wait until after the disciplinary hearing where Kelso is permanently stripped of her duties and then federally incarcerated, but he had grown impatient.

"Sorry, you don't get to where I'm at by being patient, it's all about unbridled aggression and speed. Plus, I gotta finish that bridge so that I can plug my guy in as the next mayor. He promised city council it would revitalize downtown and all that. I mean, hey, the homeless numbers are down, good stuff, right?"

"You really think you'll get away with killing us?" Det. Marano asked.

Kelso said nothing but continued to look at other nearby broken bits of stone and brick, letting Det. Marano argue with Zacks.

"It is pretty easy Detective, we'll just plant stuff on you, slick cover story. Disgraced rogue cop and Kelso is already nuclear, no pun intended, no one will bat an eye. Just like you covered up the Walla Walla deaths, right Kelso?"

Kelso began to lean near the soldier with the rifle pointed at her. She was eyeing the angles if she hit him, could the two way down on twelfth hallway get her or would their shots miss?

Det. Marano had begun to run out of negotiation tactics. As Zacks paused she heard the giggles again, louder. The soldier holding the rifle at them also turned his head a little.

"Wait wait, before you do it. Kelso, I am getting an award for donating millions to a tribal program to help the youth. And I wanted you to know, I completely appreciate your peoples sacrifices, history, and am so sorry for what my ancestors did to your ancestors. Real tragedy, people really need to pay homage to your people, this is all their land previously, right? Of course your people had their issues, private property, bad immune systems, and alcoholism. Hey we're all human right? Oh well, just wanted you to know I'll be thinking of you when I accept this award. Especially since tonight, as I'm being praised and your lifeless corpse will rot here, I'm going to do you a solid and have another team inject poison into your grandfather's IV bag. Reduce that six months to six hours or minutes. Kelso legacy wrapped up in one swoop."

"Kill me, but don't touch my grandfather please, he has nothing to do with any of this. Just take me."

"Yep! There it is. That's the look I wanted. Jesus Christ, revenge is better than heroin. Seriously. Go ahead and execute them now, I want to see if they'll scream or cry. It's like the best!" Zacks barked. His eyes glowed with joy.

As Zacks had given his final sermon to them, Kelso had caught the attention of Det. Marano. With a mini-nod, Det. Marano saw the brick behind Kelso. Marano acted like something was in her eyes using it as a wink to agree to Kelso's plan.

"Well shit, me first then buddy. Let's get this execution party going!" Det. Marano snapped.

Chad Zacks looked surprised but nodded at the soldier. He then walked over to Det. Marano while the other soldier kept the phone pointed at them in hallway eight.

As the soldier with the rifle walked up to Det. Marano the giggles became as louder, blaring through every fragment of air inside the tunnel.

"Ready or not here I come!"

A giant yellow ball, the size of a beach ball, rolled out of the twelfth hole, stopping in front of the two soldiers who pointed their rifles at it.

"What is happening? What is that?" Zacks was yelling as the two soldiers by Det. Marano and Kelso moved away from them looking down the hallway at their buddies and growing yellow ball.

It had grown to the size of a riding lawnmower. It was bright yellow like a plastic toy. Small chubby arm-like appendages were growing out of the sides with two stubby feet as well. White eyes had emerged, small pudgy nose, and a massive smiling mouth.

No one could speak. Not even Chad Zacks staring at the smiling yellow ball. It looked like a plastic smiley emoji toy with arms and legs. It began to giggle and then its smile changed. Teeth the size of swords revealed themselves as it leaned over.

"I found you!"

Before the monster could finish its words it had taken a mortal bite out of the first soldier and crunched his head in the second bite. The second soldier began to unload his rifle as did the two guards by Det. Marano and Kelso as the strange monster kept chewing his way through the first soldier.

Kelso and Det. Marano took off running from the eighth hallway, turning only to see the other soldier screaming as the monster devoured him with two dispassionate bites. The bullets weren't slowing it as the remaining guards reloaded their magazines yelling.

Kelso put up her hand and Det. Marano shot her a look.

"Wait wait, I have to check the fifth hallway. We have to get that Talon of Tears. I'm not coming back here for it. Make it out and wait for me. Just go!"

Det. Marano tried to argue but Kelso took off and dove into the dirt pile near the fifth tunnel's hole jamming her arm into the open space. Det. Marano stopped in her tracks and stood at the hallway showered in fear as she saw the yellow monster obliterate the third soldier. The fourth was pulling the upper torso out of the mouth which seemed to only make the monster madder. It was now only twenty feet away from the fifth hallway. The entire time the monster kept repeating his phrase amid gurgling bites and ingesting humans.

"Got it!" Kelso yelled. She leapt to her feet and began to sprint to the hallway as Det. Marano pointed. Kelso turned and saw that the final soldier's feet were being chewed mere feet away from their location. The monster was by them. It didn't say anything as the fourth human descended into its endless digestive tract. Kelso and Det. Marano now stood less than a foot from it. It didn't say anything but kept smiling with chunks of bone, blood, and drool. It was breathing heavily.

Kelso yelled, "I got you!" and stabbed the ceremonial dagger into the yellow monster.

EEEEK.

The peek a boo monster deflated a little and began to release a wolf like howl of pain.

"Now! Run!" Kelso shrieked.

They sprinted to the end of the tunnel and made it back into the large basement room. Both stumbled a little as adrenaline and terror mixed in their systems. They looked back as they ran for the stairs. A yellow monster hand stuck out from the tunnel entrance, it waved at them.

They barreled up to the top of the stairs, across the schoolhouse floor, and ended up outside in the dark rain. Chad's security team truck was parked next to their SUV. Det. Marano kept looking around for the yellow guy, just in case.

Well done. Bring it back after you're done. With Mayrion's jaw. I'd like it for a necklace.

The gatekeeper was at the doorway to the schoolhouse.

If you fail, so does your world. Mayrion is only the start, Leviathan is the end. Of all.

It nodded its white tomb of a face, turning away and disappearing into the dark shadows of the building.

Neither woman could say anything as they sped down the dirt road, landing onto the paved highway, heading south to Silas' hospital, as the rain berated their windshield. Det. Marano's breathing didn't calm down until they were in north Seattle. Kelso kept the Talon of Tears on the backseat wrapped in a spare roadside emergency blanket.

Chapter 60

It took an enormous amount of persuasion to get Lt. Loy on board with Kelso and Det. Marano's plan. Their plan was to track down Mayrion, use Neil, the cult leader, as familiar bait, and upon distraction, use the Talon of Tears to end this terror campaign. He agreed only with the condition that a tactical team accompany them. Kelso knew arguing would serve no purpose. She also felt that guns had not done much to the demon, but could provide fruitful distraction. She left out the part about the Gatekeeper and hide-and-seek yellow monster as Lt. Loy's suspicious looks about the Talon of Tears were enough to signal he wasn't the most receptive audience.

"You ok with this Neil kid being bait?" Kelso asked Lt. Loy.

"He didn't commit them so that is why I want the real guy behind this operation. Whoever that is."

"It's not a dude, it's a goddamn demon," Det. Marano quipped. Lt. Loy pursed his lips and winked.

"Accountability. Never in my life have I heard about a more heartless crew, so whatever it is, will answer to Seattle and America for this action. Period."

"Given what you shared with us, we think Neil and his cult crew picked up homeless and dumped them into that Attis College lair like it was a hell buffet. He watched the demon eat almost a thousand people. Without flinching it seems, then cosplayed like he was the demon king," Kelso replied.

Det. Marano shook her head and cussed under her breath.

"Oh, and he bragged to our unit that he started out torturing small animals to get a feel for his future as a serial killer. He read about that in books and watched clips."

"Oh fuck him then, he can be bait all day," Agent Kelso said.

The prisoner was loaded into the back of their SUV as Det. Marano, Kelso, and Lt. Loy sat in the front seats. Escort guards tapped the van to signal go time. Lt. Loy nodded at another guard and they radioed in the convoy, in minutes as they drove out of downtown Seattle, they were joined by eight black vans.

"So how did you get this guy on loan to us? This guy is national and world news," Agent Kelso asked Lt. Loy.

"A mix of favors, had to promise ASUA and fed teams that they get to bring the ringleader in, so you want a case that you can become a governor or U.S. Senator on, stopping the mass murderer of Seattle? Let me borrow Neil with babysitters and I'll bring you the governor's mansion or a Presidential Cabinet seat. Feds ate that up. The kid started strong but like all, he turned to shit fast," Lt. Loy said.

"What do you mean? I didn't turn to shit! Someone as important as me, in the history of our species, should be given tribute," Neil piped in from the back.

"Shit head, you are an accomplice to mass murder, not a founding father," Lt. Loy replied. He waved his hand at the kid to knock it off.

"Ok, so why did you agree to all this? Why not just let feds run the op?" Kelso asked.

"Personal reasons, if you must know. Brass is giving me twenty-four hours. Seattle PD knows how many eyes are on this."

"This sounds familiar, enjoy that disciplinary meeting," Kelso let out a sigh.

"That's right, Kelso, you know I'm ignoring that I'm bringing along someone who is technically suspended from duty. And if anyone asks, I didn't invite you here, not owning that heat. How is all that going?" Lt. Loy asked.

"Well, Mr. Zacks, that guy the feds are protecting, just tried to off me and Det. Marano last night, real fun affair. Doubt today will help my suspension nor my upcoming federal indictment. So yeah, I feel pregnant with doom."

"Don't look pregnant to me," Lt. Loy quipped.

They both laughed.

"Lt., what's the personal reason, if I can ask?" Det. Marano asked.

"My brother. He served active combat and upon return just couldn't get it together. His wife cheating on him, using kids as pawns in the divorce, and his PTSD didn't help, but no matter what I did, he preferred the streets to my apartment. Since this kicked off, I've been trying to make sure he was ok, maybe downstate in Olympia or Portland even. First time I was hoping he was getting high elsewhere. And then-"

For the first time since meeting him the persona of Lt. Loy breached, and emotions draped in his pause, unable to complete his sentence. Anguish filled in the blank from his face.

"Then you realized he was food for my demon god. Haha, fucking druggie loser," Neil stated, laughing.

Lt. Loy gripped the steering wheel and clenched his jaw so much that the bones pushed out from under his cheek, as he slowly inhaled through his nose. Long deep breaths and glares into the rearview mirror at the prisoner taunting him.

Kelso nodded in silent understanding. Lt. Loy continued.

"So we found...what was left of him...and this poser back there lacked the ability to do the murders, I will stop at nothing to find the man...thing, that did this. And bringing him to justice. For my brother and everyone's brothers, kids, parents, and such. I don't care if I lose my badge, Seattle deserves some peace. And my mom for what I had to tell her that day when we found him."

"So touching and patriotic, bumper sticker shit," Neil said as he tried to fake clap.

"We're almost there, it's right up here."

"How did you know this is the place?"

Houses sped by as the prisoner began to hum.

"Intel, we have a packet of missing persons nearby and there's a giant concrete structure. It's southeast Seattle, still on Lake Washington, and is a companion building to what we found at Attis College. Mercer Island a hop to the right, interstate highway bridge north, and pretty solid 277 acres on a peninsula. This outfit seems to like these semi-subterranean places, room for efficient mass murder."

His last words made the van go silent. They rounded a corner and pulled into the Seward Park area.

"But we could be wrong, so we'll hop out, check and if it's a no go we'll regroup and hit another packet on Mercer Island. We'll find this bastard. And then you can cut him with your magical knife or whatever, feds get to cuff him and bring him back."

"Yeah...about that, you know this is a demon, right? This isn't a bank robber," Kelso warned.

"Sure, demon, ghoul, ghost, whatever. It goes down," Lt. Loy kept his gaze on the lot.

"Master will like you, you'll taste good," Neil said.

Det. Marano rolled her eyes at the cult leader. He was trying too hard and she didn't enjoy this reunion. They pulled in past the entrance to the park and began the loop around the parking lot.

"Lots of trails, right? If there is no one here, we need to cover those trails?" Det. Marano finally spoke.

"Yeah, there's apparently a maintenance concrete bunker at the top of the peninsula where the trails end. People like to go out there and take pics of the landscape, can see Cascade Mountains, and such. The teams will sweep south and we'll take two teams to go north."

They exited the vehicles and Lt. Loy repeated his commands to the federal team who began to search nearby cars, trucks, and visitor's center for evidence of a disturbance. As Kelso clutched her backpack with the Talon of Tears inside, Lt. Loy leaned over to whisper in her ear.

"You know, you can't be armed right? That's the condition of your pending investigation. I'd become part of your investigation if I armed you in front of federal officers while you are facing like a buttload of federal felonies."

Kelso nodded. Det. Marano was checking her gun. Lt. Loy looked into Kelso's eyes and held his stare. He reached into a federal van and got a tactical shotgun.

"It's a shame how reckless those federal agents are with their weapons. That's dangerous, kids play around here. I hope someone comes along and secures that shotgun until it can be returned to a federal law enforcement agency."

Lt. Loy then laid the tactical shotgun down by the tires of their van, a mere three feet from Kelso. He began to walk north to corral the seven federal agents and Det. Marano. Kelso let out a muffled snicker and began to check the shotgun.

A truck parked behind them and the driver stumbled out. Kelso had her back turned as she started to walk and join the group moving north to help clear the park.

"Got room for one more?" a familiar voice asked behind her.

Kelso spun and her blood pressure jacked up. It was Silas!

"Grandpa, what are you doing here?"

"More than one way to beat cancer. Got bored."

"Not funny, you are seriously weak, and the doctors-"

"I didn't serve, raise you, just to sit and wait to die in that hospital bed. I want to help."

"These are FBI and task force agents, I think they got this," Det. Marano said.

"Yes, the federal government never messes up a combat op right?" Silas replied.

"Fair point, but there's still nothing for you to do here. Wait, how the hell did you find me?"

"Cell phone tracker app. I had it put on your personal cell after the radioactive monster thingy. If you needed me, I could find you."

"Oh my, after this we need to talk about boundaries and I'm turning that thing off."

"Check this out first. After I figured you'd need me, I visited my prepper buddy, bunker life has its perks."

Silas popped the trunk as Kelso held up her hand to Det. Marano. Kelso turned back and was staring at least fifty to five hundred years on gun charges.

"Yeah I know, don't worry it's all registered," Silas said.

"To you?" Kelso asked.

"No, registered in the state of patriotic defense of democracy."

"You aren't bringing that shit out, the feds will be creeped out."

Silas was rubbing a flame thrower, some rockets, a grenade launcher, and an AK-47.

"Fine I'll bring this, it's a rifle, but I'm not leaving this utility belt and vest."

"Ok, bring your 1980s AK-47 they'll love that, and that vest. For god sakes don't use those other things on your vest. Half of those incendiary devices are probably rotting. Please be careful."

"What, you don't like grenades?" Silas replied.

"For what?" Det. Marano asked.

"We're fighting a force of evil. Anything to get it is worth it."

"G-pa, just walk behind us, like way way behind, conceal that rifle as much as you can for god sakes," Agent Kelso said.

Silas dismissed her concerns and suited up. Kelso walked ahead and tried her best to spin that Silas was a Department of Defense consultant and is coming just for identification purposes. Lt. Loy figured it was bullshit but he was focused on the operation. He warned Kelso.

"Tell Rambo to not point that fucking dinosaur of a rifle at any of my men or he'll end up cuffed with that creep in the van. Or his dick shot off. Dept. of Defense my ass, my god Kelso this is why you are on suspension, shit like this. You got Father Time strapped with guns two centuries old on a mass murder apprehension op, get your shit together. Anything, I mean anything happens, I will burn you if needed," Lt. Loy replied.

Kelso nodded and waved Silas to join them, but at the back.

"Thanks kid, owe you one."

"Remember that when I need money on my books in prison."

"I'll be long dead by then, but I'll come haunt you."

"Please stop talking like that, and keep your eyes open, this thing moves fast, kills like a lion, and I have to behead it with this knife in my backpack. If that even is true, if not, I get to become a lunch for this thing," Kelso responded.

"Too skinny. I'd say you are a mid-day snack at best. Tell me you have a better plan than to shoot it like it is some circus tiger?" Silas baited.

"Not the time to discuss. I got something for it. For real, eyes sharp. We're about to leave the parking lot and hit the forest and then a concrete maintenance bunker. No idea where or what we are walking into, anything can happen."

Chapter 61

TWENTY TENSE MINUTES WENT by as the peninsula of the park narrowed. They wound their way among the trees and trails heading north, so far nothing. Joggers, cyclists, and concerned citizens were shoved away while they filmed on their phones. The south team had swept the bottom of the park and found nothing. The north team of Marano, Loy, Kelso, Silas and seven agents were approaching the northeast corner of the peninsula which included the bathrooms, viewpoint, and concrete maintenance bunker.

"Hold up, got something. Not live, but think it's blood. Checking."

Everyone moved on the position. It was a boat moored to a wooden tier a few feet away from the small restroom building.

"Confirm, blood and prints. Headed west from the trash barge towards the restrooms."

Kelso and the team moved towards the waterfront where the agent stood. It was a medium trash barge, still with rotting trash all over it. Indentations surfaced across parts of it. Streaks of blood dotted the edges of the barge.

"How the hell did no one see this?" a federal agent asked.

"Are you telling me your demon dude sails now? Yeah not human my ass," Lt. Loy said.

Lt. Loy radioed for the south team to bring the prisoner.

"Game time, we're gonna have that prick go first into anything suspect. I'll have agents block park access with their vehicles and close the park."

Just then someone radioed Lt. Loy that the press was already at the park entrance.

"Keep them out, this is an active national and regional security threat operation. No different than terrorism. They can film all day long later on. Goddamn joggers leaked us to the press. This means our timetable just got narrower before our cover is blown and Seattle news helicopters, drones, and boat paparazzi pop up. Get that prisoner up here now!"

A few minutes later two agents dragged the cult leader to Lt. Loy.

"Time to chat with your boss, daddy. Provide the introduction and then get out of the way. Do that and you'll avoid the death penalty. Head around that bathroom corner and enter that bunker."

The nearby bathroom was out of service and no prints or blood ran into it. Meanwhile a clear line of prints, human, had led to a large concrete bunker hidden behind the bathroom. It was a concrete blob about the size of a garage formed with a horizontal slot in the front. A gray door and a caved in hole stood adjacent to the left of the concrete bunker slot.

"Whoa, what is this?" Agent Kelso asked.

"World War II bunker. We were close to the pacific theater so government built a few of these," Silas replied from behind them.

"So you could watch someone drop a bomb or shoot out the concrete window slot?" Kelso asked.

"Clear that eyeline, I don't want anyone shot sniper-style. Stay out of the line of fire, low, and proceed through that door," Lt. Loy said.

"There are tales that the Nazis recruited serial killers and used them to dispense of the Jewish names they couldn't find with normal soldiers," Neil offered.

"Thanks for that, get walking," Lt. Loy ordered.

Neil led the way towards the gray door. Agents used scope cameras to peek inside the bunker from the concrete window slot and stated it was clear of any targets. They reported back that it was a two layered bunker, the top layer seemed covered in blood and trash, but no movement.

As the cult leader opened the door, an earthy woman with flowing brown hair yelled at him.

"Who goes here? Kneel or serve our master, now!" the woman screamed.

Three agents pushed Neil aside and took her down by the neck. She began to hiss and scream. She had the same mark as the cult leader on her forehead.

"It's time, nine, it's time! Let it be borne, the end of worlds!" the woman yelled.

"Ma'am, federal agents. Is there someone else in the bunker? Ma'am!"

It was no use, she squealed and just kept repeating that same line. The cult leader ignored commands to wait and ran into the bunker. Everyone but the three agents on the snarling woman ran inside. Flashlights were turned on as the sun was beginning its afternoon descent. Det. Marano recognized the odor immediately and tugged at Kelso's arm. Kelso nodded. Silas was in the back examining the walls. It was a mixture of blood and claw marks. A crude descending concrete pathway led down to a lower level. Strange and ritualistic marks were all over the upper-level floor. It looked like they were walking over a giant séance book. A large symbol Kelso recognized stood in the center with a small hole.

"Weapons live, that smell is just like Attis College. We could have victims, look out for Neil, he's the bait," Lt. Loy told the group.

As the team of now eight entered the lower level of this bunker, the smell was abhorrent. It smelled of ash, death, and a putrid sulfur smell. Their eyes adjusted to the near total darkness of the bunker basement level. It seemed to open at the back, literally opening up to the water as another entrance under the trails above. Water billowed against a dug out area.

"Master, I return to you, to serve, look at the tasty treats!" Neil yelled.

All lights moved to the sound of Neil's voice. He was kneeling down on the left side of the three-car garage room talking to a giant pile of human flesh bags. There had to be at least fifty pummeled against the wall. Kelso, Det. Marano, and Silas played the back per Kelso grabbing them. Kelso had seen this scenario play out at the Trinity nuclear plant, room to escape was a mortal requirement.

A roar emerged from the water and Mayrion appeared, storming out of the water horns first and gored one agent before he could pull his trigger. The rest began to fire their guns as it quickly tackled and tore apart two other agents. Unlike the last time Kelso encountered it, the bullets were actually lodging into its skin, causing a liquid to ooze out of the bullet holes, but it seemed unfazed in its counter attacks. Three agents had emptied their magazines and were reloading as it began to swipe at them. Agent Kelso pulled out the Talon and as she readied herself to leap at it, while its back was turned to her, it turned towards her and leaned its head down and within a mortal second pinned her into the concrete wall, its horn lacerating her arm that was clutching the Talon of Tears. It dropped, clanking to the floor as she yelped feeling the searing heat of its horn shredding her tendons and tissue like toilet paper. It looked up at her, gold eyes of hunger and mission-oriented indifference to her life. She prepared herself to die.

Silas unleashed his AK-47 as Det. Marano shot carefully at its torso and legs. Its gaze did not move from Kelso as it began to lean up to bite her head off.

"For my brother you ugly motherfucker!" Lt. Loy yelled as he unloaded his rifle into the demon's back. It turned away from Kelso allowing her to drop to the ground next to the Talon of Tears. She caught her breath and reached for it as the demon turned towards Lt. Loy. The cult leader was attacking him trying to choke him with the handcuffs as the other agents called for backup, Mayrion stomped towards the struggle in the corner.

"Master look, take him, feast!" Neil cheered.

Mayrion swung its arm down onto Lt. Loy. A sickening crunch echoed the loud bunker amid the gunfire and screams. Lt. Loy went silent as Mayrion proceeded to slam its clawed fist down until his legs were detached from his torso and he went limp, closing his eyes. The three remaining federal agents provided cover fire as everyone began to retreat, Silas, Marano, and Kelso dragged upstairs.

Mayrion did not give chase. Kelso was losing blood.

"Get us to that tree line. Just need to get my breath."

Just as Silas and Det. Marano were dragging Kelso to the nearby trees outside the bunker, the horns of Mayrion appeared as he emerged from the lower level of the bunker.

"Three. Feed me three."

"Oh yes master, here you go!" the wild lady screeched as she tried to get up.

"Don't shoot Silas, it is a waste of bullets. Just draws attention, hang back for a second," Det. Marano said ushering them away from the immediate attack zone.

One federal agent took off running into the forest to warn back-up. Police and media helicopters loomed. A police boat was sailing towards them siren bellowing into the darkening late afternoon. Various civilians in boats nearby just stared taking phone videos while others sailed away screaming.

Mayrion looked up at the police helicopters and then seized upon the three agents unloading their weapons into him. The heavy rifles only seemed to rile up Mayrion more as he tore into each of them with his horns and claws, then Det. Marano gasped as she saw his stomach exoskeleton open up and the red glowing hole with teeth emerged, sucking out the insides of the three agents as Silas covered his mouth.

Mayrion, upon eating the final federal agent a mere ten feet away from them, stared at Silas, Det. Marano, and Kelso.

"Done. Now it begins."

"What the fuck does that mean?" Det. Marano asked.

Kelso was clutching the Talon of Tears with her remaining good arm. Silas made an impromptu bandage to stop the bleeding. Mayrion slammed a hole in the bunker, turning away from the trio. They watched, along with the helicopters and boats, as the demon stalked into the upper bunker level stopping in the center of the room.

Its torso opened up and the gnawing mouth ejected out of his body and connected with the sunken hole in the altar ground.

"Leviathan, feaster of worlds, become now!"

Elim warned about us about some Leviathan thing, something about end of times. This isn't good.

"Oh no, I think we really fucked up. I didn't even get to stab him with the Talon. I can't feel my arm." Kelso stated. She was barely done with her last word as the ground shook and the rumbling knocked them all to the ground with Kelso. Even the incoming federal agents on foot and ATV were tossed to the ground.

"What the fuck is a Leviathan?" Det. Marano asked.

As soon as the words left Det. Marano's lips, Lake Washington began to swirl and spin, boats began to tilt and three capsized. Water drew back and then sucked downward like a giant drain after a bathtub plug is pulled. The water of the lake flowed down with such speed waves were crashing. And then it appeared. At first it looked like a mountain was rising out of the water, a small mountain the size of a six-story building, but then it blinked. The water mountain opened and revealed a massive mouth the size of twenty city blocks, and swallowing up ten boats including the police cruiser. The Leviathan had arrived.

Kelso stared with an empty gaze of horror. No one was staring at Mayrion anymore as the Leviathan turned its watery mouth towards the coastline of southeast Seattle, opening, and closing its galactic sized jaws onto Lake Washington Blvd., and chewing up cars, the street, and nine houses like food. It took only seconds, and the entire chunk of the coastline was gone. Screams, bullets, and running all found defeat as it took another bite consuming entire chunks of the continental earth, piping, and houses without hesitation.

For the first time since encountering it, Kelso and Det. Marano heard Mayrion laughing as it stared at its creation.

Chapter 62

"IS THIS REALLY HAPPENING?" Det. Marano asked. Silas was still staring in pure horror as Kelso and Marano debated plans.

"We gotta get back in there, each minute he isn't stopped...I mean look at it, this thing will eat Seattle in probably thirty minutes, rest of America in days, world in a month," Kelso stated.

"Military will bomb it, I bet they are scrambling fighter jets now," Det. Marano replied with a hopeful tone.

"And what will that do? This is from the end of times, do you think shooting missiles will really do it?"

"I bet atomic bombs stop it," Det. Marano said while nodding.

"Bet it swallows it, and we all die, and it keeps chewing through our civilization like candy."

Kelso stumbled to her feet. She waved at the federal agents but they no longer focused on the bunker or demon, they were getting commands to fire openly at the Leviathan. They waved Kelso away and told her to stay out of their way as they ran to the coastline that faced the Leviathan and began to pound it with bullets.

The Leviathan responded by taking a double bite eating twenty city blocks choking down entire homes, trees, sidewalks, and screaming people into the watery abyss of its underwater system. It resembled a galactic whale, black eyes the size of a school bus, two fins to swim on each side, and a body the size of the Golden Gate Bridge. The mouth opened with such width it almost seemed like a mouth with a body attached.

"Look at Mayrion, he's connected to that spot. Let's light him and up see if we can disrupt him, at least slow him down. Alex, let's go doomsday on it. Feds left their ATVs there running. Field trip to come back and give this thing a taste. Double time, each second Mayrion isn't dead more people die," Silas said while he leaned against a tree.

They sprinted over to the two ATVs, Silas alone on one and Det. Marano holding onto Kelso as they barreled across the forest trails. Ten minutes later Kelso and Silas were arriving back at the bunker. Silas hopped off and strapped the butane tanks to his back and pulled out the wand. Det. Marano pulled up a few seconds later in Silas car, branches, tree chunks, and leaves covering it.

"What the hell, Marano?" Kelso asked annoyed.

"Yeah like I could carry a fucking Browning M2 kit on an ATV. No one was on the trail. Silas if we don't die, I'll pay for the repairs from driving this baby up here."

Det. Marano and Kelso began to set up the M2 for Det. Marano.

"Now remember, don't shoot me. Don't set me on fire. I'm going to hang tight near the bunker but out of your range, the moment I see him falter I'm going in to try cut his head off. While I do that, switch to regular handguns and aim low, just keep him distracted. Get closer in case I need help cutting, I have no idea how this will be."

"Kelso, you sure? We could just retreat and let the military drop a bomb. They might anyways and kill us all. Never know, it could kill him," Det. Marano offered one last time.

"Maybe, or maybe not. Elim hinted he'll just regenerate, and Leviathan might still go onward, Tia, your family, so many innocent people. I'm not having her last moments on this planet be from being eaten by a Leviathan. And by the time that happens there might not be a Seattle or Washington left. We have the Talon of Tears, that wasn't a mistake. If we fail then sure, let's enjoy the seconds before we are bombed to death. But right now, this time, it is our chance to stop this fucker."

Silas had a tired gaze across his face.

"Grandpa, you ok? I can do this with Det. Marano. Please take cover over there. You don't have to do this. We got this."

"I'm ok. Cancer is a real bitch, but I'm set. Ready to light this guy up like a firecracker. Let me go first, I don't want to torch you two ladies."

Kelso nodded at Det. Marano as they watched the Leviathan swim towards the interstate 90 freeway bridge. Helicopters swirled following. Air Force planes swooped in firing missiles which only made the Leviathan pause, look up, and take a massive bite out of the bridge, sending cars into its mouth along with chunks of bridge. The fighter jets banked around for another attack. Meanwhile the Leviathan continued turning Seattle into his terrifying buffet, the entire earth in due time.

Chapter 63

"Go time!" Kelso yelled running with a shotgun and the Talon of Tears. She got in position as Det. Marano took a very deep breath aiming the M2 gun at the bunker window slot, aimed for the demon's torso mouth connected to the hole in the ground. Silas lit the wand and walked right up to the bunker window slot, yelling.

"A little taste of home! Take that!" Silas yelled as he unleashed the flamethrower on Mayrion. It tilted a little but kept its stance against the billowing flames across its face.

"Marano!" Kelso yelled.

The M2 erupted in ground shaking force as 50 caliber Browning Machine Gun cartridges blew chunks out of the demon's torso mouth. Silas continued to focus the flamethrower on the head, causing Mayrion to stumble. The M2's power eroded the torso mouth and Mayrion lost its balance. Under the unyielding power of Marano's WWII battle weapon, it fell down, disconnecting its mouth from the altar hole.

Kelso saw the Leviathan begin to dip downwards, half of it disappearing into the water.

"Look! If he is disconnected from the altar the Leviathan goes away, it's working!" Marano yelled at Kelso.

Kelso refocused and began to run towards the bunker, summoning fictional courage. She hopped through the cement window and ran towards the injured Mayrion. Det. Marano kept firing, knocking down Mayrion and plunging holes into its head. Kelso held up her fist and Det. Marano stopped firing. Silas threw off his flamethrower pack and readied his AK-47 as he walked towards the bunker. He was limping a bit.

Kelso pulled out the Talon of Tears and slammed it deep into the demon's head. As she began to pull the blade down into its neck, she watched in terror as the head was regenerating fast. She never saw the regenerated claw. It slammed her against the concrete wall behind them. Half of her face was cut open and blood covered her eyesight.

Det. Marano tried to fire up the M2 but it was not feeding right, and she couldn't reload more cartridges. Giving up, she ran into the bunker firing her weapon at the regenerated torso of the demon. With the power of pure hatred Mayrion stabbed Det. Marano in her stomach and tossed her like a bull throwing a kitten into traffic. As her body toppled into the back pathway down to the lower layer, she let out a long groan, dropping her weapon as she began to bleed out.

Kelso tried to sit up against the wall. Wiping the blood out of her eyes she saw Mayrion reconnect his torso mouth into the hole and heard the ancient growl of the Leviathan attacking Seattle amid screams, horns, sirens, and hovering useless fighter jets.

As she tried to get up to try one last feeble attempt to cut its head off, she saw Silas in the doorway. He was coughing badly, yet Mayrion hadn't even touched him. They caught eyes as Mayrion stared at the Leviathan in the distance leaving siege to the earth.

Kelso shook her head 'no' but Silas had that glare, the same one Gaucho gave her before he sailed away. Sweat mixed with blood on Kelso's face. Silas pointed to the grenades on his vest, he made a cutting motion at his neck. Kelso sighed knowing what had to happen. Nearby she heard Det. Marano sigh in deep pain. After a final glance between Silas and Kelso, he nodded and focused on the demon.

Silas ran up to Mayrion with his fingers on the pins. Kelso leaned down using some broken concrete blocks as cover.

"You kneel and serve, son of a bitch!" Silas jeered.

Mayrion turned to dispense with Silas and was met with an explosion that rocked the bunker. Chunks of Mayrion's arms and head shot all over the bunker. Appendage stumps and a lump of his skull remained as he leaned down, still attached to the hole in the floor. Kelso's air was knocked out of her, hearing was totally gone.

Get up. He just died for you. Now!

Kelso yelled at herself as she struggled to her feet. She drug herself across the area, reached back with her one good arm and stabbed Mayrion's residual skull chunks. She continued using her only strong arm while the weak one supported the pushing of the blade across its neck. She saw the skull regenerating on top of her blade. The demon released primal gurgles and screeches, but the grenade blast had temporarily removed any concept of hearing for Kelso.

Her injured arm started to bleed again and she felt the neck thickening as his head regenerated. The corner of her eye saw part of Silas' feet that had blown off. She gulped down her pain and used it to push the blade swiftly across its thickening neck. Its appendage arms hadn't regenerated fully so she pushed the blade across the final inches at the base of its head.

RARRRRRRRRRRRRRRRRRRRRRRRRRRRR-RRRRRRRRRRRRRR.

Mayrion's head fell off as both Kelso and its corpse toppled. Its insides exploded, covering Kelso and the bunker in viscous fluids as its body melted into the cement.

As Kelso laid on the concrete she stared up at the sky outside the bunker. Fighter jets in a large squadron were flying towards the Leviathan and fired off a small carpet bomb, exploding under the former Interstate 90 bridge where the Leviathan was descending into the water.

Kelso took a very long look at the buildings, bridges, and entire chunks of Mercer Island and Central District coastlines missing. She felt the ground shake as the Leviathan descended into oblivion under the waters, continued missile attacks by fighter jets pounding the watery abyss.

She reached into her pockets and pulled out some matches. The first two attempts were failures, but the final match caught flame with his mystical fluids, and she set Mayrion's head ablaze. She used the Talon of Tears to cut away a part of its jaw as the Gatekeeper asked. She recited the chant and the demon's skull burned faster, exploding into ash.

"Finally."

Kelso looked up to see a massive team of federal agents staring at her.

"Please tell me someone got that on video."

One agent held his hand up. Kelso gave them a thumbs up, then proceeded to collapse into darkness.

Chapter 64

Two weeks later, Kelso was waiting in the hospital visitor's area. Large sunglasses and a hoody covered her face. The doors opened and Det. Marano careened out in a wheelchair chuckling.

"Marano!"

"Sorry, I'm still getting used to this thing, new driver! I also like to blast into any hot male nurses, mistakes happen. Girl let's hit the atrium, too many ears nearby. I want the deets! Details girl!"

Kelso took control of Det. Marano's wheelchair and wheeled her into an atrium away from people. Kelso sat down next to her wheelchair on a black metal bench.

"Forget me, how are you doing? Marano, I thought you were dead in that bunker."

"Meh, my legs are goners but whatever, they got insane prosthetics now. I'm just thankful to be alive. Pain meds are helping a lot. I'll figure it out."

"Watch those pain meds, for real. Hey, you are still on the force?"

"Your fed people can play hide and seek with the truth, but no one locally is, we know what the fuck happened. We saw a monster eat our city. Duh. Despite the legs missing, I'm angling to be Lieutenant within a year, or something nice behind a desk. I'm not getting out, I'm about to shake up the entire fucking department. Now stop deflecting, how's your arm? Let me see a peek behind those glasses."

Kelso smiled for the first time in a week. As she removed the glasses the burns and explosive impacts on her face showed.

"Yeah, got some new beauty scars to brag about. They're talking about skin grafts and maybe it will be reduced a bit in time. Finally got some hearing back this week."

"Silas, like literally girl, that man is a myth now, savior of Seattle."

Kelso put her glasses back on and nodded.

"So, federal indictments and investigation status?"

"Typical bureaucratic bullshit. Despite there being some footage of the head being set on fire and demon cuts on the internet, they pushed me to sign a waiver and poof, internal investigation gone, federal charges would be dropped, cover story is terrorist attack plus earthquake, military saved the day via bombing," Agent Kelso replied.

""Wait? You saved the fucking city, state, and goddamn earth. And you can't talk about it?" Det. Marano asked. Her mouth was agape.

Agent Kelso released a slow smile. Some people walked by so she paused waiting for them to be alone.

"I refused to sign, if I wasn't willing to burn Gaucho to save my job I'm not willing to disrespect what Lt. Loy, Silas, and all of us went through, rather sit in prison than become my own Chad Zacks. They put up a fight but there is so much footage, after they were about to cuff me up, they backed off. Still, for a week, I got interrogated by a ton of the alphabet crews, CIA, FBI, Pentagon, other weirder shadowy government national security crews. They still don't believe me, oh well. Truth can't be bottled by lies anymore."

"Hah, see I told you that you were a badass!"

"Far from it, they offered me a post, FBI, Seattle. Anything I wanted."

Det. Marano's eyes lit up, she wiggled in her chair.

"Girl we're gonna tear up the town, I know a place with the best loaded nachos and margaritas."

Kelso made a face.

"Oh no, you are the worst."

"Yeah, I turned it down."

"Why?"

"I just want to be with my family, what's left of it. Without Silas around Tia and Rosa need me. I took a chill post eastern Washington, near my home sector. Just actual wildlife, hunters, and regular life. I like the slow small-town life. It is corny but I don't mind just a few stores, church, quiet, and family cookouts instead of demon quests. I'll visit, don't worry. Lucy texted me after the stories broke, you never know."

"Anytime you want, hit me up."

"Speaking of, I'm sorry but Tia has a school play I promised I'd make. It's a few hours speeding, and I agreed to take Lt. Loy's dog, its outside being watched by an impatient security guard."

They hugged bonded by surviving a darkness few could ever imagine. Kelso promised to visit in a few weeks. Det. Marano got choked up as she wheeled herself back into the hospital.

Downstairs, Kelso thanked the security guard and hopped into her truck. She sped out of the parking garage and into the crowded Seattle streets. Within hours she was trucking through the last edges of the Cascades into Eastern Washington. Rolling down the window, the Australian shepherd leaned its head out into the crisp dry wind. Tongue hanging in newfound bliss, she rubbed its fur as it sniffed new scents.

Kelso stared down at the shadows of the Cascades and imagined Silas running across the mountains of eternity. Underneath her sunglasses she let the wind blow away any attempts at tears. She continued racing across the highway outrunning dark clouds to catch the last shreds of sunlight.

About the Author

Victor Marrow was born and raised in the Midwest. Yes, he once had a mullet, and it was majestic. He has been a janitor, housekeeper, lawyer, pizza boy, and teacher. He has investigated dangerous parts of the U.S.-Mexico border, advocated for domestic violence survivors, and worked with clients on all aspects of the justice spectrum. Exploring the limits of morality, crime, and violence make him a questionable dinner guest. He enjoys canvassing cemeteries, courtrooms, and the alleyways of civilization for signs of his crew. Visit victormarrow.com to grab his first novel, The Pilgrim and the Prophet, inspired by a run in with a real-life cult, as well as track what new projects hover in the dark horizons.

Printed in Great Britain
by Amazon